Wolf Tales IV

Also by Kate Douglas:

Wolf Tales

"Chanku Rising" in *Sexy Beast*

Wolf Tales II

"Camille's Dawn" in *Wild Nights*

Wolf Tales III

"Chanku Fallen" in *Sexy Beast II*

Wolf Tales IV

KATE DOUGLAS

APHRODISIA

KENSINGTON PUBLISHING CORP.

http://www.kensingtonbooks.com

APHRODISIA BOOKS are published by

Kensington Publishing Corp.
850 Third Avenue
New York, NY 10022

All Kensington Titles, Imprints, and Distributed Lines are available at special quantity discounts for bulk purchases for sales promotions, premiums, fund-raising, and educational or institutional use.

Special book excerpts or customized printings can also be created to fit specific needs. For details, write or phone the office of the Kensington special sales manager: Kensington Publishing Corp., 850 Third Avenue, New York, NY 10022, attn: Special Sales Department, Phone: 1-800-221-2647.

Aphrodisia and the A logo Reg. U.S. Pat. & TM Off.

ISBN-13: 978-0-7582-1869-8
ISBN-10: 0-7582-1869-9

First Kensington Trade Paperback Printing: July 2007

10 9 8 7 6 5 4 3 2 1

Printed in the United States of America

Whether we accept it or not, our parents' lessons shape our lives. I can still hear my father saying, "Don't disbelieve something just because you don't understand it." Since there's a lot I'll never understand, his lesson left me wide open to accept the potential of just about anything. My mother, a writer from a long line of writers, taught me to love the written word and encouraged me to follow my dreams. Pragmatic soul that she is, however, she'll never read my Wolf Tales. "It's not the sex," says Mom. "I just can't believe stories where people can turn into animals."

I wish my father, an avid SF fan, had lived long enough to see my name on the cover of a book. I'm so glad my mother, who loves her romances, is still here and able to ask why I would want to write about shapeshifters, of all things.

Imagination and practicality. What writer can ask for more?

Acknowledgments

Thanks, once again, to my fantastic critique group, talented wordsmiths all, who never hesitate to chortle over my many mistakes. Cassie Walder, Ann Jacobs, Sheri Ross Fogarty, and Camille Anthony—I couldn't do it without you, and even if I could, it wouldn't be nearly as much fun.

Acknowledgments

Chapter 1

High Mountain Wolf Sanctuary, Colorado

If she sat very still, the wolves ignored her, even now in the failing light of dusk. Ignored her, though it was obvious they'd come searching for her. Lisa Quinn heard the zing of mosquitoes near her ear, sensed the encroaching coolness as night settled in, but she focused exclusively on the pack of seven wolves circled around the flat stone where she sat. They waited, sitting just as still as she, watching.

She recognized the alpha male and female, though even after observing this group for more than a week she still couldn't keep their four half-grown pups straight without checking the tags in their ears. An older, grizzled male sat off to one side. He was badly scarred, one ear torn and his muzzle all tinged with gray. Lisa nodded to him, giving the respect his years had earned.

The wolf blinked, almost as if he acknowledged her greeting.

There was something magical about this time of night. Magic in the way their amber eyes glowed as darkness enfolded them, magic in the silence, the sense of otherworldliness, the connection Lisa experienced as the dark bodies faded into shadow until only the shining fire in their eyes remained.

She lived for this moment in time, this sense that the beasts reached out to her, spoke to her. Though their thoughts were merely jumbled images, visual representations without language, the feeling of communication lingered long after each member of the pack finally turned away and glided silently back into the forest.

Lisa sat very still, even after the last wolf had gone. Sat with her legs folded in the standard lotus position, her hands resting lightly on her knees, her body trembling with energy and something deeper, more confusing. *Arousal?* Yes, she was sexually aroused.

It made no sense. None at all, but there was no denying the sexual energy coursing through her veins, throbbing between her legs, making her breasts ache. She breathed deeply, exhaled, took another breath, and felt the tension slowly begin to ebb.

A symphony of night sounds slowly built around her, but still she held her position, all the while reevaluating the past few minutes, considering how those minutes connected with all the years of her life. As she pondered the details, the sensual feelings faded, but the awareness remained. The sense of self, of connection.

Why now? Why here, in the midst of wolves, when she'd never found a sense of belonging among human society? Questions. Always more questions, when she'd hoped so much for answers. Dreams had led her to this place more than two years ago, dreams that took her through the forest, running with wolves, thinking as a wolf, being a wolf.

Only in her dreams.

For the first time, though, tonight they'd come to her. Come as if they'd expected her, as if they'd needed her. For what? It was more than mere curiosity about her. It was almost as if they needed answers just as she did. So many nights she'd sat here, aware of their presence as they hovered, unseen in the woods. Tonight, they'd shown themselves. Honored her with their powerful, feral presence.

Unsettled her with their disquiet. Lisa felt a small shiver run down her spine and wished it away, unwilling to lose the basic sense of this night.

Truly a magical moment. A time to savor. A memory to hold and, hopefully, to repeat tomorrow and the night after that. Finally, after a lifetime spent searching, Lisa felt as if there might actually be answers to some if not all of her questions.

The corners of her mouth twitched at the thought. There would always be more to wonder about. All was never as it seemed. For despite the sense of serenity about this place, mysteries hovered in the background.

Wolves gone missing. Four now, over the past two years. The shroud of guilt she bent beneath, that the disappearances began the month Lisa was hired, never fully left her. If only the wolves could speak. Tonight, the sense of communion Lisa felt had carried the whisper of answers.

She clung to that possibility, saw it as a destination after so many years spent wandering. Lisa's thoughts drifted from the poverty and anger of her dysfunctional childhood home to years of battling demons she'd not been able to name. The homeless encampment where she'd lived for a time under a Florida bridge was as far removed from this forest haven as she could imagine.

Caught in her unsavory memories, the questions, and her fragile hope for something better, Lisa drifted with her thoughts. She'd felt the suspicion cast her way over the missing wolves and done her best to send it back. She found comfort in the dream she'd had last night and felt her heart speed up as her mind took her on a race through the forest, running with her packmates beside her. She was miles away and years beyond when a bright beam of light cut a swath through the darkness. She blinked and shielded her eyes when it found her.

"Shit. Quinn? Is that you? What the hell are you doing out here in the dark?"

"Hal?" *Damn.* Mr. Suspicious himself, her supervisor, Hal Anderson. She gritted her teeth in an effort to keep her mouth shut.

Anderson pointed the flashlight directly at her eyes. "No one's allowed inside the pens after hours. Those gates are locked for a reason. The last thing we need is a mangled body come morning. You know the rules."

Shaken rudely out of her meditative state, Lisa slowly unwound her legs and rose to her feet. She made a big point of stepping off the flat rock and moving into Hal's comfort zone. Lisa liked the fact that she was taller than her boss. Enjoyed watching him take that involuntary step backward and duck his head in a typically submissive gesture without realizing what he'd done.

In fact, she liked the feeling as much as she disliked the man. He'd never come right out and accused Lisa to her face of having any connection to the missing wolves, but his suspicions had long been whispered about among the rest of the staff. Despite her dislike of the man, Lisa stood comfortably with hands on hips. "If no one's allowed, then why are you here, Hal?"

He stepped back another pace, apparently caught off guard by her question. Then he recovered and puffed up his chest. All it did was make him look like an irritated little rooster. "I'm in charge of this sanctuary, and I go where I damned well please." He patted the holster strapped to his side as if the sidearm gave him the authority his size couldn't. "Now get out of here. Don't let me find you on this side of the fence after dark, or your ass is gone. I'm not kidding, Quinn. You know the rules."

"Oh, I know the rules all right." She threw an extra bit of sway into her hips as she brushed by him, knowing exactly how much it would irritate the little tyrant. "I'm just wondering if you do."

She also wondered what Anderson was doing out here after dark. Had he been casting suspicion her way to take it off someone else . . . like himself? Lisa felt his gaze on her until a turn in the trail dropped her into a stretch of deep forest and the path back to the main gate. She felt the wolves as well. Felt their presence without hearing or seeing them. Knew they protected her.

Just as she knew, without any doubt at all, that they hated and possibly feared Hal Anderson.

Pack Dynamics headquarters, San Francisco, California

The printer rattled to life, and a boarding pass slowly appeared. He'd forgotten to replace the ink cartridge, so the print wasn't as dark as it should be, but what the hell. Martin McClintock, better known to his packmates as Tinker, sat at his desk wearing nothing but his worn flannel pajama pants. He watched the paper slip into the tray with the full and distinct knowledge that his life was about to change.

Tinker steepled his fingers beneath his chin and stared out the office window. It was barely six in the morning, still way too early to head to the airport. His plane didn't leave until ten. He'd been awake half the night, lying quietly in the big bed next to Tia and Luc, listening to their steady breathing, wondering what lay ahead.

There was just one more thing to do before he left, and that very thing was stalking him even now.

Tinker sensed Tia Mason before he heard her. Sensed the wildness of the forest and knew she'd most likely shifted and gone for a predawn run. The hours before day-break were the safest time to race through Golden Gate Park, a time when discovery was unlikely.

He grinned, knowing exactly why she searched him out.

For all the joy, all the glory of running as the wolf, shifting had its drawbacks, at least if one was alone. Almost unbearable arousal, a physical reaction impossible to ignore—an obsessive compulsion for sex not easily satisfied without a partner.

Among the Chanku, almost any partner would do—of either sex. It wasn't merely a way of life or a social choice. The drives and sensual needs defined who and what they were, how they lived, what they thought.

Who they fucked and why.

A constant itch that needed to be scratched, a desire that had to be filled, a hunger that must be satisfied.

Tinker recognized that need in Tia now, the arousal coursing through her veins, her pheromones a tempting aphrodisiac to any virile male with the sense to read the signs. He grinned as heat pooled in his groin, fully aware he wasn't immune.

Thank goodness. Tinker welcomed the powerful rush of blood and pounding heat. He felt his cock swell and rise within his loose flannel pants and acknowledged the arousal, the slow, throbbing ache in his balls, the tight sense of need centered along the base of his spine. It was all good, this need, this wanting.

Normally Tia would find her mate at a time like this, but Lucien was gone for the day, headed to Sacramento for an early meeting. Of course Tia would come here.

When in need, call Tinker.

He almost laughed aloud.

Tia came to him for many things—friendship, protection, sex. Tinker remembered how much he'd hoped at one time she might come to him for love, but that wasn't going to happen. Not since she'd bonded with Lucien Stone, her mate and partner for life . . . and Tinker's boss.

Tinker knew he should feel grateful that both Tia and Luc included him in their bed at night, accepted him as their partner in a thoroughly comfortable ménage. It wasn't enough, though. Not nearly enough. Their loving relationship didn't consciously exclude him, but as usual, Tinker realized he was the outsider.

The odd man out, though not necessarily at this particular moment.

Slim fingers brushed his bare shoulders. Warm lips tickled the edge of his ear. He felt her thick mass of hair brush his neck, trail lightly over the side of his face, and then sweep across his back. More hot blood rushed south as his cock reacted, swelling and tenting the front of his pants.

Tinker reached behind himself and caught the back of Tia's head in his palm, dragged her slowly around to face him, spinning his swivel chair to meet her halfway.

She tumbled gracelessly into Tinker's lap, all naked, giggling, sexy woman, and wrapped her slim arms around his neck. "I forgot Luc was leaving early. I got home and the house seemed so empty. Mik, AJ, and Tala aren't back from Maine yet, and I couldn't find you."

Tinker laughed and kissed her lightly. Tia tried to deepen the kiss, but he pulled back, teasing. "Oh damn. And the batteries in your vibrator are missing."

Tia cuffed the side of his head. "How'd you know?"

"Because I needed some for my flashlight and yours were the only ones I could find."

"Oaf." Tia nuzzled the side of Tinker's neck, nipping and licking a trail across his collarbone. "Then you owe me. Big time."

He chuckled. "I've got big. How big do you want it?"

"Big as you've got. Big as it'll get." She slipped her hand down between their bodies, tugged at the elastic waistband of his pants, and wriggled her fingers inside. Tinker sucked in a breath when she found his cock, wrapped her fingers tightly around the base and squeezed.

He tried to bite back a groan and failed. Damn, they'd fucked half the night away and he still wanted her—or at least wanted what Tia offered.

He leaned back in his chair and threw his arms up over his head. "Take me, woman. I'm all yours."

Tia snorted. "Well of course you are. You're male and I'm damned good."

As if to prove her point, Tia twisted out of Tinker's lap and slipped down between his legs. She managed to free his cock through the fly of his pants and had her lips around the crown before her knees hit the floor.

Tinker reached out to slow her down at the same time Tia swallowed him, her tongue already doing amazing things to the underside of his cock while her cheeks hollowed with each pull of her lips. Instead of stopping her, he tangled his fingers in Tia's thick waves of hair and held her close. The sight of her pink lips stretched, moist and pliable, around the dark chocolate erection sprouting from his groin took him to the edge. The visual was as sexy as the suction, like his own private porn flick starring Tia and his cock.

Tinker bit down on his lip and tilted his head back. No way in hell could he watch Tia Mason suck his cock and maintain control.

He was big and hard and filled her mouth so that the scrape of her teeth ran the length of his cock each time she pulled him in and then slowly turned him loose. Her tongue flattened against the underside, but as he withdrew, Tinker felt the tip of it curl around the crown of his penis, then dip quickly into the eye at the tip.

He wondered if she tasted the first drops of his seed, if she thought at all about Tinker or merely her search for release. Tinker opened his mind to Tia's thoughts, but for now there was merely a haze of lust without any form or feature.

Tia as woman barely existed, so trapped was she in the lush arousal following her shift, still a mindless creature of sensations, needs, and desires. Until Tia's conscious mind returned, Tinker accepted that he was nothing more to her than a means to an end, a very amenable pleasure toy to help ease the creature's needs.

He understood. He'd been that same creature so many times before.

Tia'd found a rhythm now that took Tinker closer and closer to climax. First the tightening in his groin, the tension between his legs as his balls drew up high and tight. He turned himself free, let the sensations take him. Close, so much closer to the edge, when Tia slowly withdrew until only the smooth crown of his cock was clasped between her lips.

She sucked down hard, laved him again with her tongue, and then dropped him entirely and pulled away. The cold morning air kissing his wet flesh wasn't nearly enough to cool the heat. Tia leaned close once more, swirled her tongue around the small eye at the tip, and then gave him a saucy wink. "That's all. I just wanted to make sure you were really interested."

Tinker took a moment to catch his breath and then he laughed. "Witch." He stood up quickly, grabbed Tia under her shoulders and knees, and lifted her against his chest before she had time to squawk. With his erect cock banging her butt, he carried her across the office, down the hall, and into their bedroom. Holding Tia at least two feet above the big bed, Tinker dumped her amid the tangled sheets and then rolled her to her belly.

"Oomph." She tried to wriggle free.

He held her down with one hand and slipped out of his loose pants with the other.

"What are you doing, you big oaf?" Twisting and turning under his palm, giggling uncontrollably, Tia swung a fake punch in Tinker's direction.

He dodged her flailing fist. "Finishing what you started, sweetie."

Somehow, in spite of, or because of, her struggles, Tia's legs spread apart and her hips rose up, and she was wet and ready when Tinker knelt behind her. He ran his fingers over her smoothly shaved mound, parted her swollen lips with his fingers, grabbed his cock in his fist, and found her wet and ready sex with the broad crown. One thrust took him deep; the second actually shoved Tia forward.

She practically purred.

"This is what you're looking for, isn't it?" Deeper this time, until his balls slapped against her mound.

"Maybe . . ." Her answer was muffled in her pillow, but it was obvious Tia wanted anything he offered.

Tinker's cock connected with the hard mouth of her womb on the next, hard thrust. She arched her back, cried out. Her pussy clamped down on his cock in a rippling, clenching spasm, squeezing him tighter, holding him deep inside as her entire body arched against him.

He opened his thoughts and caught her incoherent mental cries of pleasure. When he linked his mind with Tia's, Tinker felt the thickness of his cock as if it pierced his own spasming sex, felt each ripple and contraction as if his body were climaxing.

Tinker held there a moment, unmoving, mind and body saturated with sensation. His balls throbbed, a deep, dark pounding in time with his heart, the taut sense of pleasure bordering on pain as he held on to only marginal control. Tia rippled around him, her strong inner muscles squeezing and releasing, her scent rising ripe and addictive to tease his sensitive nostrils.

Slowly Tinker withdrew, teeth clenched and muscles tensing as he made his slow, steady retreat. Tia's velvet clasp tightened around his cock, attempted to hold him closer. He pulled almost completely free of her heat, then slammed into her hard and fast. Tia whimpered and adjusted her hips to take him even deeper. Her thick juices smoothed the way, her spasming sex pulled him in, and Tinker felt his hard-won control slip even more.

He slowed, rocking against Tia in a slow, steady rhythm.

Her fingers crept between their legs, tickling and scraping oversensitized flesh. He groaned when she found his sac and gently squeezed and massaged his balls in rhythm with each slow, even penetration.

Tinker slipped into a steady, leisurely cadence. Deeper, all the way in and slowly out to the very edge of her sex. His thighs trembled now, his gut clenched with need, and a slick river of sweat poured down his face and covered his chest. Almost as an afterthought, he searched for Tia's thoughts and found her once more on the edge of climax.

Close. So very close, almost in sync with him, almost there. Tinker pinched her nipples between his thumbs and forefingers, rolling the taut peaks hard enough to cause pain. Tia gasped, arched her back, and cried out. Her sound was low and haunting, more a howl than a moan.

Tinker joined his thoughts to Tia's. Not a link such as mates might have, but a simple linking of pleasure, of sensation. He leaned back on his heels and pulled Tia with him. His cock bottomed out once again, filling her. Her round buttocks pressed against his belly, and his fingers flared across her middle. He held her close. Her heart pounded beneath his palm.

Tia reached between their legs again. She scraped her nails over his sac, then cupped his balls in her palm and gently squeezed. Her thoughts in his mind turned hot, her needy flesh tightened even more around his cock, and suddenly, before he expected it, Tinker flew over the top.

Had it always been so good? Hips thrusting, jaw

clenching, and body shaking, his mind filled with Tia's climax, Tinker experienced his orgasm as Tia felt it, deep inside her body.

Exquisite, to know it from Tia's viewpoint as well as his own. He became the depth of her passion in the images, words, and sensations she shared.

Experienced the lush heat, the fullness, the desire, and even the regret. In the midst of climax, with Tinker's cock filling her, his arms holding her, his seed pulsing into her warm and welcoming pussy, Tia thought of Luc.

Missed Luc. Wished he were here with them. Wished Luc was the one loving her. Loving Tinker. Filling her sex or her mouth or even her ass. No matter. Tinker knew her thoughts and knew Tia wanted her mate.

As she should.

Would a woman ever think of him that way? Would he ever know the deep, soul-searing link of a bonded mate?

Not with this woman, no matter how much he cared for her.

Tinker slowly lowered Tia to the bed, both of them drawing deep, gasping breaths of air into oxygen-starved lungs.

Tinker kissed Tia's cheek, stroked her hair back from her face, and smiled down at her while he struggled for control of his breathing. Finally, when he felt he could speak without gasping for air, he kissed her again. It was time to let go of regrets, to think of other things. To think of the adventure that lay ahead.

He wished he knew how to plan for the unpredictable. Impossible. He'd figure this trip out one step at a time. Until he came face-to-face with his ultimate goal, he'd have to wing it.

Tinker flopped down on the bed beside Tia and turned so he could watch her face. "I'm going to need a ride to SFO. Can you take me to the airport in a couple hours?"

Tia nodded. Her chest rose and fell with each deep

breath. Her thoughts were now her own, gently yet firmly blocked. "Yeah. No problem."

Tinker sat up, but Tia stopped him with a gentle hold on his forearm. He looked down at her fingers, their bronze color still many shades lighter than his own dark skin, and thought how beautiful her fingers were, how much he liked the contrast of their skin, her deep bronze to his dark chocolate.

Her softness to his hard, muscled body. Her feminine yet forceful spirit to his Chanku male soul. Tinker covered Tia's hand with his, pushed those pointless thoughts from his mind, and glanced into her beautiful amber eyes. "What?"

"I'm . . . I . . ." She sighed and glanced away, the thought she hadn't shared left unspoken. "Do you know how long you'll be gone? Did Luc tell you anything at all? Did he find out anything?"

Tinker shook his head. "Not much more than we talked about. It's a wolf sanctuary, privately owned and funded, yet licensed by the federal government. It's in northern Colorado, up in the Rockies, though I understand the elevation isn't too high. I'll be looking for Baylor Quinn's sister. Her name's Lisa, unless she's changed it. We know that Bay's Chanku. So is his other sister Tala. It's a given that Lisa is as well. I need to find her, convince her to take the supplement and hope it works. Then we'll take it from there."

Tia slanted him a coquettish glance. "Oh, I can guess where you'll take it. Far, fast, and very, very deep."

Tinker shrugged his shoulders, but he grinned. "One can only hope. It's going to be weird, approaching a stranger who is definitely Chanku . . . and knowing she hasn't got a clue. I'll be honest and admit I'm going after her hoping she'll be the one, that she'll end up as my mate. Face it, sweetie. There are so few women among us. We have to take our future into our own hands, or someone else might do it for us."

Tia nodded, her smile fading. "I know. I want you to find someone of your very own. It's just . . ." She looked away again. Tinker grabbed her chin with his fingertips, turned her back, and was surprised to see tears on her cheeks. She sighed and covered Tinker's hand with hers. "Things will never be the same again. I feel it, and I worry about you."

"Sweetie, don't worry. I'll be fine. Everything will be okay, and I'll be home before you know it. Hopefully with someone else for you to pick on." He kissed Tia, then stood up. He had to put distance between them before he said or did something stupid. She was Luc's. Tia would always be Luc's, no matter how often she shared Tinker's bed. She loved Tinker. He had no doubt of that, but she had chosen Luc as her mate. Loved Luc on a level far beyond any feelings she held for Tinker. It might have been confusing, had they still been human.

Among the Chanku, it was the way of the pack. Thank goodness Luc knew and was cool with the relationship Tinker had with Tia. Tinker sighed. Of course, maybe that wasn't such a good thing. Maybe it made things too comfortable, all that much more difficult for Tinker to move on, to find his own mate, his own life.

Tia grabbed his hand and stretched her fingers over his knuckles, as if comparing their color differences. She looked down at their linked hands, not into his eyes as she normally would. "Do you have any idea what you're going to do when you find her? What you'll say? It's not like you can just introduce yourself and say, 'Oh, by the way, I'm a shapeshifter and I turn into a wolf.' She'd think you were nuts. You have to have some kind of plan."

Tinker laughed. "Actually, I don't. I'm just going to wing it with this one. I need to see what she's like, get a feel for how she'll deal with everything she's going to find out about herself."

Tia laughed. "I can't believe that you, of all people,

haven't got a detailed plan of action. That is so not you!" She squeezed his fingers, then dropped his hand and stepped back. "I'll miss you, Tinker. A lot. So will Luc." She pouted, glancing at him out of the corner of her eye. She looked like a pissed-off six-year-old.

He grinned. This he could deal with. "Good. You deserve to miss me after the way you manhandled me just now. A man should have some say in the matter of sex. Don't you think?"

"No way. Not when he steals my batteries. You take my toys, I get to play with yours." Tia ran her fingers lightly along his cock. Her slightest touch brought it back to life.

"Looks like you don't need batteries. This sucker's under his own power." Laughing harder, Tia jerked her hand back, jumped off the bed, and headed for the bathroom, wriggling her hips with a lot more sway than usual. "Next time, I'm gonna hide my batteries and you'll just have to deal with the dark."

Later, Tinker thought of Tia's quip as his plane crossed over the Sierra Nevadas, headed for Colorado. *Deal with the dark.* Sometimes he felt as if he spent every waking moment dealing with the dark. His own darkness, both figuratively and literally. He'd never had it easy, a black man with his convoluted background, living in a white world.

Once again he wondered what his life would have been like if his mother hadn't abandoned him. She would have carried the Chanku genes, whoever she was. Carried them, but never brought that part of herself to life, other than through the birth of her son. For all he knew, she was still alive. Tinker often wondered if he had siblings anywhere, other young Chanku men or women, living lives of quiet, or not so silent, desperation . . . but that was neither here nor there.

What would have happened if the foster family who raised him had been black instead of white? They'd loved him unconditionally and done their best, but they were a typical suburban, white, middle-class family. When they died in a car accident the year Tinker turned fifteen, he'd been thrust headfirst, unprepared, back into both the foster care system and the local black society, lacking those skills needed by a young African American male.

Add the overactive libido and chaotic thought processes of the typical undiscovered Chanku, and no idea at all how to interact with guys, much less African American girls, and Tinker knew he'd been a mess.

Literally a stranger in all worlds. A man apart and unaccepted in both black and white society, unable to fit in any world. All through the formative years in high school and college, even in the military, Tinker remained apart. The closest thing he had to a family who understood and accepted him was the pack.

Even there he was the odd man out. Luc Stone had Tia. Jake had Shannon. Hell, even AJ and Mik had Tala. There was the new guy, Baylor, but he seemed perfectly happy with Jake and Shannon. For now, anyway.

A flight attendant stopped beside his seat. Tinker glanced up and managed a smile. The woman was beautiful, tall and slim, with her black hair sleeked back into a neat bun at the back of her neck. She looked to be about his age with skin the color of coffee with cream, but he didn't encourage conversation. That was the problem with first-class seats. Flight attendants were always checking to see if you needed something, though from the flirtatious look on this woman's face, she might be the needy one.

Tinker shook his head when she asked if he wanted something to drink, and turned once again to stare out the window. He never thought of his looks one way or the other, though women always seemed interested. The attendant moved on to speak with the couple in the seat behind his. Tinker sensed her curiosity, and with his heightened Chanku senses, even scented her arousal, but it did nothing for him.

When he looked at beautiful women, why did he always compare them to Tia? He loved her, but he never thought of her as a mate. No, not in those terms. She was Luc's. She'd always be Luc's.

Which left Tinker once more alone in the dark.

Chapter 2

It was obvious the woman didn't hear him. Either that or she chose to ignore the sound of his car. Tinker had pulled in close behind the battered pickup truck, positioned his rented convertible at the side of the narrow road beneath a huge fir tree, and shut off the engine. The loud whine of a straining winch motor explained why he'd been able to park so close without notice, and he took advantage of his position in the little red car to watch the woman for a few moments.

She was tall, tan and lean, with broad shoulders and ropy muscles in her long arms. She wore hiking boots, faded jeans, and a tight-fitting faded red tank top. Though she was turned partially away from him, he could see that her breasts were high and small, the nipples sharply visible through the thin cotton. Tinker's gaze lingered there a moment before moving on to study the rest of her. The woman's dark hair was all tied up in some sort of lopsided knot that hung over her left ear. She appeared to be trying to load a badly mangled dead deer into the back of her truck.

HIGH MOUNTAIN WOLF SANCTUARY was printed on the truck door.

The winch didn't look as if it could lift the weight of the animal, which must have been killed recently because the body was limp and the front legs flopped around. The woman had tied a stout rope around the hind legs and attached it to the winch, but the motor groaned and whined, and the bloody body didn't budge.

Tinker glanced down at his freshly washed and ironed slacks, new Italian leather shoes, and crisp white shirt and sighed. It wasn't in his makeup to drive off and let any woman deal with her own problems.

Much less one who looked as good as this lady.

Tinker opened the car door and climbed out just as the winch made a loud grinding noise and stopped.

The woman kicked the animal's body in obvious frustration and muttered, "Aw, fuck."

"Need some help?" Tinker stepped forward, hand outstretched.

"Shit! Who the hell are . . . ?" She stepped back a pace, hand over her heart, eyes wide. "Oh God. I'm sorry. You scared the crap out of me! I didn't hear you drive up."

"Obviously." Tinker bit back a grin as she realized what she'd said. She slapped her hand over her mouth, blushing beet red.

Tinker nodded in the direction of the dead doe. "You sure you want to touch your mouth with that hand?"

"Oh yuck." She pulled her hand away and wiped her mouth with her forearm.

Chuckling, Tinker added, "I hope you're not planning to have that for dinner. It looks a little ripe."

The woman laughed. Tinker's head snapped up at the familiar sound. She laughed as though she enjoyed it, as if life was there to be lived. She laughed just like Mik and AJ's mate, Tala Quinn.

Sometimes it appeared his luck wasn't all bad. Tinker looked her over with a fresh eye. He'd expected small and wiry, like Tala, not this tall, healthy Amazon of a woman who checked him out with the same interest he showed her.

"Not for my table, thank you very much. I work at the High Mountain Wolf Sanctuary. We've got county permits to collect roadkill for the wolves. It's better than feeding them commercial stuff all the time. More like their natural diet."

Suddenly everything sort of fell together in Tinker's head, not to mention his agreeable cock. His assignment to find the missing Chanku female took on a whole new impetus, one that had him grinning like an idiot. He stuck out his hand. "That's where I'm headed. The wolf sanctuary. I'm Martin McClintock. Tinker to my friends."

She looked down at her filthy hands, wiped them on her jeans, and shook his. "I'm Lisa. Lisa Quinn. It's nice to meet you."

"I thought you must be Lisa. You laugh just like Tala, your sister." Tinker held on to her hand, aware of a sudden and powerful current between them. A link of souls that had to be her Chanku spirit. He sensed the wildness in her, whether Lisa recognized it or not.

Saw it in the questioning glint in her beautiful amber eyes. Eyes very much like her sister's . . . eyes just like his own.

Tinker thought of the supplements stored in his bag, the ugly looking pills that made dreams come true for those with the right genetic soup. She would recognize that wildness soon if Tinker had anything to say about it.

Lisa blinked, her lips parted in surprise, but she didn't pull her hand free of his. In fact, she tightened her grip, holding on to Tinker as if he were a lifeline. "Tala? My sister's name is Mary Ellen. You must be mistaken."

Tinker shook his head. "I'd forgotten. You're right. She told me she'd changed her name to Tala. It means 'wolf' in some Native American language. Can't recall which one. Interesting, though, that she choose that name, especially with you working in a wolf sanctuary."

Suspicion flashed across her face, but she didn't release his hand. "I haven't seen Mary Ellen or heard from her in years. Not since . . ."

Tinker nodded, still preternaturally aware of the contact running between them. He wondered if she felt it, if she recognized the link, the sense of a kindred spirit. "Your father's trial, right? That's what Bay, your brother, told us. He recently reconnected with your sister, and they've both been trying to figure out where you ended up."

The look of disbelief on her face turned to complete shock. "Baylor, too? Where? I've tried for years to find him. To find both of them. Where are they?"

"Mary Ellen's been in a little town in New Mexico where she went by the name of Tala Quinn. She had amnesia. Up until a few months ago, Bay worked for the government as a special agent. They only recently located you and sent me to track you down. Look . . ." Tinker released her hand. Immediately he missed the sense of connection. "There's a lot I want to tell you, and I imagine you'll have even more questions."

Lisa stared at her hand for a moment, then brushed both hands against her jeans. "You're right. I have so many questions, I don't know where to begin."

"We can start with this mess. Let's get your furry friends' dinner loaded, and I'll follow you back to the sanctuary."

Lisa tilted her head and looked up at him. "You're not quite dressed for the job."

"No problem." Tinker leaned over, grabbed the deer by the front legs and shoulders, flexed his muscles, and easily lifted the heavy body into the truck in one quick move, without getting any of the gore on his clothes. He slammed the tailgate shut and grinned at Lisa. He knew he was strutting, damn it, but he couldn't help himself.

She burst into laughter and clapped her hands. "Uh, never mind. Thank you."

Tinker wiped his hands on the damp towel she handed him, then helped Lisa into the cab. "How about I just follow you back?"

She looked him over, and Tinker hoped like hell she liked what she saw.

"Okay. It's only a couple miles." Lisa turned and winked. "Follow carefully. I brake for roadkill."

Lisa hoped the hunky guy in the car behind her knew she wasn't kidding when she said she braked for roadkill. She'd made three stops over the past mile and gathered up two opossums and a raccoon that hadn't made it across the road. As much as she hated the constant death along this stretch of highway bordering a small mountain lake, she welcomed the chance to feed the confined wolves fresh meat.

Doing this disgusting chore, useful though it might be, also freed her mind to think about more important things. Like who was the unbelievably sexy man who followed her? She never reacted to men as she had to him, and his touch had been absolutely electrifying. There was something about him that went well beyond the fact he claimed to know her brother and sister. Something that reminded her of the wolves she cared for at the sanctuary, a wariness that belied his easy smile and sexy good looks.

He really did look like some sort of cover model, especially with those light-colored slacks and that neatly pressed white shirt. There was something unbelievably lush and attractive about his dark, dark skin next to that white shirt, the way he wore the long sleeves rolled back to expose his strong wrists.

He wasn't wearing any jewelry. Lisa'd noticed his left hand right away, checked for that telltale band of gold or, even worse, a lighter mark left by the recent removal of a ring. Why she'd notice so much about him left her feeling flustered and uneasy. Generally men didn't do much for her, one way or another. No, she'd given up on men long ago, but that was another story altogether.

She drove through the open gate to the sanctuary's visitor's center, pulled around behind the log building, and parked beside the long, low barn where they kept the refrigerators and supplies for feeding the wolves. One of the regular volunteers, a kid from the local high school who'd started working at the sanctuary shortly before Lisa was hired, ran out to help move the bodies. He was a good kid, suffering from a bit of hero-worship, but always around to help when an extra set of hands was needed. Luckily, his class schedule seemed to give him all the free time he needed to work at the sanctuary.

"Hi, Seth. You might need the cart for this haul."

"I'll get it, Ms. Quinn." Seth made a U-turn and went back inside. Tall and lanky with dark hair that never stayed combed, he reminded Lisa of her older brother when they were kids.

Funny, she'd been thinking of Baylor today, especially considering the man she'd just met. Lisa climbed out of the truck and waved to Tinker as he pulled the little red convertible into a parking spot near the visitor's center.

Silly name for a man that size. He had to be six and a half feet tall if he was an inch, with broad shoulders and muscled thighs even his loose pants couldn't disguise. There weren't many men who made Lisa feel small, but he'd done it back there on the highway. Stepping up close to shake her hand, he'd surprised her with his sheer size, with the graceful way he moved in spite of his height and muscular build.

Seth came back outside with the wheeled cart and opened the tailgate. "Eeeww. Gross." He pulled on rubber gloves and reached for the dead deer.

"Here. I'll help you." Tinker reached for the animal's front legs.

Seth stopped him. "Mister, you're always supposed to wear rubber gloves when you handle this stuff. It can carry all kinds of diseases."

Tinker grinned at Lisa. She felt her skin grow hot. She always forgot about the damned gloves. "Oh, you are? I didn't realize that." He held his hand out. "I'm Tinker McClintock. A friend of Ms. Quinn's."

Lisa slanted a glance at Tinker. *We'll see about that.*

Yes. We definitely will.

Lisa blinked. How the hell . . . ? She had to have been imagining the sound of his voice in her head. Lisa blinked again and smiled at Seth. She had the strangest feeling the high school student was suddenly eyeballing Tinker as a potential rival. At least Seth managed to shake the man's hand without making a scene.

Lisa felt like her head was spinning when Tinker took the extra set of gloves from Seth and helped load the dead animals onto the cart. It was almost as if she and this stranger were communicating on some unspoken level. The same way it had been last night when she sat among the wolves; except then she'd seen images and now she was hearing voices.

Aware of an unexpected flash of arousal and a sudden rush of moisture between her thighs, Lisa realized communication wasn't the only thing similar to her experience last night. She caught her breath against the tide of need surging through her body.

"Ms. Quinn?" Seth was standing in front of her as if

waiting for a comment. She'd missed whatever he must have said. Lisa took a deep breath and plastered a smile on her face.

"I'm sorry, Seth. What?"

"I said, Mr. Dunlop was looking around the place this morning. I was wondering why he's here."

Lisa took a deep breath and sighed. The benefactor of the sanctuary rarely set foot on the premises, but the one time Lisa had met him, she'd felt extremely uncomfortable in his presence. Weird, really, to react like that, especially since he was the one with the money that made the sanctuary possible. "He does own the place, so I guess he can come anytime he wants." She forced a soft laugh. "Thanks for telling me, Seth. If I find out anything that's going on, I'll be sure and let you know."

"Mr. Anderson acted like it was no big deal that the owner had showed up unannounced." Seth snorted and then laughed. "He sure was bowing and scraping, though, when Mr. Dunlop's limo pulled in."

"Well, Mr. Dunlop is the reason these wolves are still alive. He spends a lot of money to keep the sanctuary viable."

Seth nodded. "Yeah. I know . . . He's just sort of a weird dude, and Mr. Anderson is a turd." With a defiant glance toward the main office, Seth lifted the handles on the cart and pushed the heavy load into the barn.

Lisa watched him until he disappeared into the shadows, then turned her attention to Tinker. She'd felt his presence, almost as if he were in her head, thinking her thoughts. Thank goodness he wasn't there now. It hadn't been an uncomfortable feeling, sharing space in her mind with someone else, but it was definitely strange.

She watched as he peeled the rubber gloves off his big hands and tossed them in the nearby trash. Stared at him and wondered just who the hell he was and why she felt this strange connection that went so far beyond mere physical attraction.

He stared right back at her. "Is there someplace where we can talk? There's a lot I need to tell you, and it's not something we can discuss in public."

Lisa blinked again, caught herself mid-question, and nodded. "We both need to wash up first. Seth wasn't kidding about the germs and stuff. Then let me check in at the office, let them know I'll be away for a while. I need to tell them the winch died . . . again. Maybe with Mr. Dunlop around we can get a new one." She flashed a broad grin at Tinker. "We can go to my place. It's just up the road. My Jeep's in the parking lot out back."

Lisa caught herself, hearing her words as if they'd been spoken by someone else. She couldn't believe she'd invited him home! Oddly enough, she trusted Tinker McClintock, a man she'd known for less than an hour. Lord knew why, but she didn't fear him. It almost made her laugh, to think she was taking a strange man into her home, she who rarely had anything at all to do with men.

Tinker parked his rental car next to her beat-up old Jeep and waited until Lisa got out and glanced his way, silently inviting him to follow. The cabin she lived in was small, set off from the road in a copse of old growth fir, almost completely hidden from view until one followed the narrow drive from the main road.

It fit her. Fit everything about her. Tinker smiled in anticipation. What he intended to tell Lisa Quinn would rock her world. Rock it, then set it upright for the first time in her life. He knew exactly what she would think, what she would feel.

He'd been there. Not all that long ago, he'd been there.

The memories hit Tinker hard and fast, jarred him more than usual. He'd just finished his tour of duty in

Afghanistan, returned to the States, and wondered what the hell he was going to do next. The military hadn't answered his questions, hadn't fulfilled the unnamed need in his life. Nothing had, until he met Ulrich Mason.

Tall, silver-haired, imposing as hell, yet with a gift of understanding that Tinker envied to this day. Ulrich had invited him to San Francisco, asked him to come to a meeting with his company, an investigative agency he called Pack Dynamics.

The irony of the name was no longer lost on Tinker. At the time, though, Mason had merely explained that he'd sensed something in Martin McClintock that no one else had seen. Something different.

Something unbelievable. Mason had talked about an ancient species of shapeshifters—men and women who could change from human to wolf in a heartbeat. Not werewolves of the horror movie variety. No, the Chanku were different. Better. Independent of the moon or seasons or hormones. Driven only by their need to be one with the pack, their amazing sexuality, their loyalty to their one true mate, to their brothers and sisters within their strongly connected family.

It had all seemed like a wild fantasy until Mason did the unbelievable. He'd shifted. Stripped out of his neat business suit right there in the front room of his Marina District home, stripped down buck-naked, and turned into a huge wolf right in front of Tinker.

Definitely one of those moments a man doesn't forget. He'd scared the shit out of Tinker. Then Ulrich had shifted back to his familiar human self, casually put his clothes back on, and explained to Tinker that he was certain they were brothers under the skin.

Chanku. Shapeshifters. Members of an ancient race born on the Tibetan steppe, creatures of those rugged plains who had spread out and moved far from their homeland. They'd gone far enough away to miss the special grasses and plants that provided the traces of specific nutrients that fed a small gland at the base of their brains, a tiny organ near the hypothalamus that allowed them to shift from human to wolf and back again.

Tinker had wanted so badly to believe, so much to belong to something remotely close to a family . . . a family where everyone was the same despite the color of their skin. He'd taken the big capsules Mason had given him, swallowed one each day and figured it was all some sort of joke, a sleight of hand so to speak. Then, after about a week, he'd noticed a difference in perception. An ability to smell things he'd not noticed before, an increase in his already overactive libido—and a desire for raw meat.

When the change had come, Tinker'd been ready for it. He'd had a more difficult time adjusting to the sense of family the pack offered than to the ability to change from man to wolf. Pack Dynamics. The company Ulrich founded as much as a cover for the few Chanku he'd been able to find as it was a venue for them to use and develop their skills as wolves—and as men.

He'd gained a wonderful code of honor from Ulrich, as well as a family and something powerful to believe in. Ulrich Mason had given Tinker the chance to believe in himself for the first time in his life.

Tinker glanced at his reflection in the rearview mirror. He saw what he thought of as an average man, dark of skin with amber eyes, a ready smile. The same thing Lisa Quinn saw when she looked at him. No one would ever suspect the beast that lived within.

Only another of his species would know, *could* know, what Martin McClintock was capable of doing. Of becoming.

Tinker grinned, opened the door of the little car, and unfolded his big frame as he climbed out. Lisa Quinn was about to learn all about Martin McClintock. And, in the process, she just might learn one hell of a lot more about herself.

Lisa held the door open and followed Tinker inside. She really loved the way he walked, sort of a loose-limbed stroll, as if he owned the ground he stood upon and feared nothing. In some ways, he reminded her of the alpha males in any of the established wolf packs at the sanctuary.

Plus, he had the finest ass she'd ever seen on either man or woman. Tinker McClintock epitomized power, self-confidence, and sex, a potent aphrodisiac as far as Lisa was concerned.

She'd never been all that attracted to men, but something about this particular male left her breathless and much too aware of their isolation in her cabin, too aware of her instant and insistent sexual need for a total stranger.

Did he really know Baylor and Mary Ellen? Did it matter? Hell, she hardly knew her brother and sister. They'd grown up in a family that defined the term *dysfunctional*. The last time they'd seen each other was at their father's sentencing for the murder of his wife.

He'd killed their mother when he caught her screwing the postman. Shot both his wife and her lover while Lisa watched, horrified, from an open doorway. She'd testified against the man who'd always denied his paternity of her, heard him threaten her life as he was led, shackled and cursing, from the courtroom.

There'd been little said among the three siblings. They'd all had the same mother, but only Baylor had looked remotely like their father.

Daughters of a whore. That's what their father had called them. Maybe he was right. It didn't matter now. Nothing really mattered. Nothing beyond the wolves. Beyond keeping them safe. At least the wolves were creatures Lisa almost understood.

She turned around and quietly shut the door, then leaned back against the frame with the doorknob clutched in her fingers at the small of her back. Tinker watched her from across the small room, his beautiful eyes wary, his smile hinting more of questions than answers. He was absolutely drop-dead gorgeous, with his close-cropped yet silky-looking black hair, long straight nose with just the slightest flare to his nostrils, and lips that looked full and firm and eminently kissable. Lisa raised her chin and took a deep breath. She felt her heart pounding in her chest, felt the trickle of sweat between her breasts.

Felt the moisture gathering between her legs, her body welcoming this man in a way her mind would never allow. His nostrils flared. Her breath caught. Did he scent her arousal? Did he know how little control she had over her libido? Thank goodness she'd taken the time to clean up in the restroom at the sanctuary, or he'd be smelling more than her arousal!

Lisa almost chuckled aloud. This was so typical of her luck. For the first time in her life she was standing within fucking distance of the sexiest man she'd ever seen, and their first meeting had been over roadkill.

Her glance fell to the front placket of his slacks. There was a noticeable bulge at his groin, a sizeable swelling along his left inner thigh that accelerated Lisa's already racing heartbeat. Obviously, the whole dead animal thing hadn't put him off a bit. She licked her lips and looked up, directly at his face, and realized she was concentrating on his mouth, on the full curve of his lips.

Neither of them had said a word, yet the room seemed full of conversation, a silent communion that was pure foreplay of the mind, totally without touch. There was no denying the fact the air was stuffed with pheromones. Lisa cleared her throat. Tinker wiped his palms along his thighs and grinned.

He took a step forward, halted, and shrugged his shoulders, then his smile grew even wider. "I have a suggestion, Ms. Quinn, that might help us with our discussion."

Lisa nodded. Her mouth was too dry to speak.

"There's an amazing amount of tension here in this little cabin of yours. It's a powerful deterrent to having any kind of adult conversation. Why don't you and I just spend some time taking care of that tension before we go any further."

Lisa swallowed. The sound practically echoed in the small room. She blinked but couldn't answer. Of course, she didn't really know the question, did she? Finally Lisa managed to find her voice. "What exactly do you have in mind?"

Tinker laughed and spread his hands wide. "Well, I think we should both get naked, rub a little, touch a little, and fuck like bunnies. I imagine it'll take care of whatever it is that's making you so nervous."

Lisa blinked. Fought down the giggles that threatened to burst out. Just like that? He wanted to have sex when they'd just met? He had to be kidding!

She took another look at the twinkle in his eyes, the sexy smile on his mouth . . . and then let her gaze slide lower. The bulge in his pants was even larger, more impressive than it had been just a moment before.

He wasn't kidding. For all the silly talk, the man was deadly serious. Lisa tried to make some appropriate quip but couldn't get the words out. The thought came unbidden—there probably wasn't an appropriate quip to be made. Not to a suggestion like that!

Tinker reached out a hand. Lisa stared at it for what felt like forever. His hand was huge, the fingers long and slim, his palm much lighter than the back. His nails were neatly clipped, and she thought he had artist's hands, the hands of a man who could create with a touch, hands capable of either strength or gentleness.

For all their artistic grace and beauty, in spite of or because of their obvious strength, she couldn't allow herself to forget these were still the hands of a stranger.

Lisa glanced up and looked into Tinker's eyes. Darkest amber with shining fire, there was no threat in them, no coercion. He stared back at her with patience and good humor, and a need every bit as strong as her own. She didn't know him. Didn't know anything about him, but looking into Tinker's eyes, Lisa felt as if she looked into the mirror of her own soul.

She chose then to listen to her libido rather than her brain. To follow her woman's instincts rather than any bit of common sense that might exist among her suddenly foggy thoughts. Lisa released her death grip on the doorknob, wiped her sweaty palm on her jeans, and, moving in slow motion, slipped her fingers into his. Tinker smiled and pulled her closer, a slow, steady tug on her hand. Lisa knew that if she didn't want what he offered, he would turn her loose, no questions asked. Knew it as if he'd spoken the words aloud.

He pulled her into his embrace as if they'd been lovers forever. Pulled her close against his body until she felt the thick length of his erection pressing into her belly, smelled the clean, masculine scent of him, tasted the flavors of the man when his lips found hers.

She sighed against his mouth and parted for him, took his tongue into her mouth the same way she wanted the rest of him. She sucked hard, drew him in deep. Tangled her tongue with his as his big hands cupped her buttocks and lifted her against him, pulling her even closer, higher, until her toes left the floor and she was weightless, caught in his strong arms, held by his mouth, his hips, his power.

He scattered kisses along her jaw and throat. Then he

lifted Lisa into his arms as if she weighed absolutely nothing and turned, scanning the small room.

She made her decision in a heartbeat, raised her hand weakly, and pointed to a doorway leading to the back of the cabin. "That way. My room is down there. The last door on the right."

Chapter 3

Tinker grunted in reply, then carried Lisa quickly down the narrow hallway, into her small bedroom. Her queen-size bed almost filled the room, but it was the biggest she'd been able to get inside such a small space.

Lisa'd never shared this bed with a man, not in the two years since she'd worked at the sanctuary. Her sexual liaisons had been infrequent, always with women visiting the sanctuary, sometimes here but generally deep in the cool, dark forest where they could find release under the open sky.

Now this man who was virtually unknown laid her carefully on the quilted spread and sat down beside her. The sense of intimacy with a stranger was almost Lisa's undoing. She felt the edge of the mattress dip with his weight, felt the heat from his body touching hers. He was a big man, huge, actually, with broad shoulders and powerful thighs to match his height; but as big as he was, he was infinitely gentle with her.

First he untied her boots and slipped them off, along with her thick socks. He spent a moment rubbing and massaging her toes and the soles of her feet, sending shivers up her legs, over her thighs, and straight to her crotch.

He pulled her tank top over her head and gently tugged

the loose knot of her hair free. It cascaded down her back in thick tangles almost to her waist, and he spent long moments arranging it over her breasts and across her belly, tickling her navel with a loose curl until she broke into giggles.

He'd managed to cover her nakedness with her hair. A simple thing, but it eased her sense of vulnerability, made her more open to his touch.

Each movement he made was a sensual caress, his touch so gentle it raised shivers over her skin. She felt no fear, no concern at all that she'd barely met him. Instead, Lisa felt her arousal growing, experienced a sense of wonder that a man—this man—could take her to such heights with nothing more than his teasing little touches, his gentle strokes, and his soft laughter.

She never wore a bra for the simple reason that her breasts were too small to need one. She wondered if such a big man would be disappointed by her relatively flat chest, dominated as it was by two sharply erect nipples.

Tinker brushed her hair aside and bared her completely to his frank and obviously admiring gaze. He stared at her for a long moment without saying a word, but the light in his eyes spoke volumes. His warm palm cupped her right breast, and then he groaned, leaned close, and suckled first one nipple, then the other. Lisa felt the suction from his lips flash like a bolt of lightning from her nipples to her clit. She arched her hips in response.

He spent a long time on her breasts, licking and kissing, pinching the erect nipples between his fingers, rolling the tips between the rough pads of his fingers exactly the way she loved, until she panted and practically wept with the pleasure. Then his lips moved lower, following her rib cage to the waistband on her jeans.

He unfastened the snap and zipper, slipped the pants down past her ankles, and then tugged them over her feet. She heard the sound of denim hitting the wood floor, the clank of her keys in the side pocket. She felt Tinker turn away from her and raised up on her elbows to watch him remove his shoes and socks.

He carefully unbuttoned his white shirt and hung it neatly over a plain wooden chair beside the bed. His chest was broad, heavily muscled and smooth. Lisa ached to touch his brown skin, wanting nothing more than to spend the rest of the afternoon learning every ridge and muscle between the two dark raspberry nipples; but the moment he removed his pants, her attention went south.

He wore tight-knit boxer shorts, the kind that hugged his thighs and ass and everything else. Right now the soft gray cotton stretched around and molded the huge package between his legs, outlining him so perfectly she saw the flare at the crown of his erection through the fabric. Much to Lisa's dismay, Tinker left the shorts on when he turned back toward her.

She forgot about his shorts the moment he knelt on the small woven rug beside her bed, pulled her legs over the edge, and gently pushed her knees apart. Forgot about everything but the hot, damp sweep of his breath as he put his face between her legs and inhaled her scent. She should have felt embarrassed to have this big, beautiful stranger in such an intimate position, but she didn't. Couldn't. Not when it was easily the most erotic moment of her life.

Make that the second . . . no, the third . . . Each touch took her higher, so high it was difficult to breathe. The very tip of his tongue found her clit and barely touched it. He acknowledged its presence, then swept between her swollen lips with broad sweeps of the flat of his tongue. He lifted her buttocks in his palms and held her up to his mouth, nipping and biting, licking and suckling, and then teased her with open-mouthed kisses on the sensitive flesh of her inner thighs.

Lost in a haze of mind-numbing passion, Lisa spread her legs wider for him. Tinker raised his head and grinned at her. He was slick and shiny around his mouth and chin, covered with her fluids, but he didn't seem to mind. He licked his lips, and she was mesmerized by the sweep of his tongue. Her pussy clenched spasmodically, the inner muscles of her sex rippling as if he were deep inside her.

Tinker nudged first one of her legs and then the other over his shoulders, opening Lisa even more to his view. Then he dipped his head and once more loved her with his mouth.

Lisa heard soft pants and louder moans, and realized the sounds were coming from her throat, incoherent cries of pleasure, building as the sensations built until she realized her voice had become one long, shimmering wail of need.

His tongue flicked over the surface of her clit and then swept deep between her folds, curling up once more to tease her unmercifully. He slipped a finger between her buttocks and pressed against her anus. Not hard, merely a persistent yet provocative pressure that increased as his tongue took her higher, as his lips and teeth drove her closer to the edge. Before long, Lisa hung by a golden thread of glittering arousal, swaying helplessly over a huge abyss. Her body hummed with anticipation. She sensed his determination to watch her fall, knew his intentions even before Tinker covered her clit with his mouth, sucked and tongued her sensitive button just as the blunt tip of his finger finally gained entrance to her backside.

Arching her back and pressing her heels against Tinker's spine, Lisa screamed. Screamed again when he sucked harder at her clit, probed deeper with his tongue and his fingers. There were two in her now, two fingers pressing deep inside her body, stretching her sensitive virgin opening, taking her through a maelstrom of sensation. Higher, more intense, more and more until . . .

She broke. The golden thread parted, turned her body loose, her soul free. Crying, sobbing, gasping for air, Lisa knew she couldn't take anymore, knew her body had reached its saturation point, knew there was room for no more sensation.

Tinker gently freed himself from the grip of her legs, laid her back on the comforter, and then slipped his knit shorts down over his lean hips. If she hadn't felt so enervated from the climaxes he'd just given her, Lisa might have run for cover. He was massive, his cock swollen and dark, a stream of white fluid spilling slowly from the broad head.

She raised her head to look at him and saw naked desire in Tinker's eyes. Amber eyes, just like hers. Like Mary Ellen's.

Like Bay's.

She wondered about that for a moment, wondered at the sense of communion she felt in their similarity, but when Tinker reached for his slacks on the chair beside the bed and grabbed a condom out of the pocket, her focus switched. Lisa watched, fascinated, as he held his cock in one huge fist and slowly rolled the condom over the broad crown and then smoothed it down the thick shaft.

What a shame, she thought, *to cover such a magnificent part of himself.* Yet in the same thought was tender appreciation that he'd thought to protect her.

They'd not exchanged any words, yet Lisa felt as if she knew more about Tinker McClintock than mere conversation might have divulged. He was a thoughtful and caring lover, he saw to her pleasure first, treated her gently, yet with respect. Now, with his need so great that his big body trembled, he still moved slowly, carefully.

She thought of the way she'd been taught to approach the wolves at the sanctuary. Carefully. Quietly, with respect. Exactly the way Tinker McClintock treated Lisa Marie Quinn.

Lisa raised her hips to meet him as Tinker grabbed his sheathed cock in his hand and directed the crown toward her sex. She choked back a moan when he touched her sensitive entrance, then bit her lips to keep from groaning as he slowly, inexorably, forced the broad head of his cock past her swollen lips. She tilted her pelvis for a better angle while Tinker pushed steadily deeper, stretching her just to the point of pain.

Expecting more discomfort as he filled her, Lisa felt nothing but heat and hard male flesh sliding carefully into her moist and swollen sex. His hands trembled where he touched her; his beautiful face was twisted with the effort to ease gently into her body.

Lisa felt awed by the control it must have taken him, to enter her this slowly when his hunger appeared so great, but he didn't rush. Nor did he stop. Lisa forced herself to relax. She consciously welcomed his huge shaft inside, aware of the potential pain of entry on one level, the pleasure he gave her on another.

Finally, panting as if he'd run a mile, sweat pouring from his face, Tinker leaned over Lisa and kissed her. "Are you okay? I'm kind of big. I don't want to hurt you."

She couldn't talk. Had to. Needed to tell him everything was fine, that it was better than fine. It was wonderful, and she wanted him to move now, wanted him to bring her back to that edge of arousal that was like a fire burning from the inside out.

It took her a moment. Lisa swallowed, reached up, and touched his face. Finally she caught her breath. "How can I need you like this? I don't know you." That wasn't what she'd meant to say at all, but she knew it was the truth. Knew she needed him more than air, more than food or water. Lisa traced the lines of his face with the tips of her fingers, touched the bead of perspiration running down his left cheek and brought it to her mouth. He tasted of salt and man, and she wanted to taste more of him, all of him.

"You know me. Better than you realize." He kissed away her confusion until Lisa forgot the question. Slowly he thrust his hips forward, pulled them back. Rocked back and forth, giving her time to adjust, picking up speed with each sway of his hips so that his heavy sac hit her butt with more force on each penetration.

She was crying. Crying so hard she could hardly breathe, but Lisa knew she was smiling at the same time because this was the first man ever to show her stars, the first one to bring her to climax with nothing more than his cock in her sex. The age-old link of man and woman was finally working for Lisa Quinn.

She felt the abyss yawning beneath her again. His size meant he dragged his length across her clit on every inward thrust, connected again each time he withdrew. Lisa thought he went deeper on each downward stroke, and she reveled in the solid pressure of his balls against her buttocks, the surprisingly silky sweep of his pubic hair over her mons. She trembled when the broad head of his cock pressed against her cervix. At that moment, he leaned close and took her nipple between his lips. Sucked hard as he pressed deep.

A charge of pure sensation raced from breast to clit to womb, a shock unlike anything Lisa had ever felt. Shuddering, she hurled herself over the waiting abyss and screamed as her world exploded.

Still Tinker filled her. Harder now, faster, his cock sliding easily through the slick walls of her clenching sex, his strength superior to that of the muscles trying desperately to hold him. Again she peaked, again her body convulsed with the powerful spasms of climax, and still he took her higher, plunged deeper, filled her completely.

Completed the woman who had felt forever fragmented.

Filled a life that had always been empty.

Showed her love, gave her completion, treated her with tenderness and respect. All new, all so unexpected on this day where all had begun as every day before it.

Everything except the memory of last night. The night she'd finally connected with her wolves. An omen? Perhaps. Later. When her mind was no longer fragmented, her body no longer caught in the rhythm of her climax. Later she would try to understand.

Exhausted, sexually depleted yet still caught in the power of her orgasm, Lisa felt Tinker's groan as much as she heard it, a deep, painful sound from deep in his chest. She wrapped her legs around his waist, tying them together as best she could, holding him close. Tinker stiffened in her embrace. She felt the pulsing energy of his ejaculation deep inside, and then something more. Something unbelievable yet magical, impossible but too real to deny.

She felt his orgasm as if she were Tinker, felt the tightening in his balls as he pumped his seed into the condom's reservoir, felt the constriction of her vaginal walls around his cock—only it was Lisa's cock, Lisa's balls, Lisa staring through his eyes, into the eyes of a woman he would love forever. His mate.

Chanku.

The sensation passed, suddenly eclipsed as if a shade had been drawn over the images flashing through her mind. She lay back, wide-eyed, as Tinker fell forward, supporting himself with his elbows before rolling carefully to one side. He slipped out of her, removed the condom, and tossed it into the wastebasket next to her bed. Then he lay beside her and covered his eyes with his forearm.

It took him a minute to catch his breath. Still breathing heavily, he tilted his head to one side, grinned at Lisa, and kissed her. She was hardly able to make her lips respond to his brief touch.

Tinker rolled back over on top of her, using his elbows to keep his weight off her, and gently trapped her legs between his strong thighs. "Okay," he said, smiling broadly. "Now that we have *that* out of the way . . ."

Lisa reached up and touched his lips with her forefinger. "What just happened? *Who are you?*"

Tinker's smile slipped away. She felt his chest rise and fall against her breasts with his sigh. "I don't know. What happened?"

Lisa shook her head slowly from side to side. Her voice sounded scratchy, foreign, but she finally managed to get her thoughts together. "The sex was . . ."

"Magnificent?" Tinker smiled and kissed her, though she noticed he still had that guarded expression on his face.

She couldn't bite back the smile that spread across her face. Didn't want to. "Well, yeah. Of course it was magnificent. Beyond that. I . . ." Lisa shook her head. It sounded crazy. "I felt like I was in . . . in . . ."

"Ah." Tinker grinned as if it all made sense, whatever it was. "We linked. I felt it but wasn't sure if you'd recognize it or not." His hand swept the tangled hair back from her forehead. The look in his eyes melted her heart. "If I needed any more proof of who and what you are, that was it."

"I don't understand. What's going on?" Lisa wriggled out from under Tinker's heavy leg holding her thighs and sat up against the headboard. She pulled a pillow against her middle like a soft shield and wrapped her arms around it. Tinker propped himself up on one elbow, tugged the pillow out of her grasp, and traced patterns on her naked belly.

This was not conducive to a serious conversation. "Are you going to explain what the fuck is happening? I really would like some answers." She folded her arms across her chest, covering her breasts. At least she felt a little less naked this way. A little less vulnerable. She really wanted her pillow back.

Tinker nodded, still smiling like the cat who ate the canary. "That's the whole reason I'm here, you know. To give you answers. Mostly to questions you've never even known to ask." He rolled over and scooted up to lean against the headboard next to Lisa. He stuffed her pillow behind his back. She felt the heat radiating off his big body, saw the pulse in the large vein at his throat, and it took all her willpower not to touch him again.

"I'll start at the beginning, okay? Just hear me out. I really am not nuts, though what I intend to tell you will convince you I must be."

Lisa grinned at his silly but serious admission. If anyone was nuts, it was her, letting a strange man into her bed only minutes after meeting him. She never did things like this. Never. "Okay," she said, nodding seriously. "I'm listening."

"Okay." He took a deep breath, and Lisa was reminded of a little kid getting ready to recite a memorized speech. She managed to keep her opinion to herself.

"Before recorded time, there was an ancient race of people who lived on the rugged plains in Tibet, an area known as the Himalayan Steppe. No one knows where they came from, if they evolved independently or were maybe part of some alien race that got stranded or planted there, but for whatever reason, they lived in that rugged area for millennia before eventually emigrating to other places. They were unique on this planet, though, because they had the ability to shift from one form to another. They called themselves Chanku."

Lisa blinked, remembering. "You called me Chanku. I heard it in my head when we . . . uh, when . . ."

Tinker chuckled softly. "When we climaxed together. That's when the bond between partners is the strongest, at the height of orgasm. I was sure then that you were one of us, that you share the same DNA as me and the other Chanku."

"What do you mean? Like shapeshifters?" Lisa blinked the minute she said that. This entire situation felt surreal, as if it were happening in some grade B horror movie.

Tinker pushed himself away from the headboard and

sat on the edge of the bed. He looked back over his shoulder at her. "That's where it gets tricky. In most situations, I wouldn't be able to tell you any of this until I was absolutely sure of your heritage, but since we know both Baylor and Tala—uh, Mary Ellen—are Chanku, we know you must be as well, and that leaves me free to be a lot more open with you than I normally might. Anyway, the gene is passed through females, so even though your mother never shifted, she had all the components of the Chanku species, as do all her children. You can pass it on; Bay can't."

"Wait a minute." Lisa frowned and grabbed Tinker's forearm. She scooted around to sit next to him, aware of a powerful need to anchor herself and at the same time to touch him. Immediately she felt the strength in him, the tension under his skin. He practically vibrated. "You're telling me that both my brother and sister are shapeshifters? That they can turn into something else besides what they are? Like I'm supposed to believe that?" She shook her head in disbelief. "If you say my mother was Chanku, why didn't she shift? And what's she supposed to have shifted into?"

Tinker covered her hand with his. His palm felt warm. Steady. Unbelievable, when her world felt like it was tilting off its axis. "There are certain grasses growing on the steppes that add nutrients to the Chanku diet, nutrients we need to help a tiny little gland unique to the species develop. Without those nutrients, the person goes through life as a normal human."

He chuckled quietly, as if he laughed at some private joke. "I will admit, most of us, before we found out who and what we are, were pretty screwed up. With the nutrients, everything changed. We're immune to disease. Chanku don't get cancer or any sexually transmitted diseases. Not even head colds. Senses become more acute, an already active libido goes into overdrive, a female gains total reproductive control and is consciously able to release an egg for fertilization—or not. It's entirely up to her. Among the Chanku, it's definitely a woman's world. Anyway, the human becomes fully Chanku. Embraces his or her heritage, the part that has always felt like a missing piece to a convoluted puzzle."

Lisa realized she'd forgotten to breathe. She'd spent her life searching, yet never knowing what she looked for. Was it a part of herself, unfulfilled and incomplete? Was Tinker explaining why she'd always suspected something very important had been missing in her life? Why, then, had her search brought her here, to this lonely outpost in northern Colorado? To a wolf sanctuary run by an eccentric, reclusive millionaire, where her only duties were finding food for the wolves, cleaning their pens, feeding them, observing their behavior?

Tinker stared intently at her, watching her as if he knew she was working through what he'd said and finding her own answers. She gazed into his amber eyes and realized how much they looked like her own. How they reminded her of something else, something wild and free.

Suddenly it all came together. Every question she'd ever had, every dream, every wish. It all finally made perfect sense. As unbelievable as what Tinker McClintock was telling her, Lisa understood exactly who and what she was. Who she could become.

She twisted around and straddled his thighs, gripping both his arms with more strength than she realized she had. "We're wolves, aren't we? We shift and become wolves. It has to be. I've dreamed of running through the woods at night, running with wolves beside me. Last night, for the first time ever, when I sat in the compound, I knew we were communicating, that somehow the wolves recognized a kindred spirit in me. That's it, isn't it? That's who I am? What we are?"

She was crying. She could hardly see Tinker through her tears, but she knew he smiled, felt it in the way his arms came around her, the way he held her against his chest and rubbed her back.

"I thought I was crazy sometimes. Thought I must be losing my mind. When I finally started to get my life together, I gave up a perfectly good job to come here because I had to be with the wolves. The need wouldn't go away. Wouldn't let me rest." She raised her head and wiped her streaming eyes with her wrist. "How? How do you do it? How can I? Tell me!"

He lifted her off his lap as if she weighed nothing, set her back on the edge of the bed, and stepped away. She watched him, her fist jammed in her mouth, blinking back tears and sniffing. She watched his face, saw his smile, realized he'd wavered, twisted, and was suddenly gone.

Lisa bit back a scream as she looked down into the amber eyes of the most beautiful wolf she'd ever seen. Without thinking, she slipped to the floor in front of him, threw her arms around his neck, and buried her fingers in the coarse black fur covering his back. Buried her face in his throat and cried again.

He made a soft *woof* and licked the side of her neck. Lisa rubbed her face in his thick fur and suddenly broke into a fit of giggles. "Oh crap." She sat back on her heels and held her hands over her face. "I'm wiping my snotty nose in your fur. That's about the tackiest thing I think I've ever done, and believe me, I've done tacky!"

The wolf shook his head, and his long tongue lolled out the side of his mouth. Lisa was almost certain he was laughing at her. She scooted back across the floor and sat and stared at him. He was beautiful. Huge, with glistening black fur that shimmered with gold highlights when he moved. His paws were big and broad, the nails tipped in black. He leaned close and licked her neck again, then backed away, shimmered, and shifted.

Once again, Tinker stood in front of her. He held out a hand and pulled Lisa to her feet. "I was afraid I'd frighten you."

"Never. My God, you're beautiful when you do that!"

"What? And chopped liver when I don't?" He laughed, a big booming sound that seemed to destroy whatever tension might have remained in the room.

"I want to do that. I want to be a wolf. How? What do I need to do?" She'd figure out the details later, figure out why she wasn't afraid, why this all seemed so logical, something that was obviously impossible and couldn't have actually happened right here in her bedroom.

Tinker pulled Lisa down on his lap as he sat back on the edge of the bed. She felt his cock pressing into her thigh, but he wasn't as big now. Not soft either, but at least not huge. She liked the way it felt, nestled there against her.

"I've got the supplements in my car," he said. "Take one capsule a day and you could have the ability to shift within the week. For Tia Mason, it only took about three or four days. Shannon Murphy did it in three, but that was damned fast. I don't know how long it took your sister."

"Who's Tia? And Shannon . . . who is she?"

"Other members of the pack. Both of them are Chanku." Tinker cupped her face in his hands. When he spoke, there was no sign of laughter in his voice. Nothing but raw emotion and a need so rich it made Lisa tremble.

"There is so much I want to tell you, so many things you need to know. Right now, though . . . now, I need to make love to you again. I have to feel your body taking mine deep inside, feel your heart beating next to mine. I realize you don't know me, that you don't have the same emotions about this, but I feel as if I've waited for you my entire life."

Lisa touched the side of his face, ran her fingers over his

closely cropped hair, then leaned close and kissed him. "I do understand, though. I feel the same way about you. It's scary, really. Very scary stuff, but I can't wait to know you better. To understand myself better. How long can you stay? Stay with me, Tinker. The bed's almost big enough."

She laughed, looked at the queen-size bed that wasn't nearly enough room for a man his size, then glanced back at Tinker. The look on his face went straight to her heart.

"Are you sure? I mean . . . how do we explain me to your coworkers? Your boss."

Lisa thought about it a minute, tapping one finger against her jaw. The answer was obvious, though it definitely went against her sexual history. "You're an old boyfriend, and I'm giving you a second chance. Does that work for you?"

"I'll make it work. Make love to me."

She laughed. Felt complete joy for the first time in forever. "That was a quick recovery."

He twisted her meaning and glanced down at his cock. It jutted out from its nest of silky black hair, as large and hard as it had been when he'd loved her only minutes ago. "I always recover quickly." He grinned when he said it. Then he set Lisa aside, stood up, and reached for his pants. He dug in the pocket for a condom. "And I'm always prepared."

He stood there beside the chair looking cocky and self-assured with the foil packet in his hand. Lisa gave him a sideways glance, dropped to her knees, and grabbed him around the thick base of his erection before he realized her intentions. She threaded her fingers through the unusually silky curls at the base and looked up into his glittering eyes. "So am I, Mr. McClintock. So am I."

When she took him in her mouth, he groaned and reached for the wall for support. The thick muscles on the tops of his thighs jumped. Lisa heard the soft thunk of the wrapped condom hitting the floor as Tinker dropped it to weave the fingers of his free hand into her hair. It still felt surreal. The entire morning carried a dreamlike quality about it.

She'd been shoveling roadkill into her pickup and now this.

Of course, hadn't her life always been a little off the wall? A bit on the edge? She glanced up and watched Tinker's face for a moment while gently licking the soft underside of his glans. His eyes were closed, his head thrown back and pressed against the wall. Dark and perfectly formed against the light wood paneling, he looked like a god to her. His body so beautifully sculpted, his taste calling her, his masculine scent weaving its own perfect spell. She stroked his thigh, ran her fingers along the ridge of muscle that stretched across the top. She felt it jump beneath her touch and heard his soft groan.

Perfect. A perfect stranger, but nothing had ever felt so right before. Lisa wrapped her tongue around Tinker McClintock's perfect cock and decided to follow her destiny, whatever it was, wherever it decided to take her.

Chapter 4

Tinker's entire body shuddered when Lisa's lips wrapped around the flared end of his cock. Her slim fingers rested first on the tops of his thighs, tickling the dark hairs sprinkled over his legs, and then moved slowly, stroking the line between his thigh and groin before skimming lower over his sensitive skin. Slowly, so slowly he almost cried, she wrapped her fingers around his sac, stroking the tender balls inside. His fingers tightened in her hair.

Tinker groaned when she lightly squeezed and then released him, mimicking the rhythm of her mouth. He practically whimpered when she held him in both her hands, fingers wrapping around his ball sac, lifting him up, stroking the base of his cock and slowly rolling each testicle between her fingers.

His knees quivered, and he knew he needed more than the wall for support; but before his legs gave out, Lisa sucked him deep, then withdrew. The cool burst of air on his hot, damp length cooled him enough to reach for a bit more control. He knew it wouldn't last.

Lisa looked up at him with glittering eyes. "Take me. I want you inside me now. Please!"

It was more a demand than a request. Lisa's fingers fumbled with the condom he'd dropped on the floor, and she finally tore the wrapper with her teeth. Tinker's chest was heaving like he'd run a mile, and his cock was hard, the blood inside pounding in time with his raging heart. He ached with need. His cock curved up until the tip of it brushed his belly. Even that simple touch made him fight for control. Glancing down at Lisa kneeling between his feet almost took him across the finish.

She was so beautiful. Her hair fell across her shoulders and curled over her small breasts. She peered at him out of those gorgeous wolf eyes and licked her moist lips with the tip of her tongue. He had to have her, had to bury himself inside her now.

Tinker reached for the condom, but Lisa grabbed his cock in her fist and slowly rolled the rubber over his length. He gritted his teeth, so sensitive now that her gentle touch and the soft pull of the rubber against his damp skin took him even closer to that sensual precipice.

Lisa grinned up at him, then palmed her breasts, lifting the small peaks up for his view.

"Oh shit. You don't have to tempt me. It's too late for that." Tinker grabbed Lisa under the arms, lifted her up, and turned her around. He bent her over the edge of the rumpled bed. Her smooth bottom was flushed, the line of her backbone running down to the crease between her buttocks; it was so tempting Tinker dropped to his knees and nipped at one perfect globe.

She arched her back and spread her legs wide for him, opening completely, showing off her swollen lips surrounded by a thick nest of dark hair. Tinker pushed her higher up on the bed so that her feet no longer touched the floor. He grabbed a pillow and shoved it under her belly, lifting her higher, opening her wider.

Then he knelt behind her once again and took her with his mouth, licking from her clit to her ass in long, slick sweeps before concentrating on her labia and the hot depths of her sex. He wished she were capable of shifting so he could become the wolf as well. He'd use his long tongue to delve deep inside her slick heat, but it seemed wrong to take her that way now.

No, she had to have made the shift herself, had to understand the sentience behind the beast or it would somehow feel like a bestial act. That wouldn't work. He didn't want anything uncomfortable between them.

Her flavors inflamed him. Tinker nipped her buttock again and she cried out. He rose to his feet quickly, unable to wait any longer. His cock was still high and hard, and he grabbed himself and pressed against the slick opening of her sex, pressed hard until she gasped with what could have been pain or pleasure or a mixture of both.

He felt the hot sheath of her pussy close around the head of his cock. Felt the ripples of clenching muscle holding him, drawing him deeper. He thrust hard, finding the perfect angle for penetration, filling her in one long slow plunge that took him as far as he could go into her welcoming body. Finally his cock pressed up against the hard curve of her womb. He pictured the tiny eye in the end of his cock meeting up with the small opening of her cervix, and the image made his balls draw up even tighter between his legs.

He wrapped his hands around her upper thighs, and Lisa raised her hips against his thrust, tightened her thighs around the hard line of his hips. He thrust into her hard and fast, driven like a wild man trying to claim her, to take her so that she'd never want another man, never need a woman in her bed, never need anyone but himself. He wanted to mark her body, her soul, her every thought, and make them his.

Tinker leaned over her back, set his teeth against her left shoulder, and bit. Lisa screamed and climaxed; her body shuddered beneath his weight, and Tinker felt himself flying off the edge as well, felt the painful pressure in his balls release in long bursts, and then he saw the brilliant light of her thoughts. As his body convulsed in unbelievable pleasure, Tinker merged with Lisa Quinn, a link more profound than anything he'd ever experienced.

It was so intense it could have been a bonding, but Tinker knew it couldn't happen. Not yet. Not until her body changed, not until the metamorphosis from human to shapeshifter was complete.

Still, he felt her orgasm as if it were his own, knew she shared the deep throbbing in his body, the almost painful tightening of his balls within their sac, even as her vaginal walls compressed and held his cock. Their sensations melded, their minds linked. With one last roll of his hips, Tinker licked the mark he'd left on Lisa's shoulder and collapsed across her back.

Driving back to the sanctuary with Tinker riding beside her, Lisa felt punch-drunk. The mark on her shoulder tingled, and she knew it would leave a bruise. Tinker hadn't broken the skin, but the implications of ownership were not lost on her. With any other person, she might have been angry, but oddly enough, his mark of possession left her feeling warm and protected.

She'd have to figure that one out later. They'd showered and grabbed a quick lunch, and Lisa had taken her first pill, a big ugly looking capsule that smelled like alfalfa and tasted worse. After she choked it down, they talked like old friends and Lisa had caught up on news of Baylor and Mary Ellen. It wasn't easy to think of her little sister as Tala, a shapeshifting Chanku now living with two men. Leave it to Mary Ellen to do things her own way!

"I don't get it," she said, glancing to her right for another quick look at Tinker. Damn, but the man was gorgeous, especially now that he'd changed into more casual clothing. His jeans hugged his legs and butt like a second skin, and the dark blue T-shirt he'd put on fit his massive chest as if he'd sprayed it on. Lisa noticed that his nipples, small though they were, left an outline on the fabric. She thought for a moment about licking him through the soft cotton, then forced her mind back to their conversation.

Mary Ellen. She'd been asking about her sister. "The guys Mary Ellen ended up with were a bonded pair, which I assume means the same as marriage, which tells me they must be gay. But they've bonded with Mary Ellen, too? It doesn't compute, if you get my drift."

"When you're Chanku, it's not all that simple. Not that cut-and-dried." Tinker twisted in the front seat and angled his big body so that he looked right at her.

Lisa glanced to her right and caught him watching her. The knowledge, the sense of possession in his gorgeous amber eyes sent a shiver along Lisa's spine, made her want to pull over to the side of the road and rip Tinker's clothes off for a quick fuck. No, make that long and leisurely . . . The fantasy was so good she actually felt her nipples harden and poke against her cotton T-shirt. Her panties were already soaked. Lisa bit the inside of her cheek, an intentional sharp nip back to reality.

Tinker chuckled. When she slanted another quick look in his direction, he was grinning, but thankfully he didn't say anything about her obvious spike of arousal. After their discussion over lunch, Lisa realized that he was fully aware when she was damp, even knew exactly what part of her menstrual cycle she was in. That was, of course, if she believed everything he told her.

So far, he'd not given her any reason to disbelieve anything, except maybe her own sanity. The sex alone was enough to make a believer out of her. She'd never experienced anything like she had today with any man or woman, much less with a man who was basically a stranger.

"Chanku, as a whole, are polyamorous, and there's no such thing as gay or lesbian or straight, though a bonded pair will only breed with each another. We can feel physically attracted to almost anyone, though never as strongly as to our bonded mate, but that relationship is bound by love as well as the bonding link." Tinker reached out and ran his finger along her right shoulder, down her arm to her wrist. Goose bumps followed his touch and Lisa shivered.

"Our sex drive is so highly tuned, our ability to arouse and remain aroused so much a part of our makeup, that we find our sexual release whenever and wherever we can. Mik and AJ bonded long before they met Tala, and while they always preferred each other, they never have been averse to sex with a willing female . . . or male." Tinker chuckled.

Lisa sensed he remembered something special. "Like you?"

Tinker nodded, completely without shame. "Oh yeah." There was a lot of feeling in his answer. The image of his perfect body sandwiched between two equally beautiful men almost made Lisa drive off the road.

"Those two are something else. You haven't had sex until you've been tag-teamed by Mik and AJ."

This time Lisa laughed. "I don't know. What we've been up to this morning was pretty spectacular. I take it they tagged Mary Ellen."

Tinker's laugh was filled with memories. "Actually, I think it was the other way around. Neither Mik nor AJ expected to fall in love with a woman because they'd already bonded with each other, but that little gal has both of them wrapped around her pinky finger. I imagine they'll be setting up their own pack at some point, though for now they're staying in the Pack Dynamics apartments, or at least they will be when they get back from visiting Baylor, Shannon, and Jake in Maine. We all live in the San Francisco apartments—me, Lucien Stone, Tia Mason, AJ, Mik, and Tala. It's a good place. You'll like it."

Lisa's head snapped around. "What do you mean, I'll like it?"

Tinker shrugged. "I want you to come back with me,

once you complete the change to Chanku and can shift. Not necessarily to stay, but I do want you to meet the others. For one thing, you'll need to talk to the women so you'll know what to expect, how your body will work once the Chanku genes take over."

Lisa took a deep breath, aware on an almost visceral level of the huge step she'd taken with that one brown pill. The fact that, when all of this finally happened, she would no longer be completely human. At least not human like she was now. She felt her heart rate speed up and wondered if she'd made a horrible mistake, wondered if . . . no. It was too late to think about decisions already made and roads already taken.

"What about you?" she asked. "Will you be going back?" Lisa drove into the sanctuary grounds and parked under a big pine tree. She shut off the engine, then turned and stared at Tinker.

"That will depend on you. Wherever you go, I want to be."

Lisa shook her head, totally confused by the powerful sense of commitment in Tinker's words. "You've known me for what, two hours? How can you say that?"

He shrugged and looked away. "I just know it. Know how I feel. You're the one I want."

The certainty in his voice was almost frightening. Lisa frowned. "What if I don't want you?"

Tinker's sigh was audible in the small cab of the Jeep. When he turned back to her, his smile was sad. "I guess I never thought of that. Is it the race thing? Are you uncomfortable with me because I'm black? I've been wolf for so long. Being Chanku blurs the racial lines for us. It makes the race thing trivial, but if my being black is a prob—"

"What?" Lisa laughed, and shook her head. "Oh God, no, I'm not uncomfortable because of your race. I actually thought we looked damned sexy together, and face it, the sex is very hot."

Lisa realized she was blushing. Now she was the one who sighed. "That's my problem. I've only had girl relationships. I've always thought of myself as lesbian. I'm not so sure about this polyamorous stuff. I honestly don't know how I'd be in any kind of long-term relationship with a man, or from what you've described, a group of men." She put her hand on his thigh and caressed the soft denim of his jeans. She felt the strength and warmth of his muscles beneath her palm, found herself staring at the back of her hand and the way her fingers molded his leg. She couldn't look him in the eye when she admitted, "Then, again, you're very convincing."

When Lisa looked up at him, Tinker was grinning broadly. "We'll just take things one day at a time," he said. "In the meantime, let's go with the old boyfriend bit." Tinker got out of the Jeep as Lisa climbed out on her side. He walked around the back and grabbed her hand, then pulled her into his arms for a kiss.

His unexpected move caught her so by surprise, Lisa met him with her mouth open. Tinker took full advantage. His lips felt mobile and warm, slanting firmly across her mouth, his tongue finding entrance with one quick thrust. One hand held her solidly between the shoulders; the other cupped the rounded curve of her ass. He ended the kiss just as quickly as he'd begun and turned her loose, then winked at her, throwing her totally off balance. "You realize," he said, his voice huskier than usual, "no boyfriend of yours in his right mind would ever be an ex. I can't imagine anyone letting you go."

She didn't have an answer for that. Couldn't do anything but stare into his dark, amber eyes and feel as if the map of her life had suddenly reconfigured itself, as if her future were no longer in her own hands.

No, it was now in the hands of this very sexy, very unusual man. Something Lisa had sworn she'd never allow. The memory of her mother and her many lovers flitted through Lisa's mind. Flitted in and shoved out as quickly as possible. Still blinking like a woman in a daze, Lisa took Tinker's hand and led him into the High Mountain office.

Hal Anderson took care of the dazed feeling the minute Tinker held open the door for Lisa to enter ahead of him.

"Where the hell were you? I've been looking all over for you, Quinn."

Lisa glanced at Tinker. His body stiffened, and he appeared ready to punch out the little jerk. She winked at him to let him know everything was under control, and then she scowled at Anderson. "I went home to shower. I needed to clean up after collecting roadkill this morning. Why? What do you want me for?"

"Who's he?" Hal glared at Tinker and pointed rudely at him.

Lisa might have laughed at the little man's posturing if he didn't piss her off so much. Millie West, the secretary sitting quietly behind Hal, rolled her eyes. Millie had never been all that sociable, but she'd worked here longer than anyone and had obviously had her fill of Anderson.

"*He* happens to be a friend—actually an old boyfriend of mine. He's here visiting for a while." She turned to Tinker. "Martin McClintock," she said, adding as much contempt as she could to her voice, "this is Hal Anderson, the sanctuary's on-site supervisor. The woman behind him is Millie West. She actually runs the place."

Anderson glared at Lisa when she mentioned Millie, who waved to acknowledge Tinker, then returned to her work.

Tinker merely smiled and waved at Millie as if there were no tension at all. "Nice to meet you, Ms. West, Hal. Call me Tinker." He held out his hand, and after waiting just long enough to be impolite, Anderson reached out for a quick shake.

"Old boyfriend, huh? Didn't think you had any of those, considering your preferences, Quinn." Lisa ignored Anderson's rude comment. He directed his next words to Tinker. "I hope you realize Lisa's got a schedule she needs to keep. She's an employee here, not one of the volunteers." Anderson glared at Lisa, and she fought an overwhelming urge to stick her tongue out at him.

Childish, but it might have made her feel better. The guy was an idiot. She'd disliked him from the moment they'd met. So unlike the immediate connection she'd felt with Tinker.

"I've been looking all over for you."

Lisa jerked her attention from Tinker back to her supervisor. "Why? I wasn't gone more than a couple hours."

"Did you leave the fenced compound like I told you last night?"

Lisa frowned, unsure what was coming. "Of course I did. And I shut the gate behind me and locked it."

"We're missing another wolf."

"What?" Lisa looked at Tinker, then back to Hal. "Which one? What pack?"

"The ones in that same enclosure where I saw you. You're sure you didn't let one out?"

The look Anderson gave her was filled with suspicion. As if he'd think she might turn a wolf loose around here? The animal wouldn't last a week, not with all the trigger-happy hunters in the area. "Of course I didn't. Which wolf is missing?"

"One of the half-grown pups. A male. The biggest of the litter. I think it's number two-sixty-one. When one of the volunteers fed them this morning, only three pups showed up with the adults. We checked the area and couldn't find the missing pup. We did, however, find fresh tire tracks near the back fence."

"Tire tracks? Like maybe someone stole him? But why?"

"You tell me."

Lisa ignored Anderson's pointed comment. She turned to Tinker and grabbed his hand. "That's the fifth wolf to go missing since I've been here. We can't figure how they're getting out. The gates are locked and the fences too high for them to jump. No one's reported a wolf running wild, and believe me, we'd be the first to hear about it."

"You neglected to tell your friend that the first wolf disappeared just after you started working here." Anderson let the comment hang in the still air, then spun around and headed back to the office. "Get to work. The temporary holding pens on the north side need cleaning. Don't say anything yet about the missing animal. I don't want word to get out until we figure out what the hell is going on." He slammed his door. The loud crack punctuated his order.

Once outside in the warm sunlight, Tinker wrapped an arm around Lisa as she let out a deep, long-held breath. He sensed her disbelief and heard a quaver in her voice.

"He's such a jerk. He's accusing me of turning the wolves free or, even worse, stealing them. He knows I hate the fact they're caged, but what other life is there for them? Most of the animals have been socialized by humans too much to survive in the wild. That pup's parents were raised in an apartment. The female was pregnant when they were brought here by animal control, and she had the four pups here at the sanctuary. That pup's never even lived wild. I'd never dream of turning him loose or taking him." Lisa turned and looked at Tinker, her face so forlorn it made his heart ache.

"You don't know for sure he's accusing you, sweetie. It doesn't matter. You know and I know you would never let them out."

"But that's the fifth wolf now. Five of them gone since I started working here. Most of these animals were kept illegally as pets or captured when they were puppies. They don't know how to survive in the wild. This sanctuary is the best place for them. Some of the wolves were kept in dark basements or tiny apartments or tied all day long in hot backyards. Damn people." Lisa pulled out of Tinker's light grasp and headed across the dusty parking lot, kicking up little puffs of red dust with every step. "I can't figure how they got out, unless someone actually stole them. It doesn't make any sense to turn them loose. Someone would report wolves running free. I don't know what to think."

"It's a big forest. Could they just disappear?"

Lisa shook her head. "This one is still a pup. He'd want to stay close to his family, at least for another year or so. I wish I knew what was going on."

"Ask them."

"What?" Lisa spun around in midstep and stared at Tinker. He grinned back at her.

"You heard me. We'll ask them. I'm not sure you can do it yet, but I might have some luck. They may not be able to communicate everything, but I imagine they've got some ideas of where their packmates go, or at least how they get out."

"You mean you can talk to them? To the wolves?" The look on her face was priceless.

"Didn't you tell me you thought you were communicating? Take that a few steps further and imagine understanding the visuals they give you. The mental images make more sense to Chanku because, once you've shifted, you understand what they mean. It's like a whole new communications center in your brain. I'm not promising we'll learn anything useful, but I'd at least like to try."

Lisa threw her arms around Tinker's neck and kissed him. "You're amazing, did you know that? Absolutely amazing."

He laughed and held her close, kissed her back. "Of course I am, sweetie. And don't you forget it."

* * *

Lisa stood silently behind him as Tinker stared at the three temporary quarantine pens lined up in a shaded area. Seeing the beautiful animals caged instead of free saddened him, though he knew this was their last chance for survival. Each one had access to its own indoor kennel, and stout chain-link fencing divided each space. One dark gray wolf paced restlessly in the first enclosure. In the second, an older animal with a white face and blue eyes sat silently in a corner, watching them. A pair of pale gray wolves lay together in the final pen, so perfectly matched Tinker knew they had to be siblings.

"I know you've got really large enclosures here. Why are these in such small pens?" He glanced at Lisa, then turned his attention back to the animals.

"They're recent arrivals. Still in quarantine, actually. The two over here were captured as pups and raised in a tiny apartment until they got too big and too dangerous for their owner. They haven't got a clue how to be wolves, much less survive in the wild. The one with the blue eyes is a crossbreed, about ten percent husky and the rest wolf, and this big fellow was humanely trapped after showing a preference for fresh lamb."

Tinker raised an eyebrow. "On the hoof?"

Lisa nodded. "Yep. Normally he would have been shot as a predator, but luckily there's at least one sheep rancher who believes in live trapping and removal. That's pretty unusual, but we'll take it. Most ranchers think the only good wolf is a dead wolf."

"They're beautiful animals. I hate seeing them in such small quarters."

"It's temporary. If they can get along penned this closely, we may be able to release them all into one of the larger enclosures together. So far they're tolerating one another, which is a hopeful sign. They are, after all, pack animals."

The wolves paid Tinker little attention. The crossbreed in the middle pen watched him, but when Tinker opened his mind to the creature's thoughts, he found nothing beyond a sense of confusion at the strange surroundings.

The older wolf continued to pace, but his mind was sharper, the images more frantic as he weighed various methods of escape. Tinker tried to catch the creature's attention with his thoughts, but the wolf merely slanted him an angry glance and continued to pace.

Lisa touched Tinker's forearm. "Any luck? I need to get them into their individual kennels so I can clean out the pens."

He shook his head. "No, though if these are new arrivals, they might not know anything. The older gray's the only one who might make any sense, but he's really agitated right now."

Lisa laughed as she dug into the bucket of scraps she'd brought with her. "They've only been here a week or so. This will calm the old guy down. They usually fall asleep after I feed them." She walked around the back of the kennels and tossed meat scraps into the first one.

The pair of wolves scented the air, stood up, and sniffed the doorway leading into the enclosed kennel, then slipped through the opening. Lisa quickly shut the door and trapped them inside. She repeated the process with the other two animals until all of them were safely inside their kennels eating. Grabbing a rake and a shovel off the wall, Lisa handed the rake to Tinker and opened the gate to the first enclosure.

The sun beat down on them as they finished up the last of the three pens. "How'd you get all the good jobs?" Tinker leaned on his shovel and grinned at Lisa.

She returned his smile with a glare. "Ask Hal. He does the assignments. So far, beyond feeding and general maintenance, I appear to be in charge of the daily search for fresh roadkill and wolf poop cleanup. Even Seth gets better assignments, and he's just a kid."

"A kid with a big crush on you." Tinker leaned the shovel against the fence, grabbed the rake, and smoothed over the gravel in the pen. "Of course, it's easy to see why he's hot for you."

"I think Seth's at an age where he's hot for anything female." Lisa laughed and then shrugged. "He's a good kid, but he's awfully immature. The job here's good for him." She rinsed out the last water bowl and refilled it. "You almost done? These guys hate being locked up."

"Is it really necessary, putting them inside kennels every time you clean the pens?"

The wolves paced impatiently back and forth inside the indoor kennels. The shadows of their noses were visible when they sniffed under the doors. Lisa sensed their anxiety, but it was a necessary part of maintenance.

"It's too dangerous for us to clean the pens with them loose in here. These enclosures are so small, and the only animals we keep here are the new ones. We can't be sure how they'll act. It's different in the big compounds. They've got lots of acres to run there, so they don't have that fear of being cornered. In here, they're just too unpredictable."

Lisa finished up and turned off the hose. Though everything was automatic, water bowls had to be washed daily and each pen cleaned and checked carefully to make sure they were secure and the wolves couldn't escape.

"It's really strange." Lisa glanced at Tinker with a new appreciation for the plight of the captive wolves. "I keep thinking I'm going to actually know what these guys are thinking, how they're feeling, before very long. Certainly gives me a different outlook on keeping these guys penned. They should be free and they're not." She checked the gates, then glanced over her shoulder at Tinker. Damn. He actually listened to her as if what she said mattered. She felt an unexpected spike in awareness. Was there anything about him that *didn't* turn her on? "Once their quarantine is over, they'll have plenty of room to roam, and even rabbits to hunt."

It might not be freedom, but thanks to Mr. Dunlop's generosity, it was the closest thing. Not many sanctuaries were blessed with as much open space as High Mountain. If only she could figure out how the wolves were getting out—or, if someone was stealing them, who the hell it was.

Her thoughts kept returning to Hal Anderson. He was always pointing the finger at her. But what if he was the one? She'd run into him out near the enclosures after dark on more than one occasion. He always claimed to be checking on the animals, but he drove a truck. She wondered if anyone had compared tire tracks?

Lisa stared off in the direction of the main part of the sanctuary, the area where the free-roaming packs lived in their ten- to twenty-acre enclosures, then glanced back at Tinker. "We need to get you into the big pens. The animals there won't be as stressed, and you might be able to read them. Besides, that's where the wolves are going missing."

"Tonight?"

"I think so. We have to make sure Anderson doesn't find out. If I get fired, we'll never figure out what's going on."

Chapter 5

A couple nights later, Lisa shivered in the darkness as Tinker scaled the chain-link fence surrounding one of the enclosures far from the main entrance to the sanctuary. She wasn't cold, not with her cargo pants and long-sleeved shirt to protect against mosquitoes, but fear of someone catching them doing what was so blatantly against the rules had her nerves beyond the edge.

Night before last, their first night out, they'd almost been caught. She still wasn't sure why Anderson had been out driving the service road after midnight. Luckily she'd hidden in time, and Tinker had been with the wolves.

The second night had gone smoother, but Tinker hadn't learned anything of importance. Maybe tonight?

Lisa focused the pale glow of her flashlight on Tinker. "This thing needs new batteries. I can hardly see you."

Tinker snorted. "Blame the bad batteries on Tia. I got them from her."

"I can't wait to meet poor Tia. You blame everything on her."

"Only because she's not here to defend herself. Actually, I can't wait for you to meet her. I think you two will get along really well." He posed in the pale beam, then turned his back, stripped off his underwear, and shook his butt for Lisa's entertainment. "In fact, you'll probably like Tia more than you like me."

"I doubt that."

"Wait until you see her. She's gorgeous and she's hot."

Lisa tilted her head and looked at him. Was he serious? "Does that bother you, that I might think she's gorgeous and hot, too?"

"Hell, no. Does it bother you that Tia thinks I'm gorgeous and hot?" Laughing, Tinker wadded up his shorts and tossed them back over the fence to her. They'd teased about him snagging something important on the sharp wire at the top. Joke or not, Lisa was glad he hadn't scaled the fence with any of his impressive parts dangling loose.

"No." Lisa shook her head. "Actually, it turns me on." She caught the warm cotton in her hands and pressed closer to the fence to hear Tinker's whisper.

"Touché." His expression went from teasing to serious in a heartbeat. "The pack must be deeper in the forest. I can sense them, but they're not close. Will you be okay until I get back? Watch out for Anderson. That dude makes me nervous. I might be gone an hour or more."

Lisa nodded and then reached her fingers through the metal links. Tinker pressed closer, until she touched his chest, just above his heart. Her fingers looked so pale next to his dark skin, almost ghostly in the dim glow of her flashlight. His heart was a steady beat beneath her fingertips, and she felt cheated not to be able to kiss him there. Tinker covered her hand with his, then squeezed her fingers, released them, and stepped away.

His thoughts came into her mind, clear now, as clear as speech. He called it *mindtalking*. Lisa had never known anything as intimate as the soft cadence of his voice in her mind.

Just yesterday he'd not been nearly as clear to her.

Six months in the life of a wolf is a long time, but they have excellent memories. Once I find them, I'll see if they can tell me anything.

She nodded, then concentrated on *sending* her answer to him. Already it was getting easier to communicate this way. More natural and absolutely mind-blowing. *A male disappeared from this pen. Full grown and very wild. He was the pack's alpha. The others should remember him.*

Tinker's grin told her he'd understood her thoughts. He'd entered a different enclosure last night, but the wolves there had been too curious about the stranger in their midst to concern themselves with his questions. When he shifted, they'd snarled and growled, then gone down on their bellies with ears laid back against their skulls in obvious submission to the huge, black wolf appearing suddenly in their midst.

Once the wolves had sniffed and whined and groveled, all they'd wanted to do was play. After a while, Tinker had taken off at a fast run with the others on his heels while Lisa waited in the shadows, watching them until they were out of sight. She'd felt the first stirrings of jealousy, watching Tinker run with the wolves. Odd, how she was more jealous of his ability to shift than she was of the mysterious Tia he talked about so often. Of course, Tinker fully expected Lisa and Tia to end up having sex. Amazing.

She'd still rather run with the wolves! Damn, how she wanted to be there, racing beside him with her great plume of a tail stroking the air behind her. She looked at Tinker now, so beautiful and yet so perfectly male, and felt an immediate response in her sex. Her body pulsed there, a low, slow clenching of muscles suddenly aroused and needy, the quick rush of moisture between her legs.

Tinker raised his head and his nostrils flared. She heard his low chuckle, saw the thickening in his cock as he responded to her scent. He flattened his palm over its rising length and forced it back down between his legs. *I'd better go, or I won't be able to leave.*

Lisa bit her lips to keep from laughing. *Just go. I'll be fine.* She wrapped her arms around her waist and stepped back. Now, after three days and three of the huge pills, after watching Tinker change numerous times from human to wolf and back again, Lisa thought she would be used to the process. She wasn't. Watching Tinker shift still sent shivers along her arms and raised the tiny hairs at the back of her neck. It was nothing short of magical, from the time he shed his clothing and displayed his truly magnificent body to the swift shimmer of form and shape and the even faster morph from human to beast.

Just as magical was the sex they shared when he returned. Lisa tried to imagine what it would be like with her own healthy libido ramped up a few more notches from the Chanku influence.

Impossible.

This entire relationship, if she could call it that, was magical. Was he the one? The one she'd always dreamed would someday come into her life?

She'd always believed there was someone, somewhere, who would love her, but she'd certainly never thought it would be a man. Lisa still remembered her first sexual experience—it had been with another girl. She'd been about twelve at the time, her older neighbor at least fourteen but obviously much more experienced. She'd made it special for Lisa, and they'd stayed friends and lovers for years. She still thought of women first when she was aroused, still found herself attracted to women.

Women were safe. They couldn't get you pregnant and were a lot less complicated. Even though she'd tried sex with men and even enjoyed a few satisfactory encounters, Lisa had never fallen in love. What was the point?

Men never hung around for long.

So why did she think of home when she thought of Tinker? Why did she find herself fantasizing that he actually meant what he said when he promised to make her his mate? He would leave her. Men always left women. Hadn't her mother beat that into her? Of course, her mother didn't really want men to hang around all that long. She was married, after all, though Lisa's father was gone more often than not. Marriage hadn't stopped her mother from a steady parade of bed partners, including the postman, who'd been in her bed when Lisa's father finally showed up—this time with a shotgun.

There'd been blood. So damned much blood, and Lisa had stood there in the doorway with her fist in her mouth to stop the screams, her ears ringing from the blast of the gun. Even now she shuddered with the image of red blossoming outward, covering the walls, the bed, the bodies of the man and woman locked together in passion, linked permanently in death.

Lisa shook herself free of the memory, took a deep breath, and concentrated on Tinker. She inhaled again, aware of something different. A difference so subtle, she wasn't sure at first if it was her imagination or something real and physical. Tinker's gaze locked with hers for a moment. His eyes seemed brighter, more feral.

Lisa watched his body shimmer and turn, a change that happened in a heartbeat. She sensed feelings beyond the shift she loved to watch and realized there was something familiar about it tonight that left her with a powerful urge to follow. A compelling need, but no map of the way, no clear instructions how to make the switch. It came to her between one heartbeat and another, a feeling so sure and sweet Lisa wondered why she'd not felt it before.

She wanted to be with the man she was beginning to love, wanted to be like him for all time, but she couldn't quite figure it out.

Not yet. But it was close. So very, very close.

Lisa noticed a strange, crawling sensation under her skin. It felt more like a trail of ants than the expected rippling of muscle and nerves. She rubbed frantically along the tops of her arms, scratching angry red furrows in her dry skin, but it did nothing to ease the itchy, crawly sensation.

She glanced up as Tinker yipped in acknowledgment and then turned and ran off into the darkness in search of the pack. Lisa stood perfectly still, absorbing the sensation of something beyond what had just happened. Yes, Tinker had become a wolf, but there was more. Some strange sense she couldn't quite grasp, some new reality just beyond her touch.

The feeling grew. Her pulse raced, and she realized she actually heard her heart thudding in her chest. She cocked her head to one side and listened for the sound of blood racing through her veins, then grinned at herself. Impossible. This was all so silly and impossible, yet she felt it, the burning energy that raised the hairs on her arms and scalp, the overwhelming awareness of her own body, of the mechanics of this bundle of flesh and nerves and bone that housed the spirit of Lisa Quinn.

She was rocking now, back and forth on the balls of her feet, alone in the darkness with the flashlight grasped in her hand and her arms wrapped tightly around her middle. She felt as if hours had gone by but knew only seconds had passed. Tinker, now in the form of a beautiful black wolf, ran in what appeared to be slow-motion across the meadow toward the forest—legs stretching out, mouth open—and time stood still.

Lisa panted, each breath bursting between her parted lips in rapid succession. This was it. This was the dream she'd held, the dream Tinker had offered with his tales of a shapeshifting species and his ugly brown capsules. She felt it, absorbed it, *became* the moment and recognized it for what it was: the birth of her new life. The first true stirrings of her enhanced Chanku senses.

It was dark, the moon not yet up, but she saw Tinker clearly beyond the feeble glow from her flashlight, so far across the dark meadow. Time resurfaced. He raced now, full tilt, slipping between the trees and disappearing in thick brush.

She shook her head in disbelief. Then, hands trembling with the power of sensations like nothing she'd ever imagined, Lisa shut the flashlight off and gasped. Darkness blossomed into stark images, and the world around her burst into life. Stunned, heart pounding, breath hissing faster in short, nervous gasps, Lisa spun in place. Her long hair had fallen loose, and it slowly whipped about her shoulders as she marveled at a night no longer dark, at individual sounds emerging, clear and distinct, from what had been a blended symphony of sound.

She picked out the croak of tree frogs and knew where they sat. She heard the high-pitched squeak of bats and the sound of their wings on the still currents of the air. An owl hooted, then another, and she knew they were different, how far apart in the woods they perched, knew when one dropped from his branch and soared low over the small meadow where she and Tinker had parked her Jeep. She saw a rabbit bound across the open meadow. Watched it pause, ears upright and swiveling to catch the sounds of the forest. An owl whooshed out of the darkness, but the rabbit was faster, darting first to one side, then the other before escaping into the forest.

She turned away from the small drama and tilted her head once more toward a new set of sounds. Mice rustled in the weeds alongside the trail, and a snake made a sinister swishing as it passed through the tall grass. When she lifted her face to the gentle breeze and sniffed, her nostrils flared, much as she'd seen Tinker's flare when he sniffed the air. Now the myriad scents of the forest told her a story. She smelled rotting vegetation where a tree had recently fallen and crushed the plants beneath it. She picked out the spoor of a buck—and Lisa *knew* it was a buck by the scent. Ancient instincts within her burst to life. Over it all, Tinker's wolven scent filled her nostrils, and her body stirred, aroused by the primitive need to mate.

Knowledge blossomed inside her mind, but Lisa remained bound to her two-legged form. Still, she knew it wouldn't be long now. Understood as well as she knew her name that the changes Tinker had told her to expect were finally happening.

She searched through this new awareness of her body and realized there was a thing she could do, a conscious act that would release an egg for fertilization, just as Tinker had told her. She searched deeper, hoping to find the means to shift, but that process still eluded her.

No matter. It would happen. She'd wanted to believe, but it had all seemed so unbelievable. Now, experimenting with the newness of her senses, Lisa sat on a fallen log to wait for Tinker. She felt the stir and shift of her muscles beneath her skin and smiled broadly into a night that was no longer dark.

She trembled with the need to laugh aloud, to shout out to the treetops that it was real. This changing body was proof. Lisa hugged herself, wrapping her hands tightly around her waist as if she needed to hold herself in place or fly off into the cool night air.

Whatever doubts she had once felt, she now knew for sure she would run with Tinker through the forest. She, Lisa Quinn, her body covered in thick, coarse hair, her tail waving gaily behind her. Feet sure and strong, legs able to carry her for miles, teeth sharp enough to bring down prey or protect herself from harm.

"Ohmygawd." Lisa panted, hyperventilating as the reality—the feral power of her new self—sunk in. She pressed her fist to her chest and held it tightly against her sternum where she felt the stretch and play of muscle and bone as she gasped for air. She wished she had a paper bag to breathe into, then giggled, imagining Tinker coming back and finding her sprawled across a rotting log, blowing into a brown paper sack.

It hurt to sit still, so badly did she want to run and shout and jump with joy, but she'd promised Tinker she'd wait. No matter how hard it was, she would be here sitting on this log when he returned.

The potential of the new life she'd embraced suddenly overwhelmed Lisa. Tears flowed freely down her cheeks, and her chest heaved with huge, gut-wrenching sobs. It wasn't all make-believe. Not a figment of her imagination, nor a tall tale told by a sexy stranger. She was Chanku. A shapeshifter like her sister. Like her brother. Like Tinker.

A sense of awe washed through her, a reverence for family she'd not experienced in her entire life—along with a new sense of who and what that family was. Her brother and sister shared this amazing ability. Tinker. The rest of his pack. Family. All of them family.

Lisa glanced up and thought of the wolves in the forest and saw them as her cousins, another branch of her exploding family. She would never be alone again. From a life lived totally on her own, she knew her family now included everyone from her true genetic siblings to her lover to the wild creatures in the forest. Now, after a lifetime of wondering, of wanting something she'd never truly identified, Lisa finally understood all her formless, incomplete dreams and unfulfilled wishes.

Needing to do something with her hands, anything, she twisted her long hair up in a knot and tied it loosely atop her head, rolling it and tucking the ends underneath. Okay . . . She looked around. The forest was dark and still, the sounds of creatures muted as the night wore on, but still the sense remained. The knowledge. She knew answers waited close at hand. If not tonight, then soon. Very soon. Rubbing at her tingling arms, Lisa waited impatiently for Tinker to return.

Tinker sensed the changes in Lisa the moment he trotted into the clearing. All thoughts of why they were here in the first place, why he'd spent the past hour chasing down a pack of totally pissed-off timber wolves, fled the instant he saw her. Lisa sat on a huge fallen log with a big grin on her face, her eyes alight with knowledge and awareness.

She spotted him immediately, slipped over the curve of the log to her feet, and came close to the fence. Watching her long-legged walk, the gentle sway of her hips, and the way her nipples pushed at the soft cotton shirt had him hard within seconds. When he shifted, Tinker's erection was almost painful.

"Here." Lisa tossed his underwear back over the fence. He snagged them before they hit the ground. "Wouldn't want you to damage anything that pretty."

Tinker laughed and slipped on the tight-knit boxers and then climbed back over the fence. Lisa held the rest of his clothes for him.

"Why would I want those?" He drew her close, kissed the tip of her nose, and nuzzled his chin against her hair. He was hard as a post, but his cock nestled easily against her belly, just above the gentle curve of her pelvis. Her scent had changed in the brief hour he'd been gone, a major clue that the supplements had worked their magic on her. Her natural perfume was still subtle but intoxicating as hell. He rolled his hips, pressing against the softness of her belly. "No point in putting my pants on. We'd just have to take them off again."

"Here? Now?" She blinked as if she'd been a long way off.

"Oh yeah." He rubbed his hands up and down her arms, and she curled her body against him like a cat in heat. "You're changing," he whispered. "I feel the difference in you." He nuzzled her neck and ran his tongue along her jawline. "I can smell the changes. Damn. It's like catnip to a cat. I want to wallow in you. Get naked and rub our bodies together until the friction sets us both to burning."

She sighed when he nibbled at her throat. Whimpered when he kissed her along the line of her collarbone, then nudged aside the scooped neck of her cotton shirt and nipped the upper swell of her breast. Lisa moaned and bent back, baring herself to his teeth.

"Submissive?" He chuckled and kissed a fresh line along her shoulder. "I've never seen a submissive Chanku bitch. They're tough . . . ball breakers, if you want the truth."

Lisa whimpered again when his tongue found the edge of her ear. Her voice came out breathy, uneven. "Never. I don't want to break your balls. I want them fully functional, okay? Your balls and that beautiful cock."

She slipped down his body, following all the angles, edges, and ridges of his with her own curves in a molten flow of feminine desire. She felt like hot wax against him, melting down his length, licking the hard muscles across his belly, nipping at the cotton band on his underwear. Her hands lingered on his butt, her face nuzzled the solid bulge trapped inside his knit boxer shorts. Tinker wanted to rip them off, but there was something almost otherworldly about the feel of her warm, moist breath melting through the cotton, blowing hot against the swell of his cock.

It shouldn't feel this good. Hell, they'd fucked right before coming out here, but he'd just shifted, and his arousal, his need after running as the wolf was at its most intense. Tinker thought his cock would explode when Lisa opened her mouth over the hard ridge and clasped him through the cotton, holding him firmly between her teeth.

Her fingers found his sac and gently massaged his balls

through the fabric. Her touch was so gentle it almost tickled, the tickle so elusive he squirmed against her hand, searching for more. Tinker bit back a groan when she pressed her fingers between his cheeks, teasing the sensitive nerves around his ass, but she made no attempt to remove his underwear. Lisa bit and licked and touched until his legs trembled. She was running her mouth along his cock now, sucking him through the knit fabric, licking and nipping at the wet cotton.

Tinker twisted his fingers in her hair, in the loose knot that always seemed to slip one way or the other. His shorts were totally soaked with her saliva, almost transparent across the front where she'd mouthed him all along the ridge of his cock, and the night air felt cold when it touched his superheated flesh through the wet fabric.

Lisa's hair fell free of its knot, spilling down her back in thick, dark ropes, coiling over his thighs as she nuzzled his groin and nipped his cock. He couldn't take it anymore, couldn't take the teasing, *almost* sense of touching through cotton that was merely an avenue for more sensation.

He tried linking. God, he wanted more than anything to know what was in her mind, but somehow she'd managed to block her thoughts, and there was nothing for him to read. He moaned as the sensations grew stronger yet not nearly strong enough. Her hands were doing amazing things to his balls and his ass, but it was all still filtered through those damned cotton boxers. He couldn't stand it another minute.

Tinker grabbed Lisa's shoulders, lifted her away, and held her, swaying, in front of him. When she blinked owlishly, Tinker knew she'd been lost in sensation, lost in a world of texture, taste, and heat. Arousal thrummed through Tinker's body, raised his senses to a feverish level. His lungs billowed in and out like a damned bull in the ring, his chest heaving with each breath and his heart thudding against his ribs. He ripped the shorts down his legs while steadying Lisa with one hand and kicked them aside. Then he picked her up and carried her the few short steps to the fallen log where he'd first seen her waiting for him after his run.

Tinker turned Lisa around and shoved her against the trunk. The wood was worn smooth from so many years lying on the forest floor. Lisa went willingly, throwing her arms over the curve and bending forward so that her breasts flattened against the curved surface.

His vision glazed, as if everything were viewed through cracked glass, as if the blood pounding in his veins was screwing with his eyes, but he didn't need to see for this. No, this was something so instinctive, so primitive that Tinker almost shifted, almost took her there in the forest as a wolf to her woman, but it was too soon—she might not understand, and he didn't want to frighten the woman who would be his mate.

There was no doubt in his mind. None at all. Lisa was his in all but the final act, the final bonding where she freely opened her mind to everything she was and had ever been, and where Tinker did the same with her. A total merging of the minds until there was no *he* or *she,* only *we,* together. A single unit forever linked.

Mates for life.

He was so close. Lisa was so close. He sensed her Chanku spirit, sensed the subtle changes taking place within her body, but subtlety wasn't important right now.

Hands shaking with lust so hot and strong he barely held on to control, Tinker grabbed the loose waistband of her baggy cargo pants and ripped them down her legs to her ankles. She wore cotton underpants. Plain white service-able panties, and they came down with a single tug. She tried to pull one foot free, but the pants caught on her boots. Tinker helped her slide the pants off over her left boot and kicked them to the right. Lisa laughed, but it was a harsh, needy sound as she spread her legs wide and lifted her ass.

There was something amazingly decadent about her pose, the fact that her body was bare from the waist down, her hiking boots still tightly laced and the heavy socks showing at the tops. Her wrinkled cargo pants lay in a tangled heap, still caught on the boot on her right foot. Half naked, she looked even more naked than if all her clothes had been removed.

Breathing hard and fast, Tinker ran his hands along her sides and traced the full curve of her hips. Her butt was round and pale in the darkness. If not for his exceptional Chanku vision, Tinker wouldn't have been able to see her at all. Now, though, he paused and ran his hands over the smooth flesh, squeezed each cheek hard enough to bruise.

Lisa moved her hips back and forth against his harsh grasp. He heard her voice, whispering so low the words were barely audible. "Now. Take me now. Fuck me, Tinker. Fill me. Now. Now. Now."

"Oh God. God damn it to hell."

It sounded more a prayer than a plea when he cursed. Tinker wrapped his hand tighter around his cock. He squeezed hard at the base, pressing with his fingertips to hold off the climax threatening to burst forth. With his free hand, he breached the tender folds of her sex, slipped his fingers deep inside, and knew she was ready when she arched her back and groaned.

"Now. Now. Now."

Her hands looked like claws, scrabbling at the smooth tree trunk. He shoved her higher over the curve and stood behind her with his cock in his hand. He'd never felt this big, this hard. Never felt his body burn and tremble with so much need or so much desire.

She was Chanku. She would be his. His woman. His bitch. He drove forward, filled her hard and fast. His thrust lifted her even higher, pushed her against the smooth trunk. She screamed. The hot flow of her fluids bathed him, the tight contractions of her sex clenched and held him.

Harder, his hips punched back and forth like a damned piston, but he couldn't get enough, could never get enough. She grunted when he connected with her cervix, arched her back, and climaxed again. Her smooth ass jiggled each time he drove into her, and he slapped her right cheek hard with the palm of his hand.

She cried out and bucked against him. He did it again, marking the left cheek with the flat of his palm. He heard her voice, the hoarse litany of "more, harder, deeper." Heard and obeyed.

Primitive. Pure sex, pure sensation. He'd never done anything like this, never felt anything so raw, so inherently powerful, so purely lush and decadent. He grabbed her hips and pulled her against him, pulled her so close they might have been one body, one entity, one person fucking.

When she dropped her mental shields, when she finally opened her thoughts, it happened.

She'd not shifted yet, never experienced the change from human to wolf, but her mind opened to that amazing level of Chanku reality that gave Tinker total freedom within her thoughts.

She was there, part of him, just as he was part of her. He'd never heard of this happening, not until a partner had shifted. He hadn't expected the exquisite loss of self, the amazing connection to be found in a total link with another.

So this is what it's like? No wonder Tia and Luc loved so deeply. Suddenly it all made perfect sense.

Lisa was there, so much a part of him she *was* Tinker, just as he was Lisa Quinn, with all the baggage, all the memories, the pain, the fear, the laughter, the needs. So many needs both of them had, so much they could do, one for the other.

He barely felt the shift coming, crawling through a nervous system completely out of control. Felt the bulge in his cock sliding into her welcoming sex as his body was suddenly more than human, more than mere beast. He'd not meant to do this, not intended . . .

His climax hit hard and fast. Unexpected and powerful, it slammed through a system in flux, as hands became paws, as mouth stretched and reshaped into muzzle. Feral lips pulled back against sharp canines, hips thrust furiously, clawed feet scrabbled for purchase in the loose earth beside the fallen log. Tinker emptied his seed deep inside his mate, aware on some visceral level that their minds and bodies remained locked in perfect union.

Just as Lisa's body was now locked to his. One human. One wolf.

Panting furiously and still connected to Lisa, Tinker collapsed into the beaten ferns at the base of the tree. Lisa screamed and fell with him in a tangle of human arms and legs, her swollen pussy clasping tightly around the hard knot of his wolven cock.

He glimpsed the look of shock on her face and growled in reaction, but it felt so damned good inside her pulsing, living heat. So perfect, as if their connection were more than mere flesh. As if they'd linked heart, mind, body, and soul.

Which they had, hadn't they? Bonded? But how, if she hadn't made the shift?

I'm sorry, Lisa. I'm so sorry. I didn't mean to shift, not during sex. Not until you're ready. Please forgive me.

His cock pulsed as his seed filled her. He'd forgotten to wear a condom, but it wouldn't matter now. He'd come as a wolf, not a man. The knot locked him deep inside Lisa's warm folds. He was afraid to look, afraid to see the disgust on her face, but her silence was even worse than her condemning words might be, and it scared the crap out of him.

Slowly, Tinker opened his eyes.

He blinked. And stared directly into the amber eyes of his mate. Tongue lolling with each rapid, panting breath, ears pricked forward and what could only be called a shocked smile on her wolven face, Lisa stared back at Tinker. Stared at him out of the eyes of a glorious, ebony-haired she-wolf.

Chapter 6

She'd watched him shift a dozen times, but until her body transformed, Lisa knew she hadn't really believed it. There was absolutely no way to truly understand the magnitude of everything involved in the change from human to wolf. Not until she'd done it herself.

She was still Lisa Quinn—but not exactly. Her mind roiled and churned with new and untried knowledge of her body and surroundings, and her thoughts felt alien and unfamiliar. Awareness of her sex tightening around a cock of unusual shape and size epitomized all that was different. The fact that the wolven cock with the swollen knot locked tightly within her body belonged to the man she loved seemed almost anticlimactic. She was a wolf, being fucked by a wolf, but she was still Lisa and he was still Tinker.

To think of him—or herself—in any other manner might tip Lisa over the edge into insanity. She realized she was staring at him, staring into those gorgeous amber eyes and seeing the man as well as the wolf. Her body was reacting to the fading ripples of her climax as a woman would react, but the relaxed sense of well-being was overwhelmed by the adrenaline rushing through her system.

She was a wolf. *Fucking unbelievable.*

It was so much more than the logistics of bone and sinew, organs and limbs reshaping, so far beyond the mere physicality of the shift. Her mind was different. Her thoughts no longer totally human; instead, she poised now on the cusp between *Homo sapiens* and *Canis lupus.*

Lisa continued to gaze steadily into Tinker's eyes, the same eyes she saw when he was human, and realized she looked far beyond his humanity. The intelligence was the same, the love she'd sensed almost from the beginning burned as brightly as ever, if not even more, but overlapping everything was a feral intelligence, an animalistic quality that gave him power surpassing his human abilities.

The beast was never far beneath the surface in this man, but now it shaped the human side, powered Tinker's humanity with the power of the wolf.

Just as that same feral quality now directed Lisa Quinn. So many things suddenly came into focus. So much was made clear to her.

His cock twitched within her sex. She felt the answering, intimate ripples along her sheath. He moved again, then leaned close and licked her muzzle. His thoughts, when they entered her mind, sounded contrite, even a little perplexed.

I'm in shock, you know. I had no idea you could do this yet.

Neither did I. It's amazing . . . so intense!

She'd watched animals mate, knew the male wolf tied to the female during orgasm, but the reality of her wolven body rippling with contractions, the fullness of her mate's cock locked inside her clenching folds—that was something else.

That and the link they'd shared. The sense of connection. She'd need time to figure that one out, to understand all she'd learned about Tinker McClintock. It mattered little to her in this form. She would have to dissect the knowledge later, when the human side of Lisa Quinn regained control. Now she tilted her head and stared at him, overwhelmed by all she'd just learned—his strengths, his weaknesses. His vulnerabilities.

Overriding everything else was the amazing sense of her own power. The differences Lisa had noticed earlier, among them the amazing awareness of her reproductive control, fluttered at the edge of her mind, and with it came a sense of empowerment she'd not appreciated before.

That part of every woman's world was so dominant— the act of reproduction. What Tinker had explained, the fact that she would be immune to all sexually transmitted diseases and would have total control of her reproductive rights, was suddenly a reality. It epitomized everything about her gender—what made women strong as well as vulnerable. But now, for the first time without any action on Lisa's part other than the power of her mind, reproduction had become her choice and hers alone. She had the power to release an egg for fertilization, the ability to enjoy sex without fear of disease or unwanted pregnancy. No one could force it upon her; no one could make that decision.

The choice was entirely hers.

I didn't give you a choice about the link. I didn't know how close you were, or I never would have . . . Tinker's thoughts burst into her head and then drifted off into a dark, silent space suffused with guilt. He looked away.

Never would have what? Focusing her attention on Tinker, Lisa tilted her head and whimpered as he slowly pulled his cock free of her body and put more space between them. Something obviously had him very upset.

Tinker lunged to his feet, but he hung his head and refused to meet Lisa's direct gaze. *We bonded. That intense link? It only happens with your true mate, with the one you commit to spend your life with.*

Aha. So that's what had him so upset. Lisa struggled to her feet, partially trapped in the shirt hanging off her shoulders and the cargo pants tangled around her legs. The boots and socks lay to one side as if her paws had slipped free during the shift.

She didn't remember any of it. She nipped at the shirt. Tinker grabbed it in his teeth and pulled it over her head as she stepped out of the loose pants. Then Lisa shook herself like a wet dog, sat back on her haunches, and wondered how she knew to make this new body work so well.

Tinker growled. As single-minded as every male she'd ever known, he went back to his topic of conversation. *I feel as if I've forced a commitment from you without your approval, without any choice on your part. I'm sorry, Lisa. That was wrong.*

I see. She tilted her head and forced Tinker to look at her. *Are you sorry we bonded?*

Tinker glared at her. Then he whined, low in his throat. *Of course not. Why would you even think that?*

If she'd been human, Lisa knew she'd be laughing by now. *Look at you. Tinker, I'm a fucking wolf and you want to argue about bonding? I don't get it.*

Tinker obviously didn't see the humor in the situation. This time he snarled. *Lisa, I love you. I knew the moment I saw you, when I realized who and what you were, that you were destined to be my mate.*

Okay. So what's the problem?

My decision shouldn't take away your rights. You hardly know me. You don't even know what this new body of yours can do. How can you possibly commit so quickly to spending your life as my mate?

Tinker! She really needed to learn to shout when they communicated like this. *Look at me. You've known me as long as I've known you. I didn't fight it. So what's the problem?* She stood up and shook herself again, eager to experiment with her new form. Resentment surged through her body. She couldn't believe they were standing here in the dark having this conversation.

She was a wolf, a beautiful four-legged wolf, and Tinker wanted to talk relationship crap? Ludicrous. Absolutely ridiculous, the two of them, two beautiful feral creatures, standing here arguing like a couple of stupid humans.

She wasn't human. Not anymore. The reality took her breath away. Made her heart pound in her newly shaped chest. She snapped her teeth. It sounded so wonderful to her highly attuned ears that she did it again, and then she nipped the air in front of Tinker. He looked much too serious, considering what had just happened. Wasn't he happy she'd managed to shift?

I have one thing to say about that link, she said, thankful their mindtalk was so clear. *If you were keeping any secrets from me before, you sure don't have them now!* She glanced at Tinker and then looked toward the narrow road leading farther into the forest.

Enough! We can talk about it later. Right now I want to find out what I can do! Lisa spun around and nipped Tinker's left haunch, then took off at a full run. Her legs were strong, her paws carrying her along the narrow road as if she flew. This was magic. Magnificent, amazing, unbelievable magic.

Power coursed through her new muscles; sounds and smells assaulted her sensitive ears and nose. The darkness glowed with an amazing amount of light, and the world felt fresh and new. The world was hers. The night belonged to the wolf.

For the first time in her entire life, Lisa Quinn knew the power of freedom, just as she knew how free the power to shift had suddenly made her. She understood answers to questions she'd never thought to ask. It was so terribly easy, after all, this shedding of her humanity. Leaving it farther behind with each lengthy stride, she ran as if the world was hers alone.

Tinker stood for a moment and watched Lisa speed down the service road. He'd never felt so torn, so angry with himself yet so completely ecstatic. He'd bonded with Lisa. He'd crept into her thoughts without thinking of the consequences, but she'd exploded into his. Her mind open, her heart filled with love.

He certainly hadn't expected her response. Still, he doubted what he'd felt, what his mind knew to be true. Lisa felt love for him along with a healthy dose of lust, but right now her entire focus was as it should be—on this new body she'd suddenly discovered.

Unbelievable. She'd shifted during the most amazing sex Tinker had ever experienced. Was her love as real as it had felt in that brief, earth-shattering moment when they bonded?

Lisa disappeared around a bend in the road. Tinker shook himself, realized he could no longer see her, and raced to catch up. Lisa ran like a dark ghost in an even darker night, but her scent alone would draw him, the rich combination of woman and wolf a potent aphrodisiac to his feral libido. Tinker caught up to her, nipped her flank in greeting, then raced beside her while still following her lead.

The night was still and windless, the forest alive with scent and sound, and Tinker ran along the unfamiliar path with his mate beside him, leading him. She was beautiful, strong and agile, with taut muscles rippling beneath her sooty coat and a sense of feminine power surging like a golden aura around her body. The true incarnation of the ultimate alpha bitch.

And she was his. Bonded to him—his mate for all time.

Lisa was the personification of every dream he'd ever had, every wish he'd hoped to fill. Tonight couldn't be real. It was all too perfect, and perfection made him nervous. Scanning the deep forest with his senses alert, Tinker ran beside Lisa.

Briefly, Tia entered his thoughts. Tia, the woman he'd been so certain he loved beyond all others. That love was a pale reflection of what he felt for Lisa. Still there, still very real, but Tinker knew there was no comparison between his feelings for Tia Mason and the exhilarating miracle of racing side by side with his one true mate.

Lisa's senses brought the world to her in a totally different light. Color, sound, smells, all of it fresh, all amazingly powerful. Her broad paws with their sharp nails hit the packed earth with a steady rhythm, her lungs drew air, and her ears twisted and turned of their own accord, listening to the sounds of the night.

Lisa was aware of Tinker racing beside her and slightly behind, giving her the lead yet protecting her at the same time. She sensed the wolves in the large enclosures on either side of the narrow service road she'd followed and knew they were every bit as aware of Lisa and Tinker as she and Tinker were of them.

She felt their curiosity as much as their acceptance. The wild ones sensed wolves. Nothing more, nothing less.

Lisa's senses were attuned to her surroundings at an almost feverish pitch. Smells, sounds, the feel of the hard-packed earth beneath her broad paws, the rush of air through her thick, black coat, all melded to create a sense of oneness with the forest, a feeling of continuity with the wolves pacing alongside, behind their wire fences.

She was wolf. She ran in the darkest night, yet clearly saw the trail ahead, a narrow service road laid out between the large fenced enclosures. She raised her muzzle and snapped at the air, clicking together teeth designed for killing.

Lisa felt the rumble beneath her feet before she heard the sound of the engines. Pausing, she turned to look at Tinker and caught him watching the trail behind them. As one, they slipped into the thick brush alongside the service road.

Three pickup trucks rolled slowly by, running on parking lights only. Lisa recognized a couple of the regular volunteers, rough men she tended to avoid. She wasn't sure, but it looked like Hal Anderson drove the first of the trucks. She wished she could get a better look, but he was on the opposite side of the road. The trucks continued on past the pens, leaving exhaust fumes in their wake.

Tinker growled, then took off through the woods in the opposite direction of the trucks. Lisa wanted to follow them, wanted to see where they were going, but her mate called to her. She put Hal Anderson out of her thoughts, whirled around, and followed Tinker through the forest.

The clean tang of fir and pine was sharply cut with the damp smell of humus and rotting wood as they ran deeper into the trees. They were beyond the inhabited pens now, past the ones where no wolves lived. Finally, in an area of forest that was open and unfenced, Tinker stopped and raised his nose in the air. Lisa followed suit. There was something tantalizing, something calling to her, and she realized she'd scented game. She slanted a quick glance at Tinker, then followed as he slipped quietly into the brush alongside the road.

Tinker moved ahead. Images flooded her mind, and she saw the small meadow, the tiny creek flowing through it. Tinker showed her with visuals, much as the wild wolves had done when Lisa picked up their thoughts. It seemed more natural to communicate with images rather than the convoluted mental speech of humans, and it made their earlier conversation about bonding all the more ridiculous.

Tinker showed her their prey before Lisa actually saw it. The small buck, ears twitching nervously, drank at a narrow stream just at the point where the water cascaded into a shallow pond. Along with the visual, Tinker showed Lisa the proper way to attack, offering her first chance for the kill.

She hesitated. Her human side appreciated the beauty of the deer, the wary manner in which it raised its head to scan the small meadow for danger. Tinker had brought them in downwind of the buck, silently and with a deadly stealth Lisa had never imagined; yet she was transfixed by the entire scene, by the fact that she hid now, within striking distance, able to appreciate the beauty of the creature she planned to kill.

There was no doubt in her mind that she was entirely capable of taking a life. The feral part of her was already calculating the distance and height of her target.

Her animal instincts burst into life. She bared her teeth. Saliva dripped from her jaws, and her heart raced. Adrenaline filled her bloodstream, and power surged through her limbs. With Tinker coming in from the opposite flank, Lisa broke through the wall of brush and attacked.

She went directly for the animal's throat just as the deer reared back on its haunches and turned to escape. Lisa's charge missed. Teeth snapping, she latched onto the thick muscle rippling across the buck's shoulder. Her weight and forward momentum brought the animal to his knees. Tinker moved quickly and with obvious skill, ripping the deer's throat in one brutal slash of his teeth. He clamped down on the animal's windpipe to ensure a quick death.

Tinker looked at Lisa over the body of the dying deer, his amber eyes glittering brightly, meeting her gaze and obviously finding what he'd hoped. She felt him in her mind, a being of pure sensation, a wild creature bringing down food for his mate.

Lisa stood across the buck's body, head lowered, breathing hard from the rush of adrenaline and the exertion of her attack. Bridging the warm body, rear legs on one side, forepaws on the other, she experienced a moment where her humanity slid away altogether.

Like Tinker, she was wolf. Her heart thundered in her chest, her muscles quivered as the adrenaline ebbed, and her nostrils flared at the rich smell of fresh blood.

She growled, low in her throat. The sound tapered off to a small whine as her human nature reasserted itself. Still in the form of a wolf, Lisa existed as well.

She shook herself and whined again, then leaned close and lapped at the blood pooling beneath the animal's torn throat. She'd never tasted anything so amazing as the hot blood now staining her muzzle.

On one level, her human self recognized the power of this moment, the first kill, the taste of blood, the nearness of her mate and his obvious pride in her, but the animal was more powerful. The wolf wanted nothing more than to feed, to tear at the tough hide and find the choice tastes.

She clamped her jaws down on the skin covering the deer's soft underbelly, ripping and tearing like the wild beast she was. A carnivore. One of nature's most powerful predators. Tinker watched while she tore the thick hide away to expose the warm flesh.

They fed together. Lisa realized if she had made the kill cleanly and on her own, she would have forced Tinker to wait, would have established her position as alpha bitch, but in this, her human side overruled her animal instincts.

Considering what little useful information her mother had actually taught her, beyond the fact that men were worthless sons of bitches, Lisa realized she'd somehow learned good manners. Which, of course, went totally counter to the natural instincts of the wolf.

Tinker showed no signs of possessiveness at all. The kill was theirs, a thing to be shared equally. The thick blood in Lisa's mouth was an aphrodisiac, arousing and exciting, filling her with strength, bringing with it an even deeper understanding of her new reality.

She was still Lisa Quinn, human, naturalist, a flawed but good woman. She was also Chanku. She had become one of the very creatures she'd loved for so long. Lisa glanced to her left, at the huge wolf licking fresh blood from his paw, and felt a surge of desire so strong, so consuming, it stole her breath.

He was her mate. Her bonded mate. The lifetime of memories Tinker had shared, the loves he'd known, the life he'd hoped for, all came flooding back. She felt her body grow tense with arousal, then languid and open. Lisa fought an unexpected compulsion to mate, to release that all-important egg and make a baby with this man.

She fought the surge of desire to reproduce, fought what was surely a most basic instinct of any creature, tamped it down and put it back where it belonged, into that part of her mind where dreams were stored. It was too soon for babies, but not too soon to once again experience that amazing bond with an even more amazing partner.

Tinker studied Lisa for what seemed a very long time. His thoughts were blocked to her, but she was aware of his desire, of the same need coursing through his veins as the almost painful longing surging through her own. He stood up and trotted away from the body of the deer to a small pond at the end of the meadow, near where the deer had been drinking.

He shifted there, standing tall and dark and magnificently aroused. Lisa didn't hesitate. She shifted as well, experiencing the change from animal to human with an increased awareness. Her first shift had been so unex-

pected and had happened so quickly, she'd not even realized what she'd done. This time, she was ready for the
change of perception as her body shifted, the alteration of
scents and sounds and even the way things looked through
her human eyes.

The way thoughts filtered through the human brain.
Lisa flashed back to the small convoy of trucks, and a
shiver raced along her spine. She raised her head to question Tinker about her worries and caught herself in his
molten gaze. Surrendered entirely to the love in his eyes,
the sense of this moment, this place, this time.

She smiled when Tinker held his hand out to her and
led her to the pool. No words were said. There was too
much to say, too many questions to ask, so she said nothing.
Merely followed Tinker's lead when he took her into the
water, stepping carefully through tangles of cattails at the
edge, finding the deepest point where the creek dropped
over a low wall of rocks.

It was cold, but the water was clear and invigorating
against her hot skin. Shivering, Lisa dipped down into the
water and tilted her head back. Her hair streamed out behind her. Long strands floated with the current, and when
she turned, they wrapped themselves around her breasts,
then flowed beyond to touch Tinker's broad chest.

He reached for her, his big hands cupping her shoulders,
drawing her back to her feet so that she stood in waist-
deep water. Her wet hair plastered to her breasts and back.
She shivered in the cold night air.

Lisa's nipples jutted out like pencil erasers, hard and
cold. Tinker leaned close, put his mouth on her breast, and
sucked. His lips and tongue scalded her. Lisa arched her
back and cried out. She clutched at the back of his head
and his neck, holding him against her breast while he
sucked and bit and lapped at her flesh. She felt every caress
as if his mouth were between her legs, felt the pull of an

orgasm building deep inside from nothing more than the moist heat of his mouth on her breast.

He didn't touch her anywhere else. His hands still clutched her shoulders, his mouth surrounding her nipple, and her sex clenched in response. She tilted her head back and moaned, offering herself to the magic of his mouth. His lips tightened around her nipple, his tongue flicked across the tip, and his cheeks hollowed with each pull as he suckled her breast.

Cold water lapped at Lisa's hips and waist, but she was on fire between her legs, and there was fire in the pit of her belly, flames reaching from breast to sex, building, a conflagration burning out of control, all from the pressure of his mouth, the suction of his lips, the sharp, insistent scraping from his teeth.

Lisa's climax ripped through her body, totally unexpected, unprecedented, even more so in she who had always loved women. She arched her back and cried out, the harsh scream centered deep in her chest, forcing air out of oxygen-starved lungs.

Her body sagged in Tinker's embrace. He lifted her up against his chest and strode from the small pool. When he lay her down in the soft bracken fern, Lisa was still trembling from the strength of her climax and her skin burned and shivered in reaction. When he nudged her knees apart and knelt between them, she felt the hot moisture between her legs and wondered why there wasn't steam rising from her body.

He thrust once, hard and deep, and she cried out again. He was a dark god, a powerful creature of the night, as much wolf as man, and he was hers. All hers. Lisa raised her knees and tilted her hips, taking him deep inside.

She put aside any lingering concerns about the trucks rumbling through her forest, saved her worries for another time. Now, she opened her mind once more, opened to the history of the man she'd already fallen hopelessly in love with, and lost herself in his past.

The link was stronger this time. Tinker hadn't thought it possible, to meld so completely with another soul. He'd shared thoughts with Tia during lovemaking, but it was nothing like this. The fact that Lisa was capable of love at all was a mystery to him. Her childhood had been a nightmare of emotional, physical, and sexual abuse; her mother, an undiscovered Chanku who had never found her true self, had been a hateful and unhappy woman.

She'd taken her frustrations out on her children and her husband and thought nothing of taking lovers throughout her marriage. Her death had been violent and unfortunate, but it was the only end possible to a miserable existence.

Tinker buried himself in Lisa's soft, slick folds, felt the firm contractions of her muscles holding him, and knew he'd come home. She'd climaxed when he suckled her breast! Now that was a first. He'd never brought a woman to orgasm so quickly before, never been with a woman so responsive. He'd never had so much trouble holding on to his own control either.

Tinker sat back on his heels and lifted Lisa with him. She wrapped her legs around his waist and locked her heels at the small of his back. She arched her spine, bringing her pubic bone up tightly against his, and her long, dark hair cascaded over both their bodies. Tinker cupped her buttocks in his palms and lifted her as he thrust, increasing the depth with each tilt of his hips.

They fit together as if they'd done this forever. He felt her thoughts, her innate curiosity as she delved into his past. With anyone else, Tinker knew he would have felt violated. He would have resisted such a thorough exploration of his life, but when Lisa traveled through his mind, he saw it as a search for understanding, a need to know even more about the man who was now her mate.

He flexed the big muscles in his buttocks and drove steadily in and out of her tight sex, marveling at their differences and celebrating the one thing they shared—their Chanku heritage.

So many contradictions. Lisa was soft and feminine folds to his hard, thrusting cock; smooth, white skin to his dark chocolate; light and laughter to his serious side. Where he was weak, Lisa had strength. Where Tinker felt strong and self-assured, Lisa had needs.

Needs Tinker fully intended to meet. Now, though, the rhythm he maintained kept both of them at the very edge of climax, kept their bodies poised on the brink. He made a conscious effort to open his mind to all of Lisa Quinn, then lost himself in sensation.

Lisa felt as if she existed on two levels. One, a woman of desire and sensation, a finely tuned instrument being played by a master. The hot, thick length of Tinker's cock, stretching her almost painfully on each penetration, sliding deep between the slick walls of her sex, then slowly pulling back, the pressure of his pubic bone against her clit, the heat of their combined bodies, all came together in a lush and sensual well of feeling.

The other Lisa was a huntress, an explorer searching through the convoluted passages of Martin Tinker McClintock's past. His first memories were of darkness and confusion, a feeling of loss and abandonment. She learned all he knew of his beloved foster parents, both of them white, both of them loving the child they considered a special gift.

She felt his grief at their deaths, his fear of being thrust into a society he was ill-prepared to handle. All the typical confusion and lack of confidence felt by any young man, compounded by racial hatred and a lack of understanding of his place in a society that didn't know how to handle him.

His bravery in Afghanistan translated as a death wish in Lisa's mind. He hadn't cared whether he lived or died. Hadn't cared about much of anything until Ulrich Mason, head of Pack Dynamics, gave him direction and purpose and an entirely new life.

A life as Chanku. Lisa's sexual fever built when she found the part of Tinker's memories where he kept those special thoughts of his packmates. Sex with men she'd never met, all through Tinker's past.

The most special memories of all, the memories that took Lisa even higher, were his thoughts of Tia Mason. Tinker's packmate's mate, the daughter of his mentor.

Were Lisa merely human, she might have been jealous. Were she not Chanku, she might have been angry.

Instead, she saw Tia from Tinker's perspective, saw the way his lips and tongue suckled her pussy, watched the thick length of his dark cock sliding carefully, slowly, almost gracefully inside the tight rosebud of her ass, felt the pressure when Tia contracted around him. She experienced sex with Tia Mason, and Lisa's world exploded.

Caught in Tinker's memories of sex with Tia, Lisa arched against his thrust, felt his cock press deep and hard, and she cried out as her orgasm slammed into her. She clutched his shoulders with grasping fingers and drew blood with her broken nails. Her thoughts remained linked with Tinker's, her body and his moving as a single entity.

Caught in Lisa's mental backlash, Tinker followed her into climax. He threw his head back, and his mouth opened in a silent howl as he filled her with hot bursts of seed. Thick streams of semen ran down her legs, leaving a scorched path behind, yet still his hips rocked against her, still his cock filled her clenching sex.

Lisa fell forward against his sweaty chest. Her legs

wrapped around his waist, and her ankles locked against the small of his back, holding them together. He tightened his arms around her and hugged her close. Lisa tucked her face against the juncture of his neck and shoulder where his skin was smooth and soft as velvet. She licked his skin and tasted salt and man.

Their bodies trembled, both of them sucked in air as if the next breath might be their last, and slowly their heart rates slowed, their gasping breaths eased, and the perspiration cooled upon their skin.

Tinker was the first to raise his head. He looked at Lisa and grinned, then cocked one dark eyebrow in question.

Lisa laughed out loud. "Wow," she said, the sexual images of other men and that one, glorious woman still so clear in her mind. "I can't wait to meet your packmates."

Tinker laughed and kissed her on the nose. "That is *not* the thing you tell a man right after he's fucked you senseless."

Lisa slipped away from him, still giggling, then stood up and held her hand out. "For one thing, I may be well fucked, but I am not senseless. And for another, now I've seen what you've been up to, I understand why you want to go back to San Francisco." She walked back to the small pool, tugging Tinker along behind her.

He followed willingly, still chuckling. His hand felt good in hers. Natural, as if it belonged there. Lisa's legs were sticky with his ejaculate. Her body still trembled from her climax, and she couldn't remember ever feeling this good after sex with either a man or a woman.

She stepped into the pool to bathe and thought how surrealistic it felt, to be here in the deep forest at the darkest time of night, still able to see with her enhanced Chanku vision, her body tingling from the best sex she'd had in her life. Surrealistic and unbelievable, yet she'd never felt so real before, never experienced life so completely.

Dipping into the chilly water, Lisa rinsed Tinker's seed from her body and enjoyed the moment. It was all good, and yet there was a sense, a feeling, that something this perfect couldn't last. She heard once more the rumble of trucks in the distance. A shiver passed over her body.

She blamed the cold water and shoved the uncomfortable sense of premonition from her mind.

Chapter 7

"Do you have to be away all day?" Lisa stretched up on her toes to kiss Tinker good-bye.

He kissed her back, his lips soft and warm, his taste more addictive each time they touched. "Most likely. I have to get in touch with Luc, have him check on Dunlop, see what he's found out about the financing on the sanctuary. I want him to look into Hal Anderson, too, among other things. Will you be okay?"

"Of course. I love you."

Tinker kissed her once more, then he left her standing on the front deck as he climbed into the rental car and drove away. She watched the empty road for several long minutes after he'd gone.

How had one man managed to upend her entire life so completely, in so few days?

Easy, idiot. He turned you into a fucking wolf.

Lisa wandered back into the cabin and paused in front of the mirror in her hallway. The woman staring back at her looked exactly as she'd looked for years. Tall, athletic, dark hair with amber eyes. Average, almost middle-aged. Slowly Lisa stripped out of her clothes until she stood naked in front of her reflection.

Then she shifted. The wolf wasn't tall enough to see its

reflection in the mirror. So much for that little experiment. Shifting back to her human self, feeling a little bit silly, Lisa gathered up her clothes and went into the bedroom to dress for work.

"Hey, Seth. How are you? I haven't seen you around for the past few days." Lisa waved to the gangly teenager. It was almost dusk, but she saw him clearly, now that her vision had grown so much better.

Seth jerked around and held something down against his leg, as if hiding it from view. "Oh, hi, Lisa. I, um, had family visiting. Had to hang around the house for a couple days."

"Whatcha doing?" This time she was certain he looked guilty.

"Just cleaning out the shed. Mr. Anderson said it was getting messy in here, and he wanted things organized."

Lisa smiled at Seth and gave him a minute to offer more information. He merely looked uncomfortable. "Any more word on the missing wolves? I haven't seen anything in the paper, and no one around here is saying much."

Seth shook his head. "No. Mr. Anderson doesn't want to make it public, so he's keeping it quiet. He's afraid the neighbors will get upset and try to close down the sanctuary if they find out any of the wolves are missing, so the investigation is staying internal."

"That's what I heard." She shrugged her shoulders, decided whatever Seth was hiding was none of her business, and turned away to head out to the parking lot. It had been a long day, especially considering how little sleep she and Tinker were getting. Between time spent learning all she needed to know about being a wolf and the amazing sex that always followed each shift, Lisa marveled she was getting any sleep at all.

"Where's that guy?" Seth stood right behind her now. For a moment, Lisa almost felt threatened. That was stupid. If anyone was a threat, it certainly wasn't Seth. He was just a kid, nothing more than a gangly teenager.

"You mean Tinker? He had some business to take care of in town. I'm meeting him back at my cabin in a couple hours. Why do you ask?"

Seth stared at her. His blue eyes narrowed; then he smiled and shrugged his shoulders. "I guess since you guys have practically been joined at the hip for the past week, I was surprised to see you here without him. He's nice enough, but he's kinda scary."

Lisa laughed. "Tinker? Scary? I don't think so! He's a marshmallow."

Seth's smile didn't go beyond the slight upturn of his mouth. "I've never seen a marshmallow that big with muscles like he's got. The guy is absolutely ripped! I guess I was surprised at first to see him hanging around here so long, and now it's weird that he's not here."

Lisa cocked her leg and rested one hand on her hip. "Now why would you be surprised he's hung around?"

Seth shrugged and had the decency to look embarrassed. "Mr. Anderson said it."

"Said what, Seth?"

He wouldn't meet her eyes. "He said Tinker's black and you're gay, so he couldn't figure out what the attraction was. It's not like there's a lot of black people around, and I didn't know you were gay, but if you are, I guess what Mr. Anderson said makes sense."

"He said *what?* I don't believe this!" Okay, so she'd figured Anderson was racist, but what the hell was he doing discussing her sex life with anyone, much less a teenager? Keeping a tight lid on her anger, Lisa snorted and shook her head. "First of all, my sex life is none of your business or Mr. Anderson's. For the record, I am not gay, and Tinker's color, besides the fact that he's absolutely gorgeous, has nothing to do with how I feel about him. He's a very nice man who cares about me."

Lisa turned to go back to her Jeep, but she couldn't let it hang there. She stopped and turned back to Seth. "Martin McClintock is also more of a man than Hal Anderson or any other male I've ever met, including you, Seth Mitchell. You might let Mr. Anderson know the next time he feels like commenting on things that are none of his business, he'd be better off keeping his mouth shut."

Seth stood there wide-eyed. Lisa spun around and headed for the parking lot. She was seething by the time she yanked open the door on the Jeep. She jerked the stick shift into reverse and popped the clutch, pulled out of her space, and shifted into first. Her old Jeep hardly knew how to respond. Damn Hal Anderson, and damn Seth, too. They had no business discussing her private life or her relationship with Tinker or Tinker's race or anything about either one of them.

Still boiling, Lisa pulled into the parking spot in front of her cabin. There was no sign of Tinker. She wondered if he'd had any luck finding a fast hookup for his computer. He'd needed to make contact with the members of Pack Dynamics and do some research on his own about the sanctuary, including some background checks on Anderson. Cell phones didn't work well here, and the cabin didn't have a regular telephone. She'd never gotten around to installing one.

There'd been no need when she had no one to call.

Now, though, they had more questions than answers after Tinker's communication with the wolves. Some of the animals did remember when their packmates disappeared, but the details were fuzzy and the visual clues difficult to decipher. There was unusual activity going on at night, but the animals only noted people passing. They didn't care what humans actually did. Tinker had an idea someone at the sanctuary was taking the animals, though he wasn't sure what the purpose could be.

One of the older males had shown him the gate where a man had come through carrying what looked like a gun. A truck had waited on the service road, not far from the place where Lisa had made her first shift. There was no sense of time in the visual, no idea when it had happened, but from what Tinker understood, someone had shot a wolf and hauled the body out in a large crate, though he couldn't be sure if the downed animal was actually dead or merely unconscious.

The truck drove away, and the wolf was not seen again. The old wolf grieved for his packmate in the way of animals. Grieved but moved on in life, dismissing the loss of one as something that diminished the whole, but a loss that would be repaired with the birth of a new cub.

It was the way of things. Life and death, birth and existence, a successful hunt or a failed one, all part of the circle of life.

Tinker had tried to communicate with others, but their lack of concern once an animal left the pack made it difficult to pursue more detailed information. Then there was the issue of trucks traveling at night, but running without lights. Another curious thing to wonder about. Tinker had wanted to discuss the problem with his boss, Lucien Stone. Luc, he'd said, had a way of figuring things out.

Lisa wondered if Tinker was merely homesick for his packmates and looking for a chance to communicate with them. In a way, she missed them as well, though she'd never met any of them. Knowing them through her link with Tinker made all of the Chanku real to her.

Already she thought of Luc and Tia as her packmates, just as she now saw Tinker as her bonded mate. She'd known him barely a week. Amazing how quickly so much in her life had changed.

Restless after a long day working with the wolves and the numerous groups of visitors who regularly toured the site, Lisa pictured Tinker as she paced around her small cabin. He'd be absolutely furious over what Seth had said today. The more she thought about Tinker, the angrier she got over Hal Anderson's comments and the fact that Seth had obviously felt no qualms about repeating racist or homophobic crap to her.

Looking for a diversion, Lisa checked the refrigerator, but the larder was empty. There'd been little reason to shop, especially since she and Tinker had hunted almost nightly since her first change.

Why cook when the forest was teeming with game? That was one of the biggest changes, as far as Lisa could tell. She'd always loved animals and hated the idea of hunting for sport. While she accepted that her beloved wolves hunted to survive, she hadn't let herself think of the details of hunting and killing for food.

Her basic nature had changed. Hunting with a gun still disgusted her. Hunting as a wolf in search of sustenance excited her. The thought of tearing into a freshly killed rabbit made her salivate, even as she paced the floor on two legs. She checked the time. Tinker had said he'd be home late this evening, but he hadn't known for certain when that would be.

There was a moon tonight. Not even half full, but it was already rising over the treetops and casting a silvery blue glow across the forest. She saw differently now. Saw with eyes that picked out objects in the dark as if it were merely dusk. It would be almost as bright as daylight for her tonight, should she run.

She'd not gone out without Tinker before. There'd been no need, as he'd never left her. Lisa stood by the large picture window that looked out over the meadow and felt the call of the night.

She would shift and run. Not far, but at least she'd burn off some of this excess energy and adrenaline that had her feeling so keyed up and anxious. It must have been that stupid discussion with Seth that had her feeling like this, but she couldn't relax, couldn't get it out of her mind that Hal Anderson was talking about her behind her back.

Even though Lisa had long thought of herself as a lesbian, at least before she met Tinker, Hal had no business discussing her sexual preferences with anyone, especially a teenage kid who'd harbored a crush on her for the last year. It infuriated her even more to know he was making racist comments about Tinker.

The more she thought about it, the angrier she got. It was good to focus her nervous energy, good to have something to think of rather than worry about Tinker. He'd been gone since early this morning. She'd expected him back before now and hadn't realized how much she would miss his mental touch, the constant awareness of her mate's thoughts in the back of her mind. Missed his mental touch as much as she missed the physical touch, the powerful realization that desire for her simmered just below his surface—much as Lisa's desire burned for Tinker.

She realized now how he'd been her constant companion since they'd met. Her companion, her friend . . . her lover. She missed him. She was lonely without him.

She'd never felt this kind of dependence on another living soul. In a way, it was almost frightening. Made her feel vulnerable, to need someone so powerfully. It would definitely take some getting used to.

Lisa glanced at the clock on the wall and realized an hour had passed since she'd arrived home. It was fully dark now, except for the almost ghostly moonlight filtering through the trees. The woods would be empty, the air cool and crisp. She could run. She had to run or she'd go nuts. If she stayed close to the cabin, stayed away from any trails where she might be seen, it should be safe.

On the other hand, maybe, just maybe, she'd spot the trucks again tonight. If she did, Lisa fully intended to follow them, if only for a short distance. Maybe Hal was merely patrolling the roads, looking for clues to the missing wolves.

Or perhaps he had his own agenda—one that involved missing wolves.

Scribbling a quick note, Lisa left the single sheet of paper lying on the kitchen table. She cast her thoughts outward in a last search for Tinker. Nothing. He wasn't close enough to hear her.

The night called to her. Questions niggled at the back of her mind. Suspicions. Setting aside her misgivings about running alone, Lisa undressed and stepped out on the porch. She stood in a pale swath of moonlight, glanced around, inhaled the myriad scents of the night, and shifted.

The night was meant for the wolf. She was wolf. Lisa checked her surroundings once more and raced across the meadow, into the depths of the forest.

"Lisa? Lisa, I'm home." Tinker pushed the front door of the cabin open and searched for his mate. The sense of emptiness was almost blinding. Where the hell was she?

He shut the door behind him and rushed through the small living room, into the kitchen. A piece of notepaper fluttered to the floor as he entered the room. Tinker leaned over and picked it up.

Shit. She'd shifted and gone for a run on her own. After asking questions around town today and talking to Luc tonight, after learning what Luc had found out about Charles Dunlop, the last thing Tinker wanted was Lisa out in the forest as a wolf, running alone.

There'd been suspiciously little information about Hal Anderson. It was almost as if the man had suddenly sprung into existence as supervisor of the sanctuary. Luc was checking on him. Tinker cast his thoughts for Lisa.

No answer. Damn. What if she ran into Anderson out there in the dark?

Shaking with a sudden rush of adrenaline, Tinker stripped off his clothing and left everything in a pile on the kitchen floor. Naked, he raced for the back door, flung it open, and shifted as he hit the deck. The huge black wolf that streaked over the deck railing snarled as it hit the ground and searched for his mate's scent.

Once he found her unique aroma, Tinker charged into the forest, praying he wouldn't be too late.

Lisa followed the scent trails of deer and rabbits, using each one as an exercise to hone her skills as a predator. She had no appetite tonight, not without Tinker beside her. She'd discovered that much of the joy of running as a wolf was lost when she ran by herself. For that lesson alone, tonight was a valuable experience. For the first time since meeting Tinker, she consciously accepted she was not complete without him by her side.

Her independent side amended the thought—at least for now, while her skills were still new. At some point, she would be more confident, more sure of herself. Less needy.

She'd been out for more than an hour when Lisa realized she was near the series of enclosures where the sanctuary's permanent wolf population lived, not all that far from the spot where they'd seen the trucks the other night. No wolves had gone missing, which meant Anderson hadn't been out here to steal one. Maybe he'd merely been patrolling, but she hated to give him the benefit of the doubt, the little bastard.

She ran swiftly past the huge fenced areas that were ten to twenty acres each. Many of the enclosures were home to entire packs of wolves, most of them threatened subspecies. Because of their endangered status, the wolves here were allowed to breed and exist in an almost natural wild state.

Nose to the ground, Lisa followed her own trail from the night before. It led to the largest of the fenced areas where a good-sized family group roamed in almost natural freedom.

Almost being the key word. They were still restrained by fences, but there was game aplenty within the enclosure, and it was the best situation that man could provide for the animals.

No matter how she felt about Charles Dunlop, at least he'd used his wealth to provide a safe place for animals unable to peacefully coexist with man in the wild. So long as humanity expanded into the wolves' territory, sanctuaries like this would have to provide the solution, imperfect though it might be.

Lisa sensed wolves nearby, knew they were curious about the female running outside their fence. This group, unlike some of the others, also sensed she was different. They knew she was one of them, yet not the same.

Could she converse with the wolves the way Tinker had? Lisa wasn't sure. She hadn't tried it yet on her own. She trotted along the service road, concentrating on the wolves, using her nose to lead her closer to the animals.

She sent her thoughts flying, searching once more for Tinker. When he answered, Lisa was so surprised she yipped.

Lisa? Where are you?

On the trail near the wolves' enclosure.

It's not safe. Come home!

Lisa stopped, halted by Tinker's frantic mental voice. Cautiously, she answered him. *What's wrong? It's quiet out. I don't hear anything.*

It's Dunlop. Luc found out he may not be what he seems.

Dunlop? The man who supported the sanctuary? Lisa opened her mind completely to Tinker. *I don't understand.*

No details yet, just suspicions. I'll fill you in later. Right now you need to come back to the cabin. Stay off the road. Get into the forest where you won't be seen.

Nervous now, absorbing Tinker's anxiety and feeling the effects of his urgent warning, Lisa slipped off the service road and into the thick brush. Silently, carefully, she worked her way alongside the road and headed back toward her cabin.

She didn't see the one who shot her. Barely felt the sting of the dart in her right hip. Turning to snap at the object, she felt a strange lassitude overtaking her body. *Tink! I've been shot with something. Looks like a tranquilizer dart. It's making me really woozy!* She stumbled, caught herself, stood spraddle-legged and panting, her muzzle almost touching the grass.

Shit! Lisa! Sweetheart, don't shift. Whatever you do, stay wolf. I'm coming. Lisa. I love you, Lisa. Don't shift.

Her legs went first, and she toppled hopelessly to the ground. Then her eyes clouded over. The night grew suddenly dark. Tinker's frantic pleas reverberated in Lisa's mind, until the only thing she was even remotely aware of centered on his beloved, anxious voice.

Don't shift. Don't shift. I love you, Lisa. Don't shift. Damn it! Luc, Tia, I need you. Lisa, don't shift!

She didn't. If she understood only one thing when the drug overtook her, Lisa knew she was still a wolf.

Tia Mason rolled over and caught herself against the firm chest of her sleeping lover. No, revise that, she thought. Lucien Stone was so much more than her lover. He was her mate, her companion . . . soon to be her husband. He was also her alpha, and sexy as hell, which was the only reason she'd let him talk her into going to bed so early. Damn, would she never fall asleep? Generally, sex with Luc left her totally wasted and ready to sleep for a month, but tonight she still felt wound tight.

Tia punched at her pillow and tried to get comfortable, but her mind wouldn't stop racing. Luc seemed distracted, too, after his long series of conversations with Tinker, and his sleep now was troubled. Maybe that was the problem. He'd been distracted during sex. Luc was never an inattentive lover. No wonder she couldn't sleep.

Damn, she missed Tinker so much. He wasn't her significant other, not her mate, but he was important to their relationship in so many ways. She wondered sometimes if Tinker's prowess in bed kept Luc on his toes—nothing like a little competition to keep a man sharp, and damn, but Tinker was amazing.

She thought of Tinker as the brother she'd never had, the companion always willing to take a chance, the one who understood Tia when she wasn't certain she understood herself. He was as close to Luc as he was to Tia, and Luc loved Tinker more than any man around. Tinker McClintock completed them. Made Luc and Tia more than what they were by themselves, completed their ménage. Now everything had changed, just as she'd feared.

"Tia?" Luc raised his head and stared at her through sleepy eyes. "What's the matter? Are you okay?"

She smiled and dipped her chin against his chest. "Just worried about Tink. Do you think he really loves this woman? They hardly know each other."

Luc's smile spread slowly across his face. "Jealous?"

Tia shook her head. "No. Just worried. I mean, I loved Tala from the first moment AJ and Mik brought her here. If Lisa is anything like her sister, she'll be wonderful. A perfect mate for Tinker, but if she's not like Tala . . . if she's not right . . ." Tia sighed. "I want him to be happy. Is that asking so much?"

This time Luc laughed out loud. "You want him to be happy and still available to use that tongue where you need it most."

Tia giggled. "Well, there is that."

Luc raised himself up over her and grinned. His eyes sparkled with love and lust and a whole lot more. "I've got a tongue."

Tia covered her mouth with her hand in mock surprise. "Well, you could have fooled me!"

Luc leaned down, moved her hand aside with his lips, and kissed her, and she knew he'd taken her jibe as a dare. She felt his tongue searching the seam of her lips, then sweeping across her teeth, tickling her sensitive palate, tangling with her tongue. Lord, how she loved this man! Tia opened her mouth wider to his kiss and sighed in disappointment when he kissed her quickly and then backed away.

Disappointment melted away as Luc nuzzled her chin and then kissed his way down her middle, licking and nipping every sensitive spot she'd ever known and finding new ones along the way. Tia almost reached for his thick, dark hair to direct his kisses, then thought better of it. Instead, she tightened her fingers in the bedding and arched to Luc's experienced touch.

His lips found her right nipple and brought it quickly to a tight, sensitive peak. Then he used the tip of his tongue to flick the taut little bundle of nerves. Shivering under his slow but steady exploration of her body, Tia felt her arousal grow, felt the rush of blood through her veins, the pounding of her heart.

So many times now, Luc had made love to her, yet each time might have been the first. Each searching kiss, each flick of his tongue, as if he'd never tasted her this way before. He licked and sucked her left nipple now, flicking the tip with the point of his tongue, then drawing the entire nipple into his mouth. The heat was incredible, the sensations sending shockwaves from her breast to her womb.

Tia arched her back, offering herself to his touch, to his lips, to his amazing tongue. Luc was right. He was every bit as skilled as Tinker.

Luc's fingers were as busy as his mouth, slipping into the moist valley between her thighs, stroking her soft and damply swollen labia. He found a rhythm between lips and tongue, his fingers, and the palm of his hand. Tia felt her peak rising, felt the climax growing deep in her center.

Once again, Luc slowed. His fingers left the soft folds between her legs and rested atop her thigh. He kissed his way slowly now, finding each rib and licking, then suckling her skin between his lips. He swirled his tongue around Tia's navel, and then nipped the sensitive patch above her pubic bone.

She cried out and arched into his bite, hovering on the edge of climax. So close. Not nearly close enough. Tia's orgasm simmered beneath the surface, waiting impatiently for more stimulation. Luc slipped lower, parting her knees and kneeling between her legs. He grabbed a pillow and shoved it under her hips, raising her for his touch. His teeth scraped the tender flesh along the inside of her thigh, and he nipped her there before gently soothing her with his tongue. He leaned close and licked her once between the legs, his tongue barely touching her clit.

She thought of begging but refused to give in, though this teasing, barely there touching had her strung tight. Luc held her in place, right below her peak, her body quivering with need wondering what would come next, what torture he had in mind.

Once again he nuzzled between her legs, licking and suckling her labia but completely ignoring her clit. Tia tilted her hips forward, blatantly begging for more. Luc sat back on his heels and grinned at her.

"Still not as good as Tinker, eh?"

"Well, he certainly doesn't make me wait around! Don't you dare stop." Laughing, Tia reached for his hand, but Luc pulled it out of her reach. "Luc, I'm so close!"

"Poor baby." He dipped down between her legs, nuzzling and licking.

Tia lay back and closed her eyes as Luc's tongue finally found her clit. He touched her gently, barely enough to bring her back to the edge. She opened her thoughts and found a blank wall where Luc's mind should have been. *Blocked, damn it!* What in the heck was he up to now?

She reached over her head and grabbed the iron headboard. Anchored now, Tia spread her legs wider in invitation just as a long, hot, rough tongue snaked from her anus to her clit, then delved deeply into her weeping pussy.

Luc's thoughts swept into her mind, the thoughts of a wolf taking a woman, and when she opened her eyes, it was the wolf who stared at her from between her legs.

She sensed his laughter, but all Tia could do was moan in response. Luc's wolven nose was wet and cold where it nuzzled her clit, and his tongue darted deep inside to stroke the inner walls of her pussy.

When he concentrated on her clitoris with that rough but mobile tongue, Tia screamed and arched her back. She reached for Luc, but he was already shifting, sliding forward now as a man, driving his cock deep inside her spasming walls, filling her with one powerful thrust that almost lifted Tia from the bed. She felt his balls against her ass on each downward stroke, felt the sweep of his rigid cock dragging at her swollen clit.

The second climax caught her by surprise, took her breath away with its power. Body shuddering, Tia gripped the headboard once again to keep from flying to pieces.

She had to turn it loose, though, when Luc gathered her in his arms and sat back on his heels. Tia wrapped her legs around his waist and her arms around his neck. This time, when her climax hit, she took Luc with her. She felt the hard jerks of his cock, the pulsating, throbbing size of him inside as he filled her with his seed. She felt his heart pounding against her chest, the hot rush of his breath when he finally drew air into his straining lungs.

Luc rolled over onto his back with Tia draped across his chest. His cock slipped free of her folds, and she felt it, now soft and pliant, resting damply against her thigh. When she finally caught her breath, Tia rose up with her arms folded under her and stared into Luc's amber eyes.

"Okay," she conceded. "I admit, you're just as good as Tinker."

He growled, then laughed out loud. "Just as good? Lord, woman. What's it going to take to impress you?" He tilted his head up and kissed her gently on the lips. "I love you."

Tia felt the tears well up in her eyes. "That's all it takes. I love you, too." She kissed Luc again and felt him stir against her thigh. This time, when they made love, there was no laughter, but there was a deeper sense of commitment than Tia had ever known.

And, at the peak of their climax, there was something more. A cry of need, a silent yet still powerful call for help.

Tinker needed them. His mate was in danger, and he needed Luc and Tia. Sobbing with her release, Tia gave in to the power of her orgasm and held on to Luc. She almost laughed through her fears when the thought hit her—Tinker'd managed to find his way into their bed after all.

Chapter 8

Tinker arrived at the place where Lisa had been abducted just as a shadowy figure shut the driver's side door on one of the sanctuary trucks. The engine roared to life, an obscene sound in the depths of the woods. Even more obscene was the metal cage in the back of the pickup. Tinker couldn't see Lisa, but her scent was strong, and he knew she was in there.

He searched for her thoughts and found nothing. The drug must have knocked her out completely. Tinker prayed Lisa had the strength to remain in wolven form. The consequences of their Chanku species being discovered were unthinkable . . . as unthinkable as harm coming to his mate. Tinker saw what looked like a heavy lock on the front of the cage. Even if Lisa were human, she'd be unable to free herself.

How the hell was he going to get her out?

The truck backed up slowly, and the driver turned it around, then headed out the service road, away from the main compound. Tinker hadn't gotten a good look at him, though his scent was familiar. He loped along behind, staying in the shadows, well aware the driver wouldn't be watching for a black wolf following.

His mind spun with plans, rejected as soon as they arrived. He needed his packmates, needed the combined logic of his brothers, but they were far away. Out of reach, not only by mental communication, but cell phone as well.

Tinker recognized the direction they were headed and knew it would take them away from the main part of the sanctuary, toward an area of sheds and storage buildings, many of them remnants of the old cattle ranch this property had originally been.

About two miles down the road, the driver pulled into a spot next to a dilapidated barn. Tinker waited in the shadows and wondered if he should merely attack the driver and free Lisa, or wait and see what the bastard had planned.

The door opened and Seth climbed out of the truck.

Seth? What the hell was the kid doing? Tinker tried scanning the boy's mind, but he'd never been all that adept at reading someone who wasn't actually projecting. Not like Tia, who could pick thoughts out of his mind as if his brain were an open book.

Right now Tinker wished he had Tia beside him. *If wishes were horses . . .* He wasn't quite sure what made him think of his foster mother, but she'd used that phrase often enough. It was time to act, and he was on his own. He couldn't change the circumstances. Tinker almost smiled. He knew exactly what Luc would say right now. It was time to adapt.

Seth lowered the tailgate, checked the cage holding Lisa, and went inside the barn. Tinker slunk across the dark road and leaped into the back of the truck to get a better look at the lock. Up close, he realized the mechanism was similar to the fasteners used by mountain climbers, just a plain old carabiner. Nothing he couldn't open with his hands. Lisa was barely visible inside the metal cage. She lay on her side, still a wolf, obviously deeply drugged. He inhaled her shallow breaths and breathed his own sigh of relief.

Tinker heard a rhythmic squeaking sound. He jumped

out of the back of the truck and dropped to all fours in the dark shadows near the rear wheel on the far side of the pickup. Seth came into view hauling a wheeled cart, much like the one he'd used to carry the dead deer. He positioned it at the end of the truck, then climbed into the bed.

Tinker couldn't see him from his hiding place, but he heard Seth's soft whistle and quiet voice. "You are a beauty, aren't you? Mr. Smith won't believe it when I tell him I got a wild wolf. I thought maybe you'd just gotten out of one of the pens, but I know I've never seen you before, and there's no tag in your ear. I bet I get a bonus for you, sweetheart. He's always telling me to look for the ones with the most spirit. If you're still wild, I bet you've got a lot."

There was a loud scraping sound as Seth dragged the cage to the end of the pickup bed; he grunted loudly as he manhandled it onto the cart. Tinker slipped around the back wheel so he could see better, then followed Seth into the dark barn.

Once through the door, Tinker realized there was a small electric lantern burning at one end. He stayed in the shadows near the door and hoped his black coat would make him invisible to the teenager.

Seth rolled the cart to the far end of the barn and checked the lock. Then he glanced at his watch and looked toward the door. He walked back to the cage and stood there a moment, looking down at his captive. "You'll be okay until tomorrow morning. Mr. Smith said he'd have someone here early." He patted the top of the cage, and Tinker could hear him sigh. "I really hate doing this. I hope you know that, but I've got no choice. Don't worry, though. You'll be okay in your new home."

Seth turned away and walked back to the door, passing within a couple feet of Tinker. "I'm sorry about the dart. I really don't have a choice. No choice at all." Still muttering to himself, Seth pulled the barn door closed, locking Tinker inside with Lisa.

As soon as the truck pulled away, Tinker shifted. Standing tall on two feet, he checked the barn door and realized the latch was simple enough for human hands. It took him less than a minute to open Lisa's cage and pull her comatose body out. Lifting her carefully into his arms, Tinker slipped out of the barn and into the night. Running barefoot and naked, he still managed to reach Lisa's small cabin in less than an hour.

"What in the hell were you thinking? Why didn't you leave me there? We might have figured out what the fuck was going on around here. Now we'll never know." Lisa paced back and forth across her small kitchen. Her head pounded from the drug in her system, and her hip hurt where the dart had penetrated. *Men. They always know what's best—even when they're dead wrong.*

Tinker leaned against the kitchen counter and just shook his head, looking more bemused than contrite. His typical macho stance infuriated Lisa even more.

"I was thinking that freeing you would be a lot more acceptable than killing that damned kid, which was my first inclination. Lisa, I was on my own. If he'd hit the highway with you still unconscious, I'd never be able to find you. That's unacceptable."

Lisa stared at Tinker as if a stranger had taken over his body. Didn't he understand the chance they'd lost? Here she'd been suspecting Anderson, and it looked like Seth was the guilty party. They needed to find out who the hell was yanking Seth's chain and what was happening to the wolves, but Tinker'd managed to screw that up big time.

He folded his big arms across his chest, and Lisa's mouth went dry. Damn, she loved the way his body looked. She really hated that it was hard to argue with a man who turned her on as much as Tinker did with nothing more than the tilt of his head and the width of his chest.

He'd taken the time to slip into jeans. The top two snaps were undone, exposing the narrow line of dark hair against darker skin, running from his navel to parts south. His chest was bare. His feet were, too. She loved his long, narrow feet, but this was not the time to be admiring either his chest or his feet or the strength of his arms. Or his hands. He had the most beautiful hands, with long, sensitive fingers that . . . *shit*.

Lisa spun away and stared out the window. "I want to go back. I want you to put me back in the cage before whoever it is comes to pick it up in the morning."

Tinker stared at her as if she was nuts. Maybe she was, but they were so close to finding out who was taking the wolves. She hated to think Seth was involved. What if Luc's suspicions were right? What if Dunlop were somehow behind whatever was going on? If it turned out the man was a criminal, the sanctuary might be shut down.

Then what would happen to the wolves?

"Absolutely not." Tinker rolled his shoulders and flexed his massive arms across his perfect chest and glared at her.

This was a side of Tinker Lisa hadn't seen before. She wasn't sure how she felt about him suddenly taking on this uber-alpha role, but her body didn't seem to have the same reservations. In spite of herself, Lisa felt a quick dampening between her legs and turned away, suddenly thrown off balance.

Tinker was always so easygoing. Lisa was never turned on by he-man theatrics. Usually. She took a deep breath and forced her libido under control. "We have to do something."

"*We* don't have to do anything. I'll take care of this."

Lisa turned around slowly and glared at him. No longer aroused, she felt anger boiling just beneath her surface. "No, Tinker. *We* will take care of this, or I will, but you're not in charge here."

"I'm your mate and I've—"

"You're my mate only because you blindsided me into linking. That's what you did, isn't it? Created a bond without telling me what I was getting into? Face it, McClintock. You're stuck with me, and it's all an accident. Well, if you regret what happened, if you want out, you figure out a way to unbond us and I'm out. Okay?"

Lisa heard the words rolling so easily off her tongue and couldn't believe she had said them. She didn't want out. Not at all. She loved Tinker and she needed him beside her. Especially now. Of all times, now.

Tinker stared at her as if she'd slapped him. In a way, she had. She'd thrown his love back in his face, but she didn't know how to call back the words. She couldn't call back the truth. He didn't control her, didn't make her rules. She'd had a chance tonight to find out what was going on with the wolves, and he'd ruined it.

Tinker's cell phone rang. He stared at the useless thing clipped to his hip. There shouldn't be a signal here. Shouldn't be anything to make it ring. Like a man moving in slow motion, Tinker unclipped the phone from his belt and answered it.

Lisa turned away, uncomfortable overhearing whatever he had to say. She flopped down in one of the kitchen chairs and folded her arms across her chest. In less than a minute, Tinker turned off the phone.

His voice sounded uncharacteristically flat. "Lucien Stone and Tia Mason are on their way. They left San Francisco an hour ago. That was Anton Cheval. He's Chanku, part of the Montana group, and the only one I know who could make a cell phone work in this canyon."

His comments took the breath from Lisa's lungs. She sat up straighter in her chair. "I don't understand. How did they know we needed help? You haven't called. You're too far from San Francisco to communicate mentally. How?"

Tinker shook his head, but now he was grinning. "I have

no idea, but I'll bet the farm that Luc and Tia were screwing each other's brains out when they got my frustrated mental call for help. We've proved that sexual arousal makes our mindtalking abilities that much more powerful. I imagine Anton Cheval picked up on what happened to you because of my frustration at not being able to help you. Frustration strengthens our communications as well, but I can honestly tell you, there is very little Cheval can't do."

Tinker leaned close and rested his hands on the arms of the wooden chair. He was so infuriatingly sexy and cocky that Lisa wanted to smack him.

"We're Chanku, Lisa. We're family. We look out for each other. We help each other. We love each other. And once we bond, we bond for life. Get used to it."

He leaned closer and kissed her hard and fast, his lips leaving the taste and heat she'd so quickly learned to crave. Then he left her there with her mouth hanging open. Just walked away. He strolled toward the bedroom door as if they hadn't had their first major disagreement since meeting. Strolled as if the only thing he had to worry about in life was strutting that perfect ass of his for her pleasure.

And damned if she didn't feel herself literally creaming her shorts. There was no denying the warm knot of desire blossoming in her womb, no denying the clenching of muscles between her legs. She needed him. Needed Tinker now in a most amazing way, just the two of them, together, finding the time and space to work through the convoluted issues of power and control and love.

They wouldn't be alone much longer. Lisa sensed that much within their relationship would change once Tinker's packmates arrived. Her packmates as well. It was weird, knowing Tinker's friends, his lovers, were on their way. *Unbelievable.* She knew they were coming to help, but Lisa found herself thinking with avid anticipation of the beautiful biracial woman who held a very secure spot in Tinker's memories.

ize--

The same memories he'd shared with her the night they bonded. Her pussy clenched once more. Lisa wasn't sure if it was the typical arousal after a shift or a reaction to her thoughts of Tinker and Tia. Both of them had become a major part of her fantasies.

Fantasies won't help the wolves. Lisa blinked away images of Tia and Tinker tangled in sex and wrapped her arms around herself. She sat alone in the kitchen for what felt like a very long time. She still felt woozy from the drug, and her head pounded as frustration over the situation with the wolves thrummed through her veins. All her worries, though, competed with arousal, with a deep yearning to merely crawl into bed next to Tinker and feel his body next to hers.

There was nothing to do now but wait.

And absolutely no reason whatsoever to wait by herself. Grinning, feeling a little sheepish and a whole lot turned on, she finally followed Tinker into the bedroom.

Tinker lay in the small room and wondered if he'd totally screwed up everything with Lisa. Should he go to her and apologize? Hell, if he had to do it again, he knew damned well he'd do everything exactly the same. He thought about the few times when Luc was upset with Tia, how his friend said he felt so helpless, as though he didn't understand a woman's thought processes at all.

For the first time, Tinker truly sympathized with Luc. There was no figuring out what went on in a woman's mind, even when you'd bonded with them, when you'd shared their innermost thoughts. Did Lisa really regret their bond? Did she honestly think Tinker would have left her lying in that cage, unconscious with no idea what that damned kid had planned?

Tinker was lying on his side, staring at the wall with his thoughts in turmoil, when he heard the door open. He felt the edge of the bed dip as Lisa crawled in beside him. A narrow shaft of light spilled into the room from the single lamp in the kitchen. He smiled to himself, suddenly much more at ease, yet well aware how much pride she'd had to swallow to join him. There was a perfectly comfortable couch in the front room if Lisa was really angry.

She snuggled close against his body, and he felt her warm breath feathering across the ridge of his shoulder. Her breasts pressed into his back, and one slim arm circled his hips. He felt the soft brush of her palm against his belly, low enough that her fingers tangled in the thick mat of black hair covering his groin.

Tinker's cock reacted immediately to her velvet touch, but his heart almost stuttered to a stop when she pressed her lips against his back and whispered, "I'm sorry for what I said, Tink. I love you. I would never wish away our bond."

He covered her hand with his and felt the pain drain away. "I know, sweetie. We say a lot of things when we're upset. Things we really don't mean. Luc and Tia will be here in a few hours. Let's get some sleep and deal with the wolves after they're here."

Her lips feathered kisses along his spine. "Do we really have to sleep? Right now?"

His cock didn't think so. Tinker grinned while he took his time answering, but he lacked the willpower not to thrust his hips forward into Lisa's soft grasp.

She laughed and ran her tongue down his spine. Her slim fingers trailed along the hard length of his cock, touching him so lightly with the very tips that he wanted to scream. His balls pulled up tightly between his legs, and his body quivered. "I might be persuaded," he said, but his voice sounded ragged even in his own ears.

"Oh . . . playing hard to get?"

Tinker shivered at the soft brush of her lips when Lisa whispered against the nape of his neck. Every muscle in his body tensed when her fingertip found the damp eye at the crown of his cock. One finger. She touched him with just one finger, but it was wet from his pre-cum, and she left a line of fire as she trailed it along the ridged underside of his cock.

Tinker couldn't remember being this hard or this turned on, and she'd barely touched him. Her body was plastered against his from calves to shoulders, her taut nipples poked into his back, and her breath was warm against his neck, but the only sign she was even awake was that one hand. One hand barely touching his cock, teasing him with featherlight strokes, the scrape of a nail, the soft pressure from a single fingertip.

It was getting hard to breathe, hard to keep his hands to himself while she teased him, but he concentrated on the pressure from that one finger, concentrated on the way she made him feel.

Her tongue caught him just behind his ear, and Tinker groaned. Lisa nipped his earlobe and tugged, then gently bit the soft skin between his shoulder and neck. This time he was prepared and did his best to ignore her.

Tinker heard her soft chuckle, felt the pressure of her breasts bouncing against his back as she laughed. "Definitely a challenge," she said, nipping him once more. "Lisa Quinn never backs down from a challenge."

She scooted away and rose to her knees, hovering over him in the darkness. Her long hair swept his side as she rolled him to his back and stretched his arms up over his head. "Hold on to the headboard and don't let go."

Curious to see how far she'd take this, Tinker did as he was told. She arranged his legs, spreading them wide so that he filled the entire bed, then sat back on her heels as if to admire her handiwork.

"Good lord, but you're beautiful. I probably shouldn't even tell you this, but I think of you as my dark god." She leaned over and swirled her tongue around his right nipple, then sat back again, totally ignoring his cock. It wasn't like the damned thing was trying to hide. No, it stood up like a flagpole, slightly curved toward his belly and so hard he ached for her to touch him.

Tinker thought about commenting on what Lisa had said, but the only sound he was capable of at the moment was a strangled whimper. In the back of his mind, the opinion that gods probably didn't whimper floated about, but he had no control around Lisa. None at all.

She licked his left nipple on her next foray, then ran her fingers lightly along his pectorals, stroking the curve of his muscles, making them jump and twitch in response to her touch.

Tinker felt as if he might explode. The pressure in his balls grew with each simple touch, and his cock was leaking a steady stream of fluid. He wondered if he might come from just watching her supple body as she leaned over to flick her tongue across his nipple or rub her fingers over his chest.

Lisa tilted her head and finally acknowledged his straining cock, but all she did was brush her fingers under the crown to catch a few drops of pre-cum. Then she raised her fingers to her mouth and sucked them between her lips.

Tinker felt an orgasm building, merely from watching the way she wrapped her lips around her fingers, the slow, steady rhythm as she pushed them in and out of her mouth. Lisa's eyes were closed, her head thrown back, her long dark hair hanging in luxurious waves over her breasts. Tinker clutched at the metal frame of the headboard and hoped the thing was strong enough to hold him.

Lisa glanced down at him through heavy-lidded eyes. Suddenly his mind filled with sensation, with the taste of his own fluids, the deep throbbing between Lisa's legs, the ache in his balls. Without another word, she turned around and licked his cock, running her tongue slowly along the full length from his balls to the crown, lapping up every drop of pre-cum.

More escaped and she licked that up as well, but he

wanted more. Needed more. Needed her sweet mouth around his cock or the tight clasp of her sex holding him, but Lisa shook her head and continued her slow, steady licking, swirling her tongue around the crown and then teasing the length of him.

Tinker tried to stop the low moans that seemed to start deep in his chest, but he had as much luck with that as he did the steady stream of fluid leaking from his cock. He didn't think he could get any harder, but Lisa slipped lower between his legs and nipped at his sac with her lips and teeth. Her fingers curled over his thighs, holding him right at the crease between leg and groin, and she sucked one ball into her mouth and rolled it around with her tongue.

He almost came off the bed.

She did the same to his other nut, and Tinker felt branded. He identified all ten of her fingers pressing into his flesh, and he burned with the heat of her mouth as she sucked on his balls and rolled them with her tongue, licking and doing her best to drive him insane. On top of it all, the sensations streaming into his mind were filled with her wickedly carnal thoughts, with the things she planned to do to him. Things she wanted Tinker to do to her.

Damn, Lisa was having way too much fun driving him mad, but he'd promised to hold on, and he did. His fingers tightened on the metal shafts of the headboard, and he heard them creak in protest. His hips lifted off the bed when she finally wrapped her mouth around the crown of his cock, but as much as he wanted her to suck him deep, she merely held the very tip between her lips and flicked at the seeping slit at the top with her tongue.

He was practically gasping, nothing more than a helpless fish out of water while she teased and tormented him, but Tinker couldn't remember ever feeling so alive before, so aware of his own body. Lost in sensation, moaning softly with the intense level of arousal, Tinker hardly noticed when Lisa switched position.

The hot, wet clasp of her sex as she directed his swollen cock inside almost took him over the edge. Perfect. She was so damned perfect, her body molding to hold his as if she'd been designed specifically for him. Tinker groaned and let go of the headboard. His hands rested first on her hip bones. Then he found her breasts.

He wrapped his hands around her sides and flicked her taut nipples with his thumbs, lifting her, easing her back down, helping Lisa settle herself astride. He raised his knees and drove into her, and she arched her back, taking him all the way.

It wasn't enough. Not nearly enough, and he'd given up control for much too long. Lifting Lisa away from his body, Tinker rolled her over to her belly and covered her from behind. She squirmed and giggled but somehow managed to end up with her arms folded under her chin and her butt in the air. Kneeling behind her, Tinker grabbed Lisa by the hips and lifted her higher, then filled her in one deep thrust. He felt resistance at the apex of his thrust and knew he'd gone as deep as he could, but she grunted and pressed back against him. She wanted more. Impossibly, she wanted more of him.

His balls slapped her in the clit. He thrust again, harder, faster, and she met him each time as if it were a contest of wills, of who had the power to hold out the longest. He reached around and found her clit with the rough tip of his finger and stroked her unmercifully. She cried out, arched her back, and climaxed, and her sex held him like a hot fist.

He wasn't through, and he wasn't going to be denied. She'd put him through hell tonight, and she hadn't understood, didn't have a clue how badly she'd hurt him, how much she'd scared him.

How very much he loved her. Tinker pulled out of Lisa's grasping sex, rolled her to her back, and thrust deep inside once more. She looked at him with tear-filled eyes, reached for his face, and cupped his cheek in her palm.

I'm sorry. I love you. I didn't think.

Tinker had had no idea he was broadcasting his feelings, no idea she might be privy to his innermost pain. Tears filled his eyes. He blinked them away and then gathered her close. He tilted his hips again, more gently this time, and slowed the rhythm of his lovemaking, taking her slow and easy, bringing her once more to the edge of climax.

When he reached between their bodies and found her clit, his touch this time was gentle, soothed by the moisture from her first orgasm. He rubbed the rounded bundle of nerves, stroking her lightly, taking her back to her peak.

This time when Lisa went over the top, Tinker went with her. He felt the climax rolling down his spine, through his balls, along the length of his cock. Felt even more this time, with her thoughts of love mingling with his own silent apology.

They had a lot to learn about being a bonded pair. A lot to learn about sharing and communicating and dealing with anger.

Tinker was glad Luc and Tia were on their way. At least those two had figured out how to get it right, and they'd started out with even more against them. Wrapping his arms around his lady, Tinker lay back on the bed with her sprawled over his body. They really needed a shower after all that sex. Really ought to go clean up or they'd be stuck together by morning.

Lisa grinned. He felt the slide of her lips across his chest and realized she'd been in his thoughts again. He'd have to talk to her about that, about reading minds without an invitation.

Of course, he did it to her often enough, but only when she practically screamed her innermost feelings.

Her voice slipped into his half-awake consciousness. *I like being able to read your thoughts. It's the only way to know what's going on in that hard head of yours. And, Tink . . . if I'm going to be stuck with anyone, I'm sure glad it's you.*

Tangling his fingers in her hair, Tinker drifted off with Lisa's scent in his nostrils and her body draped across his. He was glad she felt that way, since it looked like they weren't going to get that shower.

Chapter 9

Tink? Can you hear me yet? We're getting near the sanctuary, maybe ten miles south. How do we find Lisa's place?

Tinker raised his head and blinked himself awake. It was still dark, but Tia's voice came through loud and clear. His first thought was that he shouldn't be able to hear her so well, so many miles away, but this was Tia and she'd been working hard at developing much stronger communication abilities. Of course, being a full-blooded Chanku probably had something to do with her powers coming across such great distances. All the others he knew, including himself, were half-breeds.

Tinker answered Tia to let her know he'd heard her. Lisa was still sprawled across his chest, sound asleep. He'd been right—they were practically stuck together. Grinning at the visual that popped into his head, he gave Tia concise instructions to the cabin and then carefully rolled Lisa to one side. She grunted but didn't awaken.

Lisa was still asleep ten minutes later when Tinker got out of the shower. He watched her a moment, her long hair tangled around her arms and drifting over the pillow, and felt a surge of love so powerful it almost knocked him to his knees. Damn, she was absolutely perfect. He could have lost her.

Tinker couldn't recall ever in his life being as frightened as he'd been last night, but, then, he'd never had as much to lose before. Thank goodness Tia and Luc were almost here. He needed his packmates' support when he told Lisa she wasn't going after the bad guys on her own. Smiling at her tenacity and hopelessly proud of her stubborn pride, Tinker leaned over and kissed her. She opened her eyes and smiled sleepily at him.

He couldn't help himself. Tinker kissed her again. He had to force himself away when she reached for him. He tapped her nose with his fingertip. "Unless you want to meet your new packmates still smelling sweetly of a whole lot of really steamy sex, you might want to take a shower. They should be pulling in any minute now."

"Oh shit!"

Barely awake, Lisa pushed Tinker out of the way and ran into the bathroom. He slipped on a pair of sweats just as a car pulled up in front of the cabin. When he went to meet their guests, Tinker could still hear Lisa cursing in the shower.

The voice filled her mind, bubbling over with laughter and good wishes. *Take your time, Lisa. We're going to enjoy a cup of coffee on your lovely deck. I can't wait to meet you!*

Tia? Lisa paused with the washcloth in her hand, stunned to hear a voice other than Tinker's in her head. *I'll be out in a minute.*

It was actually closer to five, but at least she was clean and her hair tied back in a single wet braid. Lisa threw on a pair of loose cargo pants and an old sweatshirt, then padded barefoot through the house on her way to the deck. She snagged a cup of coffee on the way.

Tinker waited in the front room. He took Lisa's hand and led her out onto the back deck. Both Luc and Tia stood when she stepped through the sliding glass door.

"Wow." The words slipped out before she realized she'd said anything. Though she'd seen both Chanku through

Tinker's eyes, Lisa really hadn't a clue as to their pure, physical beauty. Luc was tall with overly long dark hair brush-
ing the collar of his shirt, lean in the way of swimmers
with broad shoulders and trim hips. Tia stood proudly beside him, her skin the color of coffee with cream, her long
blond hair falling in thick curls well past her shoulders.

Both of them greeted her with smiles. Luc held out his
arms, and Lisa slipped into his embrace as if they'd known
each other for years. In a way, they had, she thought. She
held Tinker's memories of some amazing sex with both
Luc and Tia in her mind. When she slipped just as easily
out of Luc's embrace, Lisa realized she'd like to share
more than mere secondhand memories with Lucien Stone.

Tia was next, hugging Lisa warmly. Then she kissed her
full on the mouth, chastely, but with a promise of more.
Her mental words had a sultry drawl to them.

I really want to get to know you better.

Laughing, Lisa kissed her back. *Works for me,* she said,
marveling at how easy it was to fall into this form of communication with others besides Tinker.

She sat next to Tinker on the porch swing, slipping beneath his arm as if they'd been together forever. His body
felt warm and strong, and very much as if he belonged beside her.

Tinker kissed her temple, then took another sip of coffee.
"Luc's discovered some interesting background on
Dunlop. Seems there's a chance he's involved with a big
game hunting preserve. Ownership is buried under a cor-
poration name, and we're not completely positive yet, but
it's one of those fancy places where guys with way too
much money can go hunt. Thing is, at this particular
place, they get to hunt endangered and protected species."

Lisa stared at Tinker. "Like wolves?" When Tinker
nodded, she asked, "Where is it?"

"Right here in Colorado and not all that far from us.
More than ten thousand acres of prime forest, all privately

owned. It's billed as a 'nature retreat,' and he leads private hunts. The prey is set loose and given a bit of a head start. The hunters work with dogs provided by the owners, and the entire ten thousand acres is fenced and guarded."

"Are wolves the only game?" Lisa shuddered, thinking of the pup that had disappeared. It was too used to people. There was no way he would know the danger behind men with guns.

"No. Rhino, big cats, bears, even elephants when he can get them, but wolves are their specialty. The ads for the preserve claim they can get any animal a hunter wants to add to his trophy collection, for a price. I imagine the wolves are popular because they don't have to pay top dollar for them, if we're right about Dunlop's connection. He's got his own wolf sanctuary, and it essentially doubles as a breeding farm." Tinker hugged her close against him. "I've told Tia and Luc about the situation here, about the wolves disappearing and that you were darted last night by the kid who works for the sanctuary. As far as Seth knows, he's caught a wild wolf and still has it caged in that old barn."

Luc jumped into the conversation. "Obviously, whoever picks the wolves up is taking them to this hunting club and charging hunters the big bucks to get the chance to hunt one of our nation's smartest predators. What we'll do is substitute me for you in the cage. Tinker thinks our coats are about the same color and—"

"Absolutely not." Lisa shot to her feet and glared at Tinker. "If anyone goes back in that cage, it's me. I know the players, and Seth may be young, but he's not an idiot. He knows he darted a medium-size female. When he sees a large male in there, he's going to know something weird is happening."

"You're not going back in that cage." Tinker stood up and set the swing swaying wildly back and forth. "No way in hell are—"

"Don't you dare tell me what I can and cannot do."

Lisa's angry shout cut through Tinker's words. She rolled her fingers into fists.

"I still think—"

"Wait a minute. All of you." Tia cut into Luc's comment and held up a hand for quiet. Amazingly, both men shut up and listened.

Lisa flashed her a grin.

"I agree with Lisa. She's the one the kid tranked; she's the one who needs to follow through on this. We've brought tracers with us, and it shouldn't be that hard to stay in contact." Tia turned to Lisa. "It's your call, hon. How do you feel about it?"

Lisa plopped back down on the swing, secretly amazed at Tia's power within the group. Tinker hadn't been kidding about the role of the alpha bitch. "Thank you. It's the only solution, but we need to hurry. I have to be back in the cage before daylight. I just need to be there long enough to find out who picks up the wolves and where they take them."

Tinker crossed his arms over his chest and glared at Tia. "Traitor." Then he turned to Lisa. "I don't like this. I don't like it one bit. You have absolutely no plan. No idea how you're going to get out once you get in."

Tia lightly punched his shoulder. "As I recall, when you said you were coming to Colorado and I asked what your plan was, you said you were going to wing it. Exact words. If you can wing it, so can Lisa."

Tinker shoved his fists against his hips and glared first at Tia, and then at Lisa. For the first time, Lisa saw his anger for the emotion it truly represented. He was worried he might lose her. He really was afraid for her. It wasn't all macho posturing as she'd first thought.

Lisa grabbed Tinker's hand and pulled him back down to sit beside her on the swing. She touched the side of his face and forced him to look into her eyes. His sparkled with amber lights and what looked suspiciously like tears.

I love you. I won't get hurt. I need to come back to you as much as you want me back. Maybe more.

Tinker's chest heaved as he drew in a huge breath and then let it out on a gusty sigh. Then he grinned, though Lisa realized there was no humor in his smile. "I know," he said aloud. "I still don't have to like it."

"You'll have to hold the transmitter in your mouth, down in that little pouch that forms behind your back teeth after you shift." Luc held a tiny plastic disk between his thumb and forefinger. "If we try and attach it to your body, someone will find it. I wish we could insert it under your skin."

"Ouch." Lisa shuddered at the thought. Tinker squeezed her arm for comfort.

Luc just laughed. "Except the minute you shift, it would fall on the ground. You've probably noticed you can't wear any jewelry or clips in your hair. When you shift, they're gone. I sure hope you didn't have any fillings in your teeth!"

Laughing, Lisa shook her head. "Nope. Perfect teeth. They'd fall out, too?"

Tia snorted. "Yeah. Like Tala's IUD. I just about choked when your sister told me about her first shift. She said the little coil fell right out on the floor! Good thing we've got that controlled-egg-release thing going, right?"

"Her IUD fell out? I haven't seen Mary Ellen in ten years, but that sounds exactly like something that would happen to her." Lisa held out her hand. "Let me have the transmitter. What's the range for this thing?" She studied the tiny plastic disk.

Luc grinned when he launched into an explanation. It was obvious he loved the techno-toys. "It's a GPS—global positioning system—so your location will be relayed to us via satellite no matter where you go, though it's not quite as effective if you're inside a building. It's a prototype, developed for tracking migrating birds and such, which is why it's so tiny."

Tia poked Luc in the side with her elbow. "Tracking birds. Yeah, right. That's why it was developed by the Department of Defense."

Luc flashed a broad smile at Tia and poked her back, but he spoke directly to Lisa. "If you hadn't noticed, my mate and I tend to differ politically. Anyway, if you're absolutely positive you want to go through with this, we need to get moving so we can have you safely back in your cage before anyone comes to retrieve the wolf."

Lisa didn't expect to feel so nervous when Tinker closed the door on her in the metal cage. The sky had begun to fade from black to the pale mauve of early dawn, but the barn was pitch black inside. Even with her Chanku vision, it was difficult to see. When the metal door slammed shut and she heard the latch fasten into place, her heart suddenly began to pound.

She whimpered and flicked her tongue through the slats in the door. Tinker reached through the bars and stroked her ears.

Luc waited in the rental car with Tia. He'd wanted to be the wolf who helped Lisa and was totally frustrated at being away from the main part of the action, but Tinker refused to let himself be separated from his mate. There wasn't really much he could do for her, but neither Luc nor Tinker would allow her to wait here alone. Even Tia had agreed it was a good idea to have one of the men close. Just in case.

With all three of them ganging up on her, Lisa agreed. Now she was glad she hadn't fought the idea enough to win. She wriggled her tongue around until she felt the small transmitter tucked down in the corner of her mouth. Lodged in the natural pouch between her cheek and back teeth, it felt fairly secure and barely noticeable.

Tinker squatted down in front of the cage. Lisa could

barely stand up inside the metal walls, but she stood as best she could, if only to get a better look. It said something about her increased Chanku libido that she would feel aroused right now, considering her situation.

Tinker was absolutely beautiful, and there wasn't an ounce of anything superfluous on his entire body. The fact that he squatted naked in front of her cage, balanced on the balls of his feet with his knees spread wide didn't hurt either, especially with all his attributes visible. Prepared to shift and follow her once someone came to pick up the wolf, he'd left his clothes with Lisa's in the car with Tia and Luc.

Lisa couldn't help but notice Tinker was totally unaroused right now, though he was still larger than any man she'd ever seen hard. It gave Lisa a good idea just how stressed he was by this entire situation. She'd rarely seen him flaccid, even after sex. *This is a new look for you,* she teased.

Tinker frowned. Obviously he didn't get it. Before Lisa could explain, her wolven ears picked up a distant rumble.

Tinker spun his head around and looked toward the closed barn door. "Damn it, Lisa. You be careful or I'm going to be so pissed at you." He winked at her to take the sting of his words away, and shifted. Tinker was even more beautiful as a wolf than he was in human form. Lisa watched him drift silently into the shadows toward the back of the barn.

An errant thought flitted through her mind: The few days since she'd first shifted had been so busy, she and Tinker still hadn't had sex as wolves. The first time didn't really count, since her shift had occurred in the midst of her climax.

As sexy as he looked as a man, he was even more luscious as a wolf. She stared into the shadows where he'd disappeared, imagining his wolven body covering hers, wondering what the difference would be, what it would feel like to have that powerful wolven cock fill her. It certainly gave her something to look forward to, once this whole mess was cleared up.

You guys okay in there? Sounds like someone's coming. Tia's soft voice filled Lisa's mind.

Luc's mental voice was firm and powerful. Lisa recognized the traits of a natural leader in everything he said and did. Now that she'd seen Luc in action, Tinker's love and respect for the man made even more sense. *Even if you're a long way from us,* Luc said, *Tia and I will be able to pick up your mental voice, so don't forget to project. We've learned to work together to increase our power to both read and transmit.*

We're fine, Tinker said, his words echoing in Lisa's mind. *Lisa's in her cage, and I'm in position. Tia, have you got a read on the transmitter?*

Working perfectly. Be careful, Tink. We love you both.

I love you, too. Can't wait until Lisa gets to know both of you a whole lot better.

The sexual innuendo in Tinker's slow comment took some of the pressure off Lisa. If he was back to thinking about sex, he must not be as concerned as she assumed he was about potential problems.

Tinker's soft voice wiped out that reassuring thought. *I love you, Lisa. Now, please, don't worry. I'm doing enough of that for both of us.* His laughter rolled through her mind, a gentle balm to her suddenly ragged nerves. *Remember,* he said, *we're professionals. Pack Dynamics does covert government work all the time, and we're damned good at our jobs.*

Do you wing it on those jobs?

No, sweetie. Never. We always have a plan. You come up with one yet?

I'm working on it. Lisa sensed Tinker transmitting his thoughts to her on a tighter range, unheard by either Luc or Tia. She'd have to learn how to do that. There were so many things about this body she didn't understand. For now, though, she felt warmth blossom in her chest at the concern in his voice as she crouched down in her cage and waited.

Lisa tried to spot Tinker on the far side of the barn, but he stayed to the shadows where he blended completely. Luckily there was enough junk in here to give him plenty of hiding places. If she couldn't see him with her enhanced Chanku vision, she doubted anyone else could either.

The sound of a vehicle grew closer. Lisa realized she was shivering, whether from fear or an excess of adrenaline she wasn't sure. She hoped Luc and Tia were hidden well enough. They'd parked off the road, but in an area where they should be able to get out quickly enough to follow whatever vehicle hauled Lisa away. Tinker would follow close behind, staying to the woods and relaying directions to Luc and Tia; then, when they finally got out of the maze of fire and service roads and reached a main route, he planned to get in the car with them while they followed Lisa's captors as closely as possible.

The barn door slid open, creaking loudly on rusty hinges. The sun had risen, and the two men coming through the door were backlit by the bright rays. Lisa couldn't see them well, though the silhouette of one of the men looked vaguely familiar.

Once they stepped beyond the glare, she quickly recognized Charles Dunlop by the style of his stride and the shape of his protruding belly. He appeared to be armed. When he passed through the door into the barn, she saw the gun more clearly but had no idea if it was loaded with bullets or darts. The other man wasn't familiar, but he was large and powerful-looking and made the hair on Lisa's neck stand up. She growled, a low threatening sound that rumbled up out of her chest.

It sounded so great and felt so good, she did it again.

"Look at this, Bill. The kid was right." Dunlop squatted down in front of her cage. "This one is wild. Beautiful. See, there's no tag in the ear. I had no idea there were any wild wolves left in this part of the country. Someone's going to pay top dollar to hunt this little bitch."

Hunt? Lisa sent her comment to Luc and Tia as well as Tinker. *You were right, Luc. It's Dunlop and one other guy. That's why the wolves have been disappearing. They're prey.*

Remember what I said about Dunlop's hunting preserve? You'd fetch a lot of money from some jerk who wants to hunt a wild predator.

Oh, Luc . . . you're such a sweet talker. Lisa relaxed a bit more when everyone laughed at her silly comment.

Bill, the large man with Dunlop, kicked Lisa's cage. She snarled and threw herself at the metal door, assuming that was the reaction he wanted. Dunlop grabbed his arm. "Hey, don't do that. I don't want her pelt damaged. These guys pay the big bucks for a good trophy."

"I wanted to see if she had any spirit."

"She's wild. What do you expect? Back the truck up to the door so we can load the cage. It's heavier than it looks." Dunlop walked away, headed in the direction where Tinker hid in the shadows.

"Yeah. All right." Bill squatted down and stared at Lisa for a long moment. She pressed her nose against the bars and stared right back at him, but kept a low, threatening rumble emanating from her gut.

"You think you're so tough." He punched her through the slats so quickly, Lisa didn't have time to move. She yelped in pain when his big fist connected with her nose.

Tinker charged out of the shadows and grabbed the man by the back of his neck. He had him down, throat bleeding, before Lisa had time to react.

Dunlop raced across the barn, aimed his gun and fired. The dart caught Tinker in the left shoulder. He released his victim's throat and snapped at the dart, but he wasn't quick enough, and he couldn't reach it.

While Lisa watched in horror, Tinker snapped ineffectively at the dart, snarled, and lowered his head, and then slowly folded in upon himself. She cried out, silently, to Luc and Tia. Her plea was met with a stunned silence.

Lisa threw herself at the locked gate, biting and snapping at the metal, fighting the need to regain her human form and merely open the lock.

Dunlop yelled at his assistant to quit griping and help him. The man rose slowly, holding a hand over his bleeding throat. "What the fuck do you want me to do?"

Dunlop glared at him. "I told you to leave her alone, damn it. Find the spare portable kennel. It should be big enough. One of those for carrying dogs on planes. Should be in one of the stalls at the back of the barn."

"That damned wolf almost tore out my fucking throat, and all you can think of is a carrier?"

Dunlop laughed. "Quit bitching. There's a bonus in it for you if we get this beast caged before the tranquilizer wears off. Do you have any idea what one of our great white hunters would pay to hunt a male wolf in his prime? This animal is gorgeous. I've never seen one this big and healthy."

"He fuckin' tried to kill me. What if he's rabid? The fucking thing might be rabid!"

"I'm more concerned about what he might've caught from you. Get moving!" Dunlop laughed as his wounded assistant lurched toward the back of the barn in search of the carrier. Lisa snarled and bared her teeth, but both men ignored her. She searched frantically for Tinker's thoughts and found nothing except the profound lack of his presence. Whatever drug coursed through his system had knocked him completely unconscious.

Don't shift, Tink. Whatever you do, don't shift.

Lisa stayed in his thoughts, hoping her voice would be the first thing he heard as consciousness returned. He couldn't shift. She wouldn't let him.

The cage holding Lisa along with Tinker's oversized carrier were loaded in the back of a newer four-wheel-drive pickup, then covered with a blue tarp. The first part of their trip along the service road was fairly rough, but Lisa felt the change immediately when they turned onto the highway.

Luc? Tia? We're on the main road. I think they turned left. Can you follow?

Luc's voice filled Lisa's mind. He sounded calm, self-assured. *We've got you. Is Tinker still out?*

I think he might be coming to. I hope he is. I hear him panting in the cage next to me, but I can't see or read him. God, Luc . . . do you think he's okay? What if they gave him too much of the drug? What if he doesn't wake up? He doesn't hear me when I try to communicate. If he tries to shift, he'll kill himself. His cage is too small, it's—

It's okay. I see the truck. You're about a half mile ahead of us. Hang in there. Keep talking to him. Let him know he can't shift now. We won't let anything happen to either one of you.

Tinker sensed the walls of the carrier first, the closeness of the space that held him, and immediately recognized it as one of those portable kennels for transporting large dogs. He almost shifted but figured he needed a clear mind before attempting anything.

When in doubt, don't. He would have grinned if he'd had lips instead of a muzzle. Ulrich Mason's oft-repeated words of caution popping into his head were stronger than his desire to touch the world with human hands.

He saw vague images of two men in his mind's eye, and the taste of blood was rich and coppery in his mouth, but he couldn't recall why. His memories were cloudy and indistinct. Awareness drifted away, then returned, like ocean tides carrying little bits of clarity back with each wave. Faintly, as quiet as the beat of a butterfly's wings, Lisa's voice spread over his consciousness.

He felt her love, felt the strength of her fear. Heard her warning in time with the beating of his heart.

Don't shift. I love you, Tink. Please don't shift.
Lisa?
Tink! You're awake! I've been so worried. Are you okay?
Yeah. I think so. He tried to stand up, but the carrier was too small. He stretched his legs as best he could, discovered his parts all worked, and curled back up into a fairly compact ball for a wolf his size. *Everything seems okay, but I've got really tight quarters. Doubt I could shift even if I wanted to. How long have I been out?*
Not long. Maybe a half hour or so. Luc and Tia aren't very far behind us.
Good. What direction are we heading?
North, I think. Maybe northeast. I can't tell for sure because the tarp they threw over us blocks out the view. Is that where Dunlop's hunting club is? At least now we know for sure it's Dunlop.
Yep. That we do. That's the right direction. It's about an hour's drive from the sanctuary, according to Luc. Luc?
I'm here, bud.
Tinker felt himself relax. *Good.* There was no need to say more. His packmates were close by. They would help him keep Lisa safe.
As if she sensed his thoughts, Lisa's voice filled his mind. *You did that on purpose, didn't you, Tink? You got yourself captured on purpose. How could you?*
Tinker almost laughed. He might need Luc and Tia to keep him safe from Lisa. She sounded totally pissed right now.
Well, that bastard made it so easy. No point in denying it, I guess, but think, Lisa. How could I not? I love you. He crossed one leg over the other and rested his chin on his front paws. No way in hell would he let her do this on her own. She was his mate, even if she didn't understand the rules. One of these days she'd figure out what the whole bonding thing meant.

Chanku mated for life. Lisa was his, and he'd die protecting her before he'd let anything happen.

Tinker felt confirmation from his packmate. Luc understood, though Tia's grumbling was almost audible in the background. Tinker imagined she was talking privately with Lisa, most likely complaining about the bossiness of men. He sighed. Lisa on her own was bad enough. Add Tia Mason to the mix and he was in deep shit. Sighing again, Tinker rested his chin on his paws and listened to the sound of the wheels on the pavement.

Chapter 10

Lisa couldn't believe she'd actually fallen asleep, but the sound of tires on gravel awakened her to the reality of thirst and stiff muscles and the fact she was still a wolf.

Tinker? Luc? Tia? Are you guys there?

Right next to you, sweetie. I wondered if you were going to wake up.

Tinker! I can't believe I fell asleep. Are Tia and Luc close?

About a mile back. I think we went through a security gate a while ago. They have to hide the car and come in on foot. Luc said the property is heavily guarded and fenced, but they'll figure out a way to get inside.

Lisa sighed and wished she could stretch. It was hot in the cage, and she worried about Tinker, shoved into a pet carrier much too small for his large wolven body.

The truck rolled to a stop. A minute later, the blue tarp was pulled off the back of the truck. Lisa almost sighed with the welcoming blast of cool air. They'd stopped in front of a large shed, and she immediately quit worrying about the size of the carrier and lack of air.

Two men came out to the truck hauling a large cart. Lisa and Tinker both growled. The men came to a halt. "Two? I thought you only needed one."

Dunlop walked around the side of the truck and stepped into view. "They're wild. Seth darted the bitch last night, and the male was in the barn this morning. I have no idea how he got in. Must be a loose board somewhere, but he's probably her mate. We can charge five times the regular rate for this pair, and I bet we'll have a waiting list."

"When do you plan to turn them out?"

Lisa recognized Bill, the one Tinker had bitten. He'd joined the other three near the back of the truck. She noticed he wore a blood-soaked scarf tied around his throat.

"Not right away. I want them used to the area. Plus they'll need enough time for the drug to get out of their systems. Put them in the holding pen for now." Dunlop turned away and moved out of Lisa's line of vision, but his voice carried. "And, Bill, keep your hands off those two. I don't want anything to happen to either one of them. Any injuries, any problems, you're out of here."

Tinker snarled, as if adding emphasis to Dunlop's words.

One of the two men with the cart yelled out to Dunlop. "You want them in separate pens?"

"Nah. It's obvious they're a pair. Put them together. We can advertise the chance to hunt a pack. Make sure they get fresh water."

Is there any time limit on how long we can stay in wolf form? Lisa braced herself as the two men unloaded her cage and placed it on the wheeled cart. She was facing away from the truck, though, and couldn't see Tinker when they moved his carrier.

I don't think so. Oof. Jesus, you think they'd be a little more careful with my precious hide.

Lisa heard a deep snarl. *You okay?*

Yeah, they just tilted it wrong. Anyway, I've been on assignment with Luc where we worked the whole job on four legs. Two, sometimes three, weeks.

"Be careful with the big one. He looks really pissed."

Lisa heard laughter, but she couldn't see who was talking.

"Wouldn't you be, too, if someone stuck you in a carrier this small? Ya know, I sure wish we didn't have to do this."

Lisa felt the cart jerk forward.

"You're not getting cold feet, are you? I told you exactly what this job entailed, and you sure seemed excited about it when you started."

"They're just so damned beautiful. I hate to think of some rich bastard blowing them away just for the thrill of killing something smarter than he is."

"Hey, you got the money, you can do whatever you please. Look at Dunlop."

"It's even worse with him. He's already rich. He just likes killing stuff."

"Nah, he just likes the power. Likes having something other rich guys want. In this case, it's endangered species to hunt. C'mon. We'll put them in the pen on the north side. It's big enough they can stretch their legs, and there's plenty of shade. Ya never know. Smart as these critters are, they might just get away."

Laughter rang out. "Yeah, or kill the son of a bitch who ends up hunting them. Did you check out Bill's throat? I'm kind of sorry the wolf missed."

"He's such a bastard." More laughter. Lisa heard grunting and groaning as her cage was shoved up against a wire kennel door that appeared to open into a small room of some sort. The door opened just as someone banged loudly on the back of her carrier. Lisa was out of the cage, through the shed, and standing in a large fenced enclosure before she even realized she'd moved.

Tinker joined her a moment later. They both turned around at the sound of the door slamming shut. *Come on. Wild wolves would run. Look nervous.*

Shit. That's easy. I am nervous. Lisa took off after Tinker. He raced into a small grove of trees, then came up short on the other side when he reached the fence. Head down, feet pacing a steady rhythm, he followed a well-worn track around the perimeter of their pen.

Lisa followed, though she managed to glance around at their surroundings. Their pen was fairly large, the size of a typical suburban backyard. An eight-foot-high chain-link fence surrounded it, and there were at least two gates with padlocks on them and on the door into the enclosed shed where they'd first been released.

Even in human form, Lisa knew she'd have a tough time getting out of this one. She sniffed the air and realized there recently had been other animals inside their pen, not all of them wolves. Lisa didn't want to think of their fate. She wondered where Luc and Tia were, wondered how long Dunlop planned to hold them before turning them out for the hunt.

Tinker suddenly veered off track and headed toward the shed. Lisa followed and realized it was the large bowl of fresh water that caught his attention. They both lapped up their fill. Lisa almost lost her little transmitter, but she managed to tuck it back in the pouch in her cheek.

What now?

Tinker tilted his head and looked at her. She could almost swear he was laughing. *I take it you're asking if I've got a plan?*

Lisa growled.

Tinker took another drink, then trotted off. Lisa followed. *Now we wait until nightfall,* he said, *and get out of here. Then we contact the authorities and let them know about Dunlop's little project. He's got other big game on the premises. I smell large cats and possibly a rhino. Not sure about that one. Only smelled one once before on an assignment in Kenya.*

Where are Luc and Tia? I haven't heard from them for a while.

I did, while you were asleep. They're on four legs, cutting cross-country right now, headed this direction. I think they distracted a guard and slipped in through a security gate.

Is it safe?

Safer than trying to come in as humans. Tinker lifted his nose to the air and sniffed, then whirled around. Bill, the man he'd attacked, stood just outside the chain-link fence.

Lisa snarled and backed away from the fence. Tinker stood his ground. He growled, a low, menacing sound that raised the hackles on Lisa's back.

Bill's knuckles were practically white, he'd clenched his fists so tight. He didn't say a word. Just stood there and glared at Tinker.

You rotten bastard. Dunlop thinks he can keep me away from you. Damned fool. You're gonna pay. Nothing goes after me like that and gets away with it.

Lisa jerked her head in Tinker's direction. *Did you hear that? He's practically shouting in my head.*

Hear what? Tinker glanced back toward Bill, then looked at Lisa. *You can hear him? Mindtalk?*

I did. Not right now, but he was really clear. He was threatening you.

Missed that. Tia can hear some humans as well, but Luc can't always pick them up.

Whatever. I think he's planning to do something to hurt you. Be careful.

C'mon. Let's move to the other side of the pen. There's only access along this front section of fence.

The two of them turned as one and trotted back across the pen. Bill stayed where he was, staring at them until they disappeared behind the small group of trees.

I wish we could have brought the receiver. Tia trotted along behind Luc, following him through the thick forest.

Yeah, that would have looked really cool. Two wolves carrying a GPS receiver. Explain that one to Dunlop's guards.

Are you sure we're going the right direction? I didn't think it would take so long.

Luc's laughter echoed in her mind. Tia nipped his flank in reply when he said in a whiny, child's voice, *Are we there yet?*

I'm worried about them. Tinker hasn't answered me.

They'll be fine. Keep trying to reach him. Try Lisa, too.

Tia didn't answer that she'd been trying, but neither one had responded. She worried they might be going away from the area where the two were held, but without the receiver, they couldn't know for sure.

Suddenly Luc stopped. He sniffed the ground in a small clearing they'd just entered and looked back toward Tia. She stopped beside him and shuddered. The grass was beaten down and covered with dried blood. Bits of hair, boot prints. A wolf had died here, in the not too distant past.

It hadn't died cleanly. There was evidence of thrashing and torn earth, as if the animal had been in horrible pain. Luc shook his head. *Not all hunters are good shots.*

We have to find them. Why couldn't we just call the authorities?

We have to protect our Chanku identity, and besides, we need more proof. Dunlop has a lot of powerful friends. I imagine more than one congressman has hunted here as a guest.

That's disgusting.

Luc turned and licked her muzzle. *Sweetheart, that's life.* He whirled around and took off in a ground-eating lope with Tia right behind him. She continued calling out to Lisa and Tinker.

It felt as if they'd traveled for miles and raced for hours, and by the time they finally reached the compound without any word from the other two, even Luc had begun to show signs of worry. A muffled snarling caught their attention. Luc glanced back once at Tia and carefully worked his way through the heavy brush surrounding the pens with Tia close behind him.

They broke through the thick underbrush and crept over freshly turned loam along the edge of a low fence until they could see the first of a series of pens. One wolf lay on its side in the pen, unconscious. Tia was almost certain it was Lisa. Another, just outside the enclosure, was tied to a short stake. A wire muzzle held its jaws closed while a huge man beat the wolf with what looked like an ax handle. The animal twisted and turned to avoid the blows, but with such a short line, it had nowhere to go.

There was no doubt the man was trying to kill Tinker.

Luc didn't hesitate. He jumped the fence and went straight for the man's throat. There was a single shocked cry, the gurgle of air from a slashed windpipe, and the man went down. Blood from his severed carotid artery painted a crimson arc as he fell. More blood continued to flow, spurting out now in slow, steady jets of red, staining the gravel around his body.

Luc stood over the body, growling low in his throat as the man died. Tia shifted. Naked, she raced to the pen and opened the unlocked gate. She grabbed Lisa by the front legs and dragged her across the gravel. Luc forcefully shook off his bloodlust and shifted. Quickly he unfastened the rope holding Tinker and removed the muzzle.

Tinker shifted the moment he was free. He helped Tia lift Lisa's limp body over Luc's shoulder. Still in wolf form, she hung loosely, eyes closed, mouth agape. Tia grabbed Tinker's arm to help him, but he shrugged it off. It was all Tinker could do to walk, but it was obvious he intended to do it on his own.

He absolutely radiated anger. His body was bloodied and bruised, but at least he was alive. Tia glanced back and saw the man's body lying near the pen, the blood-stained ax handle on the ground next to him. Killing prey for food was one thing. Killing a man was something else.

She shouldn't have this sense of satisfaction to see him lying dead, but she did.

The three of them slipped around the edge of the paddock, keeping to the gravel to avoid footprints, and raced back into the woods. Not a word was said. No communication was necessary. There'd been no one around and very little noise beyond the solid blows of wood against bone and flesh, but the man's body wouldn't go undiscovered for long.

They'd gone close to a mile before Tinker finally spoke. *He darted Lisa and me. Not too heavy a dose in mine, but Lisa went down hard.*

Luc merely nodded at Tinker's information and continued his quick pace. Tia shifted and raced on ahead. Her Chanku senses would alert them to any problems. She glanced back at Tinker. He walked like a man possessed, his hand resting on Lisa's shoulder, his eyes glittering with anger. She had a quick thought: The man had been lucky Luc killed him as cleanly and quickly as he had.

She doubted Tinker would have been as thoughtful.

Charles Dunlop knew he was grinning like a Cheshire cat when he hung up the phone, but it was even better than he'd hoped. The senator and his party would be here within the hour, willing to pay top dollar to hunt a mated pair of North American timber wolves and unwilling to wait another day.

He grabbed his cell phone and keys and headed for the pens. Time to turn his little moneymakers loose and give them a good head start. The senator enjoyed a challenge.

Dunlop liked the money. It made for a wonderful business arrangement.

"Hey, Bill? You out here?" Dunlop climbed out of the cab of the pickup and searched the area around the pens. The sound of flies and meat bees buzzing caught his attention. Slowly, he walked around the side of a pen. Bill's body lay in a pool of drying blood in the noonday sun. His throat gaped open. Insects had settled in the blood, and others buzzed around his body. Dunlop's first thought was that Bill looked like a freshly killed deer he'd once seen, one they figured had been taken down by a wolf.

Dunlop fingered the pistol he wore strapped to his side. It had always been more affectation than necessity, but for once he was glad he carried it loaded. He tried to make sense of the scene. The rifle they used to dart animals was propped against the wall with a couple of empty syringes nearby. The bloodied ax handle, short rope, and muzzle told a big part of the tale. Bill had always had a mean streak. He should have known the idiot would try and get back at the wolf that bit him.

"Looks like the wolf won this one, Bill." Dunlop circled around the side of the pens. Two sets of tracks coming into the compound? He knelt down and looked closer. One large, one small, running loose. The pair he'd captured, or another set? Dunlop stood up and scratched his head. There were no tracks on the gravel, but a long swath of disturbed gravel in the pen made him wonder if other wolves had dragged the female out.

Bill had obviously managed to tie the male and get in a few good whacks, if the bloodied ax handle was any indication. Whatever happened, it was too late to do anything for Bill, but the senator's hunt might not be a loss.

Dunlop grabbed his cell phone and dialed in the guards' station on the western side of the property. "I want double patrol duty for the next couple days. Make sure the gates are locked and there's no way a wolf can get off-site. We've got two, possibly four loose for a hunt right now. I don't want them getting away."

He flipped the phone shut without waiting for an answer and glanced back toward Bill's body. The man was an idiot. Correct that—he'd been an idiot. The gene pool was suddenly much improved. Dunlop shook his head in disgust, aware now even more of the stink of death. He wasn't quite certain why he'd even hired Bill Smith. Hell, he wasn't even sure that was the man's real name. No matter. It wasn't all that difficult to dispose of a body. Not when you had big cats to feed.

What was more important was the senator's hunt. Dunlop had no idea if other wolves had somehow gotten in, and he couldn't imagine them smart enough to actually save the two who'd been captured. Somehow the bitch had freed herself, killed Bill, and freed her mate. It almost seemed a shame to hunt such a resourceful animal, but she'd definitely give his clients a run for their money.

Lots of money. Grinning over the amount he'd be collecting at the end of this weekend, Dunlop went to fetch the cart to haul Bill's body away. He'd store him in the freezer for now, chop him up next week once the hunt was over. There were plenty of predators on-site, always hungry for fresh meat. Maybe he'd even check to see if the senator was interested in hunting any of the big cats.

They were damned expensive to feed. Whistling to himself, Dunlop dragged the cart across the yard toward Bill's body.

"They've got the entire perimeter covered, as far as I can tell." Whispering quietly, Luc knelt in the thick band of brush that ended about a dozen feet from the chain-link fence. "When Tia and I got in, there was only one guy guarding the gate, and we managed to distract him long enough to slip through without being seen. No way can we get past this."

Tinker knelt next to him, shaking his head. "I agree. I'm not about to risk Lisa's safety. We'll have to find another way out."

Lisa lay curled up in the grass beside Tinker. She still felt woozy from the strength of the drug that idiot had shot into her. She had no memory at all of Tinker's beating, though the dark bruises and bloodied contusions that marred his beautiful skin made her glad Luc had taken care of the problem in his own manner.

Tia slipped into the brush beside them. Like Lisa, she'd remained in wolf form. She'd been checking the perimeter for the past hour, racing to the north and south along the western edge where they'd hidden the car. Now, though, she shifted to make her report. There was something almost regal about her, the way she held herself, the confidence and poise that was integral to her as either human or wolf.

"We're stuck, guys," Tia said. "They've cut a twelve-foot break between the fence and the forest, so there's no cover at all. There're a lot of guards at regular stations and cameras posted along the way. It's obvious security has been increased, and I hadn't even noticed before, but that looks like an electric fence. I suggest we rest until nightfall, get some sleep, and then try and slip out at one of the smaller roads where the gates aren't as secure. All the gates are too well guarded to attempt anything in daylight. I found a nice spring and a small meadow. I think we'll be fine there for now."

They shifted and followed Tia back to the spring. Lisa walked behind with Tinker, moving at a slower pace. Even as a wolf, he moved as if every muscle hurt, and Lisa still felt groggy. *Are you okay? Did he break anything?*

Nothing's broken. I'm just pissed off that Luc got to rip the bastard's throat out. I'd love to have done it myself.

Maybe you'll get your chance with Dunlop.

Tinker looked at her, and his laughter bubbled up in her mind. *I kind of like the way you think.*

Thank you. I kind of like you, too.

The meadow they found was cool and quiet, with fresh water from a bubbling spring. After they all drank, Tinker submerged himself in the clear water for a few minutes to ease the pain of his bruises. Lisa thought he looked a hundred percent better when he climbed out and lay in the sunshine next to her. His ebony coat gleamed with red fire in the sunlight.

Still in wolf form, Tia and Luc lay curled up together, probably still trying to figure out how to get out of here. Knowing the reason all of them were stuck within this fenced enclosure rested fully on her shoulders, Lisa could hardly look at them.

Guilt perched on her like a ten-ton weight, especially with Tinker covered in bruises, not blaming anyone but himself. Finally Lisa stood up. She couldn't take it anymore. *I'm sorry*, she said, hanging her head in shame. *This is all my fault. I never meant for anyone to get hurt. I just wanted to find out why the wolves were disappearing.*

Luc raised his head. He looked every bit as regal as Tia when he was a wolf, his eyes gleaming, his coat shining. *You did the right thing and made the right call. We'll figure something out.*

I guess Tinker was right. I should have had some sort of a plan.

Tinker raised his head. *Can I get that in writing? Tinker was right?*

Lisa snorted, but smiling felt great. *Where's that wizard of yours when you need him, eh?* Her mental mumbling seemed to catch everyone's attention.

What did you say? Tia sat up.

I said, where's that wizard. He made Tinker's cell phone work at my cabin, and cell phones never work there.

That's brilliant! Without warning, Tia shifted and began to pace. Obviously, she needed her hands to make her point. Tall and lean and gloriously naked, she immediately had everyone's attention. "Lisa, you're new to the pack, so you weren't part of my father's rescue when he was kidnapped, but a bunch of us were able to make contact with Dad even though he was well over a thousand miles away."

Lisa shifted. "How?" As far as she knew, mental contact of a few miles was exceptional.

"Anton Cheval, that wizard you just mentioned, he had us work together—"

Luc shifted and interrupted his mate. "He actually had us all get horny as hell together, but we couldn't do anything about it. He wanted us frustrated."

"Well, it worked, didn't it?" Tia glared at him, but it was obvious she was enjoying the moment. "Besides, I love it when you're horny and frustrated. You're much easier to control."

Tinker raised his wolven head, sighed, and shifted. "He's never easy to control. He's a pain in the ass."

"Only when the sex gets rough."

Tinker slanted Luc a suggestive look and stroked his cock. It immediately grew longer and thicker beneath his palm. "I thought you liked it rough."

Luc laughed and Tinker shoved him in the shoulder. Lisa looked at Tia, and they both rolled their eyes, though Lisa was aware of a spike in her own libido, a sudden clenching in the muscles between her legs. How could she not react in a situation like this?

At the same time, her immediate reality slammed into her. She couldn't believe she was sitting here, stark naked, in a quiet little meadow with three of the most sexually attractive people she'd ever seen in her life. Two gorgeous men, one of them who assured her he was her mate, and Tia, who took her breath away with just the slightest provocation.

People who were not only intelligent, beautiful, and sensual, but capable of shifting from human to wolf. Totally unbelievable.

Lisa was still contemplating the odd direction her life had taken when, giggling, Tia held up her hand and the laughter fell silent. "Okay, enough, guys. This is serious. What we're talking about is a form of sex magic, if you will, but it worked. There's no reason it won't work for us."

"You're talking about contacting Anton, right?" Tinker's gaze slipped from one to the other. "We let him know what's going on here and he calls the authorities. There are enough threatened species on this property to gain some legal attention, and if there's a hunt planned for the escaped wolves, so much the better."

Lisa shook her head. "I still haven't got a clue what you're suggesting, but I'm all for trying whatever works."

Tia stroked Lisa's shoulder in a touch that was both comforting and inviting. It raised shivers along Lisa's spine. "I think what works might be just the two of us. Luc, Tinker, and I are accustomed to sexual intimacy with one another. You're new to the group, yet familiar with us through Tinker's memories. Because you're new, you bring a different dynamic to our mix, one both Luc and I are curious about. A dynamic we're eager to experience."

She leaned close and kissed Lisa, a gentle meeting of lips filled with promise. "I find you terribly attractive. So does Luc and we all know how Tinker feels. Now, imagine their frustration if they have to watch us explore each other, touching, kissing, tasting . . ."

The sentence slowly drifted off on a whisper. Lisa felt the moisture gathering between her legs at the soft, sensual promise in Tia's voice. Her nipples puckered into tight, jutting points.

She glanced toward Tinker. His cock jutted straight out in front of him, almost as if he aimed it at the women. It continued to grow harder and darker as she watched. Lisa knew exactly what he was capable of, and the memories made her sex clench and her stomach muscles tighten.

Her mouth watered in anticipation, and she licked her lips. Tinker responded with a frustrated groan.

Shifting her glance away from temptation and moving it in Luc's direction, Lisa's mouth went dry. He was hard as well, his cock curving upward until it brushed against his belly. It was beautiful and perfectly formed, and she wondered how it would feel to have him inside her. To have both Tinker and Luc taking her at the same time, two perfectly beautiful men in her bed, inside her body.

Tinker cleared his throat. "Uh, Lisa? You're broadcasting, sweetie. Not sure if Luc and I can take it."

Lisa groaned and covered her eyes with her hand.

Luc reached down and cradled his sac in his palm. Tia leaned close and grabbed his wrist. "Uh-uh. No touching. Frustration, remember? Build the power."

Luc frowned. "You fight dirty, woman. How much power do you need, anyway?"

Tinker shrugged. "Anton's not all that far away. A few hundred miles at most." He sounded hopeful.

"Doesn't matter." Tia laughed. "We need to build up as much frustration as possible, and we have to do it fast. No touching. You can look, though. Look all you want."

Lisa took her cue from Tia. Everything about the blonde fascinated her, and she didn't hesitate now. She rose up on her knees, spreading her legs apart in open invitation. The dark curls over her pubic mound were wet with her arousal, and she lifted her small breasts in her palms as added incentive. When Lisa flicked her own nipples with her thumbs, both men groaned.

Tia knelt in front of her and leaned close. Her body was slim and muscular, her pubic mound completely bare. Lisa licked her lips, imagining Tia's flavors, imagining the smooth skin beneath her tongue and the damp folds of her sex.

Tia's full lips parted, her tongue swept her own lips first, then swirled around the tip of Lisa's left breast. She sucked hard, nipped gently with sharp teeth, then moved to the right.

Her thoughts slipped unobtrusively into Lisa's mind. *I hope this is okay with you. We need to give the guys a show. Make it hot and fast, okay?*

Lisa had to bite her tongue to keep from laughing out loud. *Works for me.* Tia scooted closer and rubbed her full breasts against Lisa's. Lisa gasped and arched into Tia's touch. *Works really well, if you want the truth.* She almost cried out when their nipples touched and rubbed together. So much sensation, so much desire, enhanced by their audience. There was something wonderfully decadent about sex with Tia while the men watched, especially here in the open with the risk of capture hanging over them.

Tia slipped her fingers down Lisa's right side, then stroked over the smooth curve of her buttock. She trailed lightly up and down the tight valley between Lisa's cheeks, pausing only briefly to press against her anus, teasing that sensitive ring of nerves before moving lower, dipping slightly inside Lisa's moist sex.

Lisa moaned. She huffed in and out in short, sharp gasps. Hot and aroused, she knew her climax was only seconds away without Tia ever even touching her clit. Lisa backed away, moving out of Tia's reach and breathing hard.

"Your turn. I don't want to come." Lisa laughed, shaking her head. "Well, actually I do, but I think that would screw up the whole purpose of your experiment. Lie down."

Tia did as she was directed, lying back on the soft grass with her knees raised and her legs parted. Lisa crawled over her, settling herself between Tia's thighs as if she were a man, her hands flat on the ground on either side of Tia's breasts. When she touched her pubic hair against Tia's cleanly shaved mons, both women sighed.

They were both damp, both aroused. Lisa pressed against Tia, then lay over her so that their breasts touched, nipple to nipple. Tia lifted her hips, obviously frustrated by the pressure of Lisa's sex against hers. Lisa didn't move. She held her position, their nipples touching, mouths mere inches apart, and then she slowly worked her way down Tia's body, kissing here, nipping there, until Tia squirmed and twisted beneath her.

"Damn, you're so bad, woman."

Lisa ran her tongue lightly around Tia's navel. "Yeah. I know. I'm especially good at bad. Or something like that. Ask Tinker."

"I don't have to ask him. Just look at the poor man. In fact, look at both of them."

Lisa twisted around and laughed out loud. Both Tinker and Luc sat with hands tightened into fists to keep from touching their cocks or maybe each other. "Well, as much as I'm enjoying myself, I imagine it's about time we try and contact your wizard. Any longer and I'm afraid one of them might explode."

Before Tia could answer, the air began to vibrate with the pulsing roar of two helicopters. Without thinking, all four Chanku suddenly shifted.

When the two choppers passed overhead, four large wolves stood their ground and watched. One of the helicopters peeled off from the other, then circled around and hovered overhead. As one, Tia, Luc, Tinker, and Lisa melted silently into the forest. They watched through the leafy canopy as the helicopter hovered a moment longer, then turned and followed the first one toward the hunting lodge.

Chapter 11

Shit. This is horrible. They saw us!

No, it's great! Lisa wondered how one wolf calmed another. Tia looked absolutely frantic. *Now they know we're here, and they'll definitely be hunting. We need to contact your wizard.*

Should we shift? Tia took deep, slow breaths in an obvious effort to calm herself down. *He had us hold hands before.*

Tinker stepped forward. He was absolutely beautiful and already moved as if his bruises weren't quite as painful. *Our mental powers are stronger when we're Chanku. And if sexual frustration adds to that power, I could probably reach the guys on the space station with a message right now.*

That's for sure. Luc stood next to Tia, but he watched Lisa intently. *When we get out of this mess, I want a replay of what you guys were doing. I really loved that nipple-to-nipple thing.*

Lisa couldn't believe they were teasing at a time like this. *You've got it. So long as I get to watch you and Tinker.* She flashed a quick grin at Tinker. He looked a little bit shocked at her suggestion, which made it sound all the more interesting. To think she'd actually left him speech-less gave her a rush of feminine power.

Now, she said, cocking her head in Luc's direction, *we need to call Anton or we're all going to end up as pelts on some jerk's wall.*

That idea definitely got their attention.

Tia lay down on her belly and spread her front paws wide. *Anton had us hold hands. I think if our paws touch, we'll get the same effect.*

Tinker shook his head to clear the buzzing in his brain. Whether from the blows he'd taken earlier or the rush of power when all four of them reached out to Anton Cheval, he wasn't sure, but at least they'd succeeded.

Now they merely needed to stay alive for however long it took to get the authorities on-site, and that was assuming Anton could expedite the search warrants. It definitely helped that Anton had lots of friends in high places, all of whom probably owed him something.

That was amazing! Lisa looked as shaken as Tinker felt. Luc and Tia weren't in any better shape.

Definitely cool. Tia stood up slowly, shook, and stretched her front legs out until her nose practically hit the dirt. Her butt went into the air as she worked the kinks out of her wolven body. She was so sexy in this form, but it was the one way Tinker would never know her sexually. Open sex was reserved for their human bodies. Wolves belonged to their mates.

Tinker wondered if they all still felt as horny as he did. Reaching out to Anton Cheval hadn't burned off one bit of his sexual frustration. He kept picturing the girls together, the way their nipples beaded up when they made contact. The visual actually made his own sensitive nipples ache. The fact that Lisa wanted to see him with Luc was even more of a turn-on. Damn, they had to get out of this mess soon or he was going to explode!

Luc stood up, stretched, and shook himself like a big dog, then shifted. His body gleamed, and his muscles were pumped as if he'd been lifting weights. When he looked this way, it was hard for Tinker to keep his hands to himself, especially with images of Tia and Lisa joining Luc and Tinker in bed. He was going to have to do something about this driving need, and soon.

Lisa, Tia, and Tinker shifted. Luc was already walking barefoot down a narrow trail. "I say we move as humans to another part of the woods. They're probably going to hunt us with dogs, and our human scent should confuse them, at least for a while. You guys okay with that?"

Tinker grunted and grabbed Lisa's hand. Tia followed. "How long do you think it'll be before the authorities arrive?" Lisa's fingers had a death grip on Tinker's. He squeezed her hand, then pulled her close so he could wrap his arm around her waist.

"As long as it takes," he said. "Don't worry. We'll be fine. It's going to be dark soon, and I doubt they'll hunt at night. They're probably up there at the lodge right now having cocktails and bragging about what brave hunters they are. We need to find someplace to bed down until the authorities show up."

They'd walked for maybe a half mile before Tinker spotted the cave beside a small creek. It was warm and dry inside, though scattered debris from high water littered the floor. Still, it was just large enough for four wolves who didn't mind sharing body heat. Their feet were sore from walking along the path barefoot, but they'd left a human trail instead of wolf scent, which should help confuse the hunting dogs.

Lisa peered in through the opening, then turned back to Tia. "I don't know about you, but that looks to me like snake heaven. I am so not cleaning out that mess."

Tinker gently moved her out of the way. "Tell you what. Luc and I will handle the housekeeping; you and Tia find something for dinner."

Lisa slanted him a questioning look. "I take it you want us to trot on down to the local supermarket and pick something out at the deli?"

"Remember how good that deer tasted? You didn't mind fresh meat the other night." Tinker swept Lisa's hair back from her eyes. It seemed almost permanently tangled with all the shifts they'd done. She hadn't even attempted to tie it into a knot.

Lisa blinked. "I keep forgetting. I've got a whole new set of options now, haven't I? Fine. You clean house, and Tia and I will shop . . . if you can call it that."

The women shifted and trotted back into the woods. They had their noses to the ground, their tails waving like silken plumes behind them. Luc shook his head as the men watched them leave. "They're both gorgeous, aren't they? I swear, if we don't get out of here soon, I'm gonna . . ."

Tinker laughed. "Me, too, Luc. Me, too." He glanced at his packmate standing thoughtfully beside him, naked and obviously as aroused as Tinker, and thought of suggesting they ease each other's discomfort. Lisa's request that she be able to watch them slipped into his thoughts, and Tinker's erection grew even more painful.

No, it was better to wait. He willed his libido to take a break and followed Luc back to the small cave. Damn, he hoped Lisa was wrong. Tinker really hated snakes.

Lisa wondered if she'd ever get used to the thrill of the hunt. Her human side totally despised the thought of killing any living thing, but her Chanku instincts won out when she and Tia scared up a couple of fat rabbits.

They fed immediately. There was no question of eating first before finding game for the men. Lisa was hungry, and the rabbit's body was warm and tender. It filled the emptiness in her belly. She scraped her bloodied muzzle in damp grass alongside a creek, then waited while Tia finished gulping down her meal—bones, fur, and all.

They hunted along the creek where the grass grew tall and green, and managed to catch a couple more rabbits without going too far from the men. Carrying their prey in strong jaws, the women turned and trotted back the way they'd come.

Sort of the wolf equivalent of grocery shopping, right?

Tia's amber eyes sparkled. *Almost like takeout.*

If they hadn't been trapped in a hunting preserve as the main attraction, Lisa might have thoroughly enjoyed herself. As it was, she trotted along the trail, wary of every sound and nervously wondering how the hell they were going to get out of this mess.

It was all her fault, no matter how she looked at things. She glanced at Tia trotting beside her, the dead rabbit clenched in her jaws, and ached to think Tia'd put herself in danger, coming to the aid of someone she didn't even know.

Tia turned and looked at her. *That's not true, you know. We're packmates. When you bonded with Tinker, you bonded with Luc and me. We have no alternative but to help you. You would do the same for us. Don't waste your time on pointless guilt.*

Tinker said it's rude to stomp around in people's heads.

Tia's mental shout of laughter rolled through Lisa. *Yeah, well, no one ever accused me of not being rude. Besides, you're broadcasting on an open channel. C'mon. The guys will be starving by now.*

It's cloudy. Getting dark early. Luc bolted down the last of the meal his mate had brought him, then shifted and walked back to the creek. He knelt beside it and washed himself. Lisa and Tia sat nearby, talking quietly. Both of them seemed exhausted after the rush of adrenaline, their hunt, and the long day.

Tinker sensed Luc's tension and knew it was worry for their women more than anything. On their own, he and

Luc could probably figure out how to get over the electric fence or through one of the gates without any problem, but they weren't willing to risk Lisa or Tia's safety.

Maybe after dark? He wished he knew what was going on with the authorities, when to expect some activity. It was hard to plan, harder to wait. Lisa stood and came up behind Tinker. She put her arms around his waist, lay her head against his back, and sighed. "I love you. If anything else bad happens to you because of my stupid idea, I'll never forgive myself."

"Hey, I got myself captured. That wasn't your fault." Tinker turned around within Lisa's embrace and kissed her. "I want you so badly right now I hurt."

"I want you, too, but I want us out of here just as much." She glanced nervously over her shoulder at a sound in the woods. A pinecone dropping through the branches.

Suddenly Luc stood up. "Here, take my hands and link. I think I sense Anton."

Once their hands were joined, the wizard's voice was as clear as if he stood nearby. Tinker watched Lisa's face as Anton Cheval's words filled their minds. Everything was still so new to her. Hearing the voice of a man she'd never met must be unnerving, to say the least.

Both local and federal law enforcement agencies are gathering at the gates along the west and south sides of the preserve. You've got a fairly well-known senator on-site. He's paid a lot of money to hunt the four wolves he spotted on the flight in today. The incident commander knows there are four operatives inside the gates who need to get out undercover. I've told them you're trained wolves with Pack Dynamics. Ulrich's crew is well known among the upper echelons of law enforcement, and the information didn't raise an eyebrow. Be at the southernmost gate on the western side in one hour. It should be fully dark by then. When the authorities rush the gate, get the hell out fast. They'll be watching for four very well-trained wolves, so you should be okay.

A senator, eh? Luc raised an eyebrow and glanced toward Tinker.

Yes. And he's very popular around that part of the state. It could get ugly, so you'll want to be far away when all hell breaks loose. You know it's going to get real messy when they find the body and realize the man was killed by a wolf, since, as far as we know, you're the only live ones on-site. Take care.

Lisa couldn't stop shivering. She figured most of it was from nerves, but for some weird reason her body still hummed with desire and sexual arousal. It was almost as if the adrenaline coursing through her veins from a combination of nerves and fear excited her as well. For whatever reason, for now she made a very nervous wolf. Considering the circumstances, nerves made perfect sense. Arousal didn't, but she actually welcomed the sexual need. It took her mind off some of the things scaring her half to death.

Hiding with the others in heavy undergrowth near the gate, she'd been listening to the barks and howls of the senator's hunting dogs for the past ten minutes. They'd heard the first sounds of the hunt just after Anton's message.

Tinker's only comment to Luc, aimed, of course, directly at Lisa, was that this must be what she meant by "winging it."

No one had expected the senator to take off at dusk to hunt, but the dogs wouldn't be out on their own, which meant men with guns were close behind. The sound of the hunt grew closer. Neither Tinker nor Luc seemed all that concerned. Tia glanced occasionally toward the forest, though she appeared to be a lot more relaxed than Lisa.

Tinker's long tongue swept across Lisa's shoulder.

When she turned to look at him, the love in his amber eyes left her reeling. Overwhelmed by all that had happened in the past week, she took strength from the wolf beside her.

Lisa's trembling eased. Her arousal didn't, and Tinker's proximity certainly didn't help. She concentrated on the gate just twenty feet away, illuminated under bright spotlights. The sound of the dogs grew closer, then once again faded as they changed direction.

Another sound intruded—the low rumble of vehicles. The two men guarding the gate stepped out of their guardhouse and stood in the middle of the road. They seemed confused by visitors coming this time of night.

The first car pulled into sight. An older man got out, dressed in a state trooper's uniform. Other vehicles pulled in behind. More men got out, some dressed all in black, others in various agency uniforms. One of the guards grabbed his radio and made a call. The other tried to stop the sheriff from raising the gate, but three men with rifles stepped up, and the guard lowered his gun and moved aside.

Someone went into the guardhouse and flipped off the power to the electric fence. Another took both guards back to a van waiting off to one side, cuffed them with plastic ties, and helped them into the van. The small caravan rumbled through the gate.

They left it open. Lisa was one of four dark wolves that slipped through the gate and dove into the forest on the other side. Dark shadows among darker shadows. They'd made it. She'd left behind the senator and his hunting dogs, Charles Dunlop, and all his horrible deeds.

It seemed almost anticlimactic to be trotting down the edge of the gravel road while all hell broke loose behind them. Lisa heard a commanding voice over a bullhorn, giving orders to someone to drop their guns. The chaotic sounds of dogs barking and men shouting. Gunshots.

Luc and Tia trotted ahead. Both of them glanced back

toward Lisa, as if acknowledging the success of their mission. A feeling of warmth spread throughout her body. The trembling had long since disappeared, replaced instead by a sense of belonging, of camaraderie. Of family.

They reached the car in less than ten minutes, and all of them shifted. Lisa leaned back against the side of the car while Tia sorted through the pile of clothing in the backseat. Tinker flashed a grin at Lisa and held out his hand.

She frowned, then realized what he wanted. She spit the little plastic disk out of her mouth and handed it to him. "You thought I'd lose it, didn't you?"

"Never doubted you. Not once." Tinker's fingers closed around the disk, and he handed it to Luc. "She's a natural if she can carry a transmitter through that many shifts. I think the Pack's got a new operative."

Luc took the transmitter as he leaned over and kissed Lisa very gently on the mouth. "I agree. One of these days you might want to ask Tinker how many of these things he's lost."

The taste of his mouth on hers lingered. Lisa touched her fingertips to her lips and looked at Tinker. He smiled warmly at her, but, then, he knew exactly what Luc's kiss felt like.

Tia crawled out of the backseat and handed each of them their clothing. After they'd dressed and Luc took the wheel, Lisa finally felt the tension ebb.

It was replaced by absolute exhaustion.

"I can't wait to get home." She tied her tangled hair into a loose knot on top of her head and then snuggled close to Tinker in the backseat.

"Me neither," he said, "but as late as it is, I think we'll get a room for the night. That okay with you?"

She nodded. "As long as there's a bed and a shower, I'm fine."

"A bed," Tinker muttered. "There most definitely will be a bed."

"One big enough for the four of us."

Lisa raised her head when she heard Luc's quiet statement. He sounded deadly serious. She glanced at Tinker. He wasn't smiling either. There was an unusual intensity about him, a steady determination that changed his entire appearance from the handsome sexy man she loved to someone powerful, focused. And relieved. Tinker looked very, very relieved.

She loved him so much she ached. Wanted him so badly she burned for him. Lisa pressed her face against his solid chest, inhaled his familiar scent, and realized she had never felt so certain about anything before as she did about her love for Tinker McClintock. Feelings so powerful they frightened her.

Her life would never be the same again. She'd known that from the first time Tinker shifted and showed her what was possible. Still, she felt even more change was coming, sensed the need from both Tia and Luc and knew she returned that same need.

These were her packmates. Strangers to her just hours ago, now as much a part of her life as the man she clung to. Lisa raised her head and realized Tia had turned around in the front seat. She was smiling. *That okay with you?*

The image Tia shared with her, of Luc and Tinker together, both of them lost in passion, took the wind from Lisa's lungs.

Things were definitely not the same. *Oh yeah. It's great with me.*

Tia turned around in her seat and faced forward. Lisa snuggled close to Tinker and let her thoughts float free. After all the shifting back and forth, the adrenaline and the tension of the past twenty-four hours, she felt as if she'd left her own reality behind.

Nothing was really settled yet. Dunlop would be arrested, but what about Seth? Was Hal Anderson involved?

Was everyone at High Mountain part of the scheme? If so, how had she remained so oblivious?

"Let it rest, sweetie. We can't solve everything tonight."

She tilted her chin up to look at Tinker. "You're in my head, aren't you?"

He chuckled. The sound came from deep in his chest, and she loved the way it made her feel. "I don't have to be. You're broadcasting anxiety all over the place. Relax. We'll figure things out in the morning."

"I'm sorry." Damn, there was so much she needed to learn. "Sounds good in theory. I wonder if I'll ever figure anything out at all." Lisa yawned. "I'm exhausted."

Tinker kissed the top of her head and knocked her loose knot of hair askew. She felt his fingers tangling in the mess, separating the long strands, rubbing her scalp in a gentle, sensual massage. "Don't plan on getting all that much sleep," he whispered. "We have other plans."

Lisa's exhaustion fled. It was replaced by a warm bubble of expectation, a steady flow of desire that grew stronger with each moment. Smiling, recalling the memories she'd found in Tinker's mind and the ones Tia had just shared, Lisa settled back against his warmth and let her imagination run free.

"This okay with you, girls?" Luc held the door open to the room in the small motel he'd spotted just a few miles southwest of the hunting preserve. Tia walked in ahead of Lisa, then opened the door to the adjoining room, a mirror image of the first.

"They're clean, the beds are big, and the bathrooms have all the stuff I need. Works for me." Tia headed straight for the shower.

"What about you?" Tinker lifted Lisa's chin with his finger and kissed her.

She kissed him back, even as she swayed with exhaustion. Tinker swept her up in his arms and set her very gently on the king-size bed. Lisa trailed her fingers along his muscular arm as he sat beside her. "I'm fine," she said. "I'll feel a lot better after a shower."

He kissed her again. "Good. Luc's going across the street to that little deli he spotted. He'll pick up something for all of us. I'm going to help you with your shower."

Lisa looked at him and blinked. He wasn't kidding. Tinker slowly tugged her T-shirt over her head, slipped her shoes off her feet, tugged her jeans down, and helped her step out of them. There was nothing remotely sexy about his undressing her, but it was terribly sensual. He lifted Lisa up like a child, cradled her against his chest, and carried her into the bathroom.

There was nothing special about it, just a regular-size shower with a plastic curtain, a sink, and a toilet, but the water was hot, and there was plenty of pressure when Tinker stood behind Lisa, underneath the spray. She leaned against him as he soaped her breasts and belly.

His hands left behind trails of pure sensation as he washed her, going down on his knees to bathe her legs, her butt, her sex. Then he leaned her forehead against the back wall of the shower and poured shampoo into his palm. The gentle massage of her scalp almost left Lisa whimpering.

Tinker rinsed and conditioned her hair, then rinsed it again. He ran his fingers through the long strands, working the tangles out, then moving lower across her spine, trailing his fingers over the globes of her butt, tracing the valley between her cheeks.

Lisa shivered, but not from cold. The water pounded against her body, her heart pounded in her chest, and she felt each fingertip wherever Tinker touched her. He left her there with the water flowing over her back and took a moment to wash himself.

Lisa rolled slowly around to watch him. He was turned partly away from her, his face lifted to the warm spray, the sheets of water cascading over his broad shoulders. His skin looked darker than the darkest coffee against the white-tiled shower. Lisa looked carefully for bruises from the beating he'd gotten, but his skin was virtually un- marked.

She reached out and touched his side, trailing her fin- gers over his ribs. "I'm so sorry he hurt you. I'm sorry I couldn't help."

Tinker leaned down and kissed her very gently. "I'm fine. Chanku heal fast. He pissed me off more than he hurt me, but he's dead now. Not our problem anymore."

"Will there be repercussions? The authorities know wolves were there. It's going to be obvious he was killed by a wolf."

Tinker finished rinsing the soap off his back and chest. He turned then and smoothed her wet hair back from her forehead. The look in his eyes was gentle and yet, at the same time, fierce. No one would harm her so long as Tin- ker breathed. Lisa knew that. Felt it with every beat of her heart.

"Dunlop will have to deal with the repercussions. No one in law enforcement will mention Pack Dynamics. That's sort of an unwritten rule. They know we show up with our wolves when there's a problem, so long as word doesn't make it into the media." He leaned close and kissed her. His lips moved over her mouth, gliding on the beads of water covering both of them. He ended the kiss and sighed. "So far," he said, "we've been lucky. C'mon."

Tinker turned off the water and grabbed a thick white towel. Lisa stood there like a child while he dried her off and wrapped the damp towel around her hair. There was nothing childish, though, about the look he gave her when he finished drying himself and hung his towel over the shower rod.

There was pure, unadulterated hunger in his gaze. Lisa realized she wasn't nearly as tired as she'd thought. Her nipples tingled in expectation, as if a current ran from Tinker's amber eyes directly to her breasts.

She felt the rush of moisture between her legs, the hot shaft of heat that signaled her own rising need. The towel slipped off her head and slid to the floor. She hardly noticed.

Tinker lifted her as if she weighed nothing at all, and set her on the counter next to the sink. The tile felt cool beneath her buttocks, but Lisa leaned back against the mirror and spread her legs wide.

There was no need for foreplay, no need to raise her level of arousal in search of that elusive orgasm. Her body trembled on the cusp of climax, aroused to a feverish peak by the need in Tinker's eyes. It grew in her with the hunger in each breath he took, grew with the solid weight of his erection pressing now against her inner thighs.

Tinker grabbed Lisa's hips and pulled her forward, impaling her perfectly on his cock, sliding all the way inside in one smooth thrust of his hips. She clasped her ankles around the small of his back and pressed her breasts against his chest. He filled her, burying himself entirely on the second thrust. Lisa imagined the moist tissues of her sex parting gladly for his entry. Her rippling muscles clasped his cock, holding him even as he tried to withdraw for yet another thrust.

Once more, and then again, and that was all it took to carry her screaming over the edge. Lisa's climax didn't build; it exploded in a rush of heat and light, flashing behind closed lids. Shaking like a leaf, she clung to Tinker as he let go of all vestige of control, his hips pumping in and out as he climbed his own peak.

Sobbing against his chest, Lisa felt the anxieties and tension of the past hours drain away with each pulse of her sex, each deep penetration her lover made. Tinker finally tensed in her arms, threw back his head, and groaned.

His hips continued pumping as if of their own accord, slower now as he filled Lisa with his seed.

Finally, Tinker leaned forward and draped his arms over her shoulders. He rested his forehead against hers and kissed the tip of her nose. "I love you. I've never been more frightened for anyone in my life as I was for you tonight. Nor have I felt more proud. Don't you ever put me through anything like this again!"

Lisa would have laughed if she'd had the energy. "I felt the same about you. It's not going to be easy to watch you go off on your missions. I'll have to go with you."

Tinker nodded in agreement as he slowly withdrew, leaving her feeling somewhat replete and only partly satisfied. Her sex still clenched with the last traces of her climax. She glanced up at him and wondered how she could possibly want more.

"You are Chanku. You've been in and out of your wolven self today without any sexual release. This is normal. Get used to it." Laughing at her, Tinker grabbed a washcloth, rinsed it under warm water, and proceeded to bathe her between her legs. Embarrassed, Lisa reached out to grab his wrist and stop him.

Tinker pulled the cloth away. "Uh-uh. I like to do this. Besides, I hear Luc and Tia in the other room. You want to be nice and ready when we crawl into bed with them, don't you?"

Stunned, Lisa raised her head and looked into Tinker's glittering eyes. He might sound as if he was teasing, but it was obvious he was serious. Whatever fantasies Lisa might have held close to her heart were about to come to life.

Chapter 12

Tia and Luc were stretched out on the bed in Lisa and Tinker's room when the two of them stepped out of the bathroom. Tia lay on her back with the sheet pulled up to her waist. Luc leaned over her. He was propped on one elbow and twirled a tendril of her long blond hair around her left nipple. They both looked up and smiled when Lisa and Tinker entered the room.

"We're trying to figure out a fair way to do this," Luc said.

"He wants to watch us make love, but I told him you want to watch the guys." Tia scooted up on the bed and shoved a pillow behind herself. "I figure, you're the new kid on the block, so it should really be up to you."

"She gets her way too much." Tinker wrapped his arms around Lisa's waist to take the sting out of his words. He kissed her on the back of the neck, raising shivers along her spine. "I really think it would be inspirational for Luc and me to watch you girls."

Lisa slipped right into their teasing banter. "You need inspiration? I thought that was inspiration poking me in the behind." She wriggled her hips against the solid length of his cock. "I imagine Tia and I can give you lots of inspiration." Once more, Lisa rubbed her fanny against Tinker's growing erection. He pressed back. She moved out of his reach.

Tia winked. "Well, if that's the way you want it. I guess we can oblige."

Lisa shrugged. Did it really matter? She felt light, freer than she'd ever felt in her life. As if some long-imprisoned part of her were suddenly flying. Flying high and free with the three beautiful, perfect entities in this room. Not only perfect to look at, but also brave and loving friends . . . soon to be lovers. "What I really want is all of you."

Tia grinned. "I think we can manage that." She rolled off the side of the bed and reached for Lisa's hand. "That is, if you're willing to give up a little control."

Lisa wrapped her fingers around Tia's and nodded. With Tia's firm grasp in hers, all of this suddenly felt very real to Lisa, as if everything leapt into focus. She swallowed, and the sound echoed in her own ears. Tia led her to the bed and helped her lie down. Luc moved to the upper corner and took her right hand. Tinker held on to her left, all of them moving as if this had been choreographed. Tia slipped down between her ankles and spread Lisa's legs wide, then knelt and propped her calf against Lisa's left leg, holding it there.

The room seemed so quiet. Lisa closed her eyes and listened to the sound of Luc and Tinker breathing, heard the springs in the bed groan as someone shifted position. Her own heartbeat thudded in her chest, and she waited.

Nothing happened. No change in air currents to signify movement, no squeaking springs in the bed, nothing beyond the growing tension in Lisa's body. Then, light as the brush of a butterfly's wing, Tia's fingers touched the tops of her thighs. Lisa smiled and felt her body relax. She'd been waiting for something, anything to happen. Now that it had, her nervous energy settled into a warming sense of expectation. She kept her eyes closed, concentrating on the silence, on the slow movement of fingers from her knees to the crease between thigh and groin.

The mattress dipped as Tia moved closer. She pushed Lisa's legs farther apart with her knees while she used her thumbs to rub deep into the muscles of Lisa's inner thighs, touching the sides of her labia on each downward stroke. Teasing, touching lightly, and then moving back to massage her legs.

Tia slid her thumbs closer. She touched the stretchy hood protecting Lisa's clit, then slid the skin down, exposing the moist bundle of nerves to the air. Lisa fought a strong need to raise her hips when a small gust of hot breath washed over her clit. The lightest touch of Tia's tongue.

The pace of the breathing behind her picked up. Lisa wanted to open her eyes, but the fantasy behind her closed lids was too lush, the feelings too powerful. Luc's grip tightened on her wrist, as did Tinker's. Lisa could only imagine the looks on their faces. She wished she could see their cocks, but she didn't open her eyes. Couldn't.

She'd moved beyond reality, into a place of pure fantasy, a place where only her pleasure mattered. Tia's palms slid under her buttocks, lifted her high enough that someone—Luc? Tinker?—slipped a couple of pillows beneath her. They'd raised her very high, exposed her, and her legs fell limply to the sides.

Tia's fingers continued to massage her buttocks, slipping occasionally between her cheeks to touch her ultrasensitive ass. Lisa loved the sensation. She'd always loved sex-play with dildos and such when she'd been with women, though she'd never taken a man that way.

Tonight? Later? She wanted only to think about now, about Tia and the wonderful, lazy, loving things she was doing to Lisa's body. There was an odd shift to the bed. Lisa heard the cadence of the men's breathing change, as if they revved up a notch or two, sensed Tia moving closer between her legs.

She felt the unexpected brush of stiff hair on her inner thigh. The tongue that swept from her ass to her navel almost took Lisa over the top. Her eyes blinked open of their own accord just as a heavy paw pressed down on her upper right thigh. It was Tia, but not as Lisa expected her. Tia's dark brown coat sparkled in the pale light from the bathroom, her reddish highlights giving her an otherworldly appearance.

Her amber eyes glowed with feral delight, and her long, pink tongue snaked out and wrapped partially around her muzzle. Then she tilted her wolven head and disappeared once more between Lisa's legs.

Tinker had taken her this very same way, but it was different now: This was Tia. She knew instinctively where to lick, how deep to penetrate with her amazing tongue, licking and lapping at Lisa's flowing juices, running the coarse flat of her tongue not so gently across Lisa's exposed clit.

There was hardly any warning. Lisa's orgasm slammed into her trembling body. Shocked by its power, she arched her back and screamed, pulling at the hands holding her wrists, writhing beneath the unbelievable sensations of tongue and sharp canine teeth, of cold nose and whiskered muzzle.

It was wrong and delightful, bestial and Tia, and beyond every fantasy Lisa had ever imagined. Two beautiful men held her captive. Their fingers plucked at her taut nipples, pinching and rolling them in perfect sync, one with the other.

Lisa felt the solid pressure of their cocks; hot, silky skin covering ironlike shafts, smooth and powerful pressing against her shoulder on one side, her arm on the other.

She wanted to taste, to compare first one and then the other, to move from Tinker's cock to Luc's and back to her mate's, but the beast between her legs held Lisa's full attention. The woman who pleasured her had complete control.

Tia gentled her sensual assault, licking and nuzzling between Lisa's legs, sweeping her tongue along the tight crease between her buttocks, taking Lisa closer and closer to another mind-blowing climax.

Her legs trembled, her inner muscles clenching with each penetration of that amazing tongue. Lisa hovered at the peak, once more riding the wave of sensation, so close to orgasm that she cried out when the fingers left her breasts, whimpered when, without warning, the men lifted her up and away from that amazing tongue. Her body tensed, searching for the myriad sensations that had taken her higher with each swirling lick, each sharp-toothed nip. The men turned Lisa completely over, moving her effortlessly to lie atop the pillows, her ass in the air, her arms once more securely held in position.

Lisa giggled as the air returned to her lungs. Luc and Tinker moved to her sides and each grabbed an ankle along with her wrist. She was well and truly trapped, stretched out, helpless, in the grasp of two beautiful men. Her heart raced, and her sex convulsed as Tia entered her again, licking and stabbing her with that long, mobile tongue. She licked Lisa from clit to ass and back again, concentrating now on the sensitive ring of her anus, licking, probing, harder, deeper until the sensations seemed to roll over Lisa in a tidal wave of need for more.

The men released her hands and ankles, and she lay there on her stomach, her ass in the air, trembling, waiting to see what they would do next. No one had said a word, no one whispered or opened their thoughts. Had the other three been communicating all along? Discussing each move outside of Lisa's consciousness, each separate act they chose leading to a single spear of need? Lisa realized she'd been so caught up in her own arousal, she'd not even searched.

Now she did, opening her mind and finding more than she'd expected, a convoluted mental overload of sensation and sex, of immeasurable arousal and powerful desire. All of them, caught up in the extreme, overtly sexual cravings of Chanku after shifting, each one of them seething with adrenaline and hormones and desperate, overwhelming need.

The combined sexual desires of Luc, Tia, and Tinker slammed into Lisa, ramped her already heightened senses into overdrive. She began to shake, violent tremors, a desperate need for more sensation, more touch, more sex.

Something cool and moist was spread across her buttocks. She jumped at the contact and then shivered again as the fingers moved deep along the seam between her cheeks, spreading a cool, sweet-smelling cream. In her heightened state, Lisa moaned and pressed against the thick finger that slowly circled and probed her ass. Not enough, not nearly enough as it pressed slowly but surely inside. Was it Luc? Was he the one making her breath catch in her throat, making her heart slam against her ribs? Mind whirling, body a seething mass of sensation, she struggled to identify the one who would take her this way.

Tinker! She caught his thoughts with hers and felt tears behind her eyelids. When the tears slipped free, they scalded her cheeks, left trails of cool fire to her chin, but she was glad, more pleased than she might have expected. It seemed only fitting that Tinker take her one remaining bit of virginity. She loved him, though Lisa realized that, through Tinker, she loved Tia and Luc every bit as much.

She was worrying her way through that concept when Tinker added another finger and pumped slowly in and out. The image of his erect cock, his massive size made her squirm. Desire or fear? She didn't know. Couldn't tell, beyond the fact that his fingers weren't enough, beyond the fact that she wanted more, wanted it deeper, harder.

Would anything ever be enough? She pressed back against

Tinker's fingers as he slowly stretched her and knew she could take more, could take all of him. Then Luc lifted Lisa and draped her over his body. She felt the hard, hot length of his cock stretching long beneath her belly, the hot brush of his lips on her throat and chin. Tia was there as well, sitting close beside Lisa and stroking her shoulder, offering her silent encouragement.

Tinker knelt behind her, settled himself between her legs and Luc's, and stroked her back with one broad palm while he continued slowly thrusting in and out of her ass with two fingers. Luc touched her breasts and shoulders as he settled her on top of him.

Lisa almost laughed out loud. It was so unreal, to picture herself sandwiched between two of the most beautiful men she'd ever seen, but the solid pressure of Tinker's cock against her ass, the heat of Luc's against her belly, made it all too real.

Tinker entered her first. Slowly, with whispered words of encouragement, he stretched her tight muscle with the broad head of his cock. It burned like fire, and Lisa's first instinct was to fight him, but his thoughts were in her head, and he was telling her to push back, to relax, and she felt his broad crown slip past her sphincter, slip deep inside her passage.

It was amazing, like nothing she'd ever experienced in her life—somehow dark and forbidden, unbelievable pleasure verging on indescribable pain. She moaned and pressed harder against Tinker, forced him deeper inside that final virgin passage, until she felt his silky pubic hair rubbing against her buttocks, felt the weight of his sac lying heavy and hot against her perineum.

He was inside her. All the way inside, and she knew this was just the beginning, knew that every sexual fantasy she'd ever had was about to come true. Practically quivering with expectation, she waited . . . waited while Tinker seemed to gather control, waited for more.

After a few moments of slow, steady breaths, Tinker reached around Lisa and grabbed Luc's cock in his fist. In what seemed like a surrealistic part of an amazingly vivid sexual dream, Lisa lifted herself enough to allow Tinker to guide Luc inside her sex.

She was swollen and wet and impossibly turned on, but the thought uppermost in Lisa's mind was that there couldn't possibly be room, not for two men as big as these guys. Very quickly, though, it was obvious they'd had more than enough practice. In fact, from the answering thought in Tinker's mind, she knew they'd done it many times.

She turned her head and looked at Tia, tried to picture her slim, bronze body between Luc's light skin and Tinker's dark. They would look beautiful, the three of them, all graduated color and slim, healthy bodies. Then Lisa wondered briefly why there was no jealousy in this room. Tia had been Tinker's lover, had shared her bed with both men on a regular basis. Had given herself to others within the pack, all with Luc's encouragement.

Now she encouraged Lisa, with both her smile and the love in her amber eyes. Beautiful eyes. The eyes of a wolf. A brief shiver crawled along Lisa's spine. Tia had the eyes of a wolf. Eyes just like Lisa's. Like Luc's and Tinker's. All of them alike.

Packmates.

Lisa sensed the differences between the men who surrounded her, who filled her. Their size and shape and the way they moved, their scent, the way they touched her, kissed her skin, held her and encouraged her. Still, no matter how different they might be, they still managed to enter her together, slowly and carefully, until she felt as if she might either burst or fly.

It seemed awkward at first, getting all their parts in sync, but they found a rhythm with Luc's cock slipping past Tinker's, in and out in opposing strides. Tinker invited Lisa into his mind, into the sensations of wet heat and tight muscles and unbelievable arousal, the feel of Luc's cock slipping along his, the fact that he could feel every bit of Luc's shape and texture through the thin wall between her rectum and her vaginal wall.

Experiencing what Tinker felt, knowing how much he loved both her and Luc, took Lisa higher, closer to the edge. Each time Luc slipped inside, each time he drew back, the top of his cock rubbed against her clit. When Tinker thrust forward, he pushed Lisa closer to Luc, and their bodies slipped over one another, wet with their own sweat and each other's.

Hot and wet and so turned on, Lisa thought she might explode, but the ultimate climax eluded her. So caught up in the magic of three bodies fucking, three lovers sharing, it took a moment to realize Tia was no longer part of the mix.

Lisa turned her head and looked directly into Tia's amber eyes. Propped against the headboard with her long, blond hair cascading wildly about her shoulders and her legs spread wide, Tia slowly thrust her fingers in and out of her swollen sex. Her nether lips were dark red and clung greedily to her fingers. Her bare mound glistened with moisture as she pleasured herself, rubbing slow circles around her clit, then pressing deep inside in a steady rhythm. Lips parted, she watched her three packmates through hooded eyes.

Watching, Lisa heard the wet sounds Tia made and imagined her taste, earthy and fresh, and wanted her mouth where the fingers of Tia's right hand now traveled. Luc reached out and took Tia's left hand tightly in his, and Lisa knew his strong grip kept his mate physically connected to Tinker, Lisa, and himself. Now it truly was the four of them, each growing closer to the edge of release, each one linked through touch as well as love.

This time when Lisa scanned the thoughts of the others,

she found them all open and waiting for her, maintaining control until she reached for them, joined with them in the most intimate sex of all, the sex they shared in their minds.

Bombarded with sensation, she felt her climax rushing forward, felt her body rising up from Luc, from Tia, and most especially from Tinker. His was the love that bonded the four of them, his was the emotion that grounded them, made them whole.

His love was the power that sent them flying into tiny pieces as orgasm claimed each of them as one. Tinker drove deep inside Lisa at the same time Luc filled her. Tia arched, her fingers deep inside herself. Lisa wanted to watch, couldn't help but want to see another woman in the throes of orgasm, but she was shaking and crying, and still the pleasure continued to build. Hotter, higher, clasped in Tinker's arms, held close by Luc, Lisa reached her peak with a scream, and then slid effortlessly over the top.

She lay sprawled across Luc's chest, aware of his pulsing cock still deep inside her sex. Tinker covered both of them, clasped tightly by her spasming body. Tia lay sprawled just as limp against the headboard, still holding on to Luc's hand. The only sound was the chuffing of deeply drawn breaths, the rapid beat of Lisa's own heart echoing in her ears.

The fantasy peeled quickly away as people walked by just outside their door, talking and laughing, and their voices came through the thin walls as if the sound passed through cardboard.

"Oh. My. God." Lisa tried to raise her head and couldn't. How noisy had the four of them been? Had there been an audience while they moaned and screamed and groaned in ecstasy? She tried to imagine a stranger walking in on them about now, and the visual of tangled, sated bodies twisted and sprawling atop the big bed was too much. She started to giggle. She slapped her hand over her mouth and tried desperately to stop, but she only laughed harder.

Her arms felt like rubber, and Luc's chest was beginning to bounce beneath her as he tried to hold back and couldn't. Tinker snorted into her ear, and that set Lisa off again.

Tia had managed to slap a pillow over her mouth, but even though she rolled over and buried her face in the fluff, it didn't muffle all the sound.

Tia's antics set Luc off once more, and Lisa, still squashed between Tinker and Luc, laughed even harder. By the time they got the giggles under control, the four of them had managed to disentangle themselves, but none of them seemed able to move beyond the big bed.

"That was fun," Luc said, deadpan.

And of course, that set them off again. Finally Tinker crawled off the bed and dragged Lisa with him toward the shower. She followed behind on rubbery legs. Tinker had to help her into the shower, but it felt wonderful to wash all the stickiness and sweat off her body and the ejaculate from two men from between her legs.

She didn't really think about what she'd just done, that she'd had sex with two men while another woman watched. It had been wonderful, and she sensed that it was so right and knew they were going to do it again. And again.

But Lisa wasn't quite ready to think about it. It was as if she'd lost that part of her brain that should be telling her what they'd done was wrong. Maybe that was part of being Chanku. Maybe all the rules changed along with that ugly looking capsule she swallowed every day.

Would the rules reverse if she stopped taking it? Lisa tilted her face toward the hot spray and smiled. No way in hell would she ever want to go back to her life before Tinker.

Before Luc and Tia.

Tinker took great care with her, treating Lisa as if she were made of spun glass. He bathed her gently, kissed her shoulder, her cheek, the indentation on her lower back. Once he'd soaped and rinsed her, he washed himself, but he was quick about it. It was all Lisa could do not to tumble to the tile floor, but at least Tinker had propped her against the wall of the shower so she wouldn't fall over.

This time when they went back into their room, Tia and Luc were gone and the bed put back to rights. Lisa crawled between the sheets and Tinker followed. He pulled her into his embrace and kissed the top of her head. She didn't think she'd ever felt so loved before. Or so tired.

"Tomorrow, okay? I'm really sleepy tonight." Tinker's deep voice rumbled in her ear. Lisa snuggled her butt up against his belly.

"Tomorrow what?" She really had no idea what he was talking about.

"Luc and me. You girls wanted to watch. Tomorrow, okay? Before we head back to the sanctuary. Your bed at the cabin's too small. We're big boys. We need big beds."

He wrapped his arms around her waist and pulled her up close against him. Lisa had been ready to fall asleep. Now she lay there in Tinker's embrace, picturing the two men she'd fallen so desperately in love with making love to each other.

Odd, she thought, how she now included Luc in her feelings of love. Tia as well. She'd always been so terribly monogamous in her relationships, even if it was serial monogamy. Tinker was right. The changes in her body and mind since becoming Chanku really did extend to her basic sense of relationships, her physical reaction to sex, to love.

Tinker's cock rose up to fill the crease between her buttocks. Pondering the entire concept of packmates and more than one sexual partner at a time, Lisa finally fell asleep with her mate tucked up close against her, holding on as if he'd never let her go.

Luc woke them before it was even light. He was already dressed, and Tinker heard the shower running when Luc opened the connecting door between their rooms.

"Ulrich just called. There's a raid planned at the sanctuary at dawn, all part of the hit on Dunlop's hunting preserve last night. It more than got ugly. According to Ulrich, the senator took a couple potshots at the cops. Guess they'd been drinking and decided to do a night hunt. That's why we heard them out after dark. Got the attention of a whole lot more folks than it might have otherwise. It's a little after four right now. If we hurry, we can be there when the authorities arrive. I really want Lisa on hand in case anything comes up." He leaned over and kissed Lisa fully on the lips. "Good morning, sleepyhead. Hope you slept well."

She blinked owlishly and kissed him back. Tinker swung his legs over the side of the bed. "Looks like that guy-on-guy sex gets put off a bit longer. Damn." He grinned at Luc. "I was really looking forward to that, too. Sorry, sweets." Tinker leaned back over and kissed Lisa, then laid one on Luc for good measure. "I'm going to take a quick shower."

Laughing, Luc headed back to his room, but he paused in the doorway. "Lisa, if anything comes up, you're an employee of Pack Dynamics. You've been working undercover for almost two years at the sanctuary. Got it? Ulrich already has the books adjusted."

He closed the door behind him. Lisa flopped back down on the bed. Tinker turned on the shower and wondered how much of the conversation she'd even remember, as sleepy as she looked.

Tinker finished his shower in record time. Lisa took hers while he gathered their few things together. Luc had saved the deli sandwiches he'd bought the night before but never got around to eating. They bundled into the car, stopped for coffee to go, and headed back to the sanctuary with Tinker at the wheel. They'd only had a few hours' sleep, but he was buzzing with an adrenaline rush. One look at Lisa, sipping her coffee, munching on a sandwich and staring thoughtfully at the road ahead told him she worried about the repercussions of Dunlop's arrest.

Luc and Tia appeared to have fallen asleep in the backseat, so Tinker kept his voice low. "You okay, sweetie? You look worried."

She turned and smiled at him, still obviously half asleep. "I guess I am worried, a little. What will happen to the sanctuary? Dunlop supported it but he won't be able to now, I imagine. Not if he's in jail. I'm concerned that Hal Anderson is involved, and I know Seth is, the creep. Other than me, all who are left are Millie West, Hal's secretary; a couple of part-time employees; and a bunch of volunteers. I worry about the wolves. I feel as if they depend on me."

Tinker brushed the loose hair back from her eyes. "They do depend on you, but don't forget, Pack Dynamics has a lot of resources. If it's money, we might be able to help. Just hang in there and don't worry until you know for sure there's something to worry about."

She laughed quietly. "Tink, some of your other packmates don't even know me. How can you be so sure they'd want to help? I'm a stranger to them. My problems aren't theirs. Besides, if there's one thing I've learned in my thirty-four years, it's that there's *always* something to worry about."

"That's my job, sweetie. I'll take care of the worrying. You try and get some sleep." He flashed her a grin, and she smiled back, but Tinker could tell she wasn't convinced. Still, she leaned her head back against the seat and closed her eyes.

Thirty-four? Tinker grinned at the road ahead. Damn, he'd gone and fallen in love with an older woman. She looked younger than he did, but he was just twenty-seven. Hell, age meant nothing. Her worries were his, though. He hoped the next few hours weren't going to turn out badly. If there was anything he could do to protect her . . . The thought made him grin. The last thing Lisa wanted was protection. She was tough. As tough as Tia, if not more so.

There was nothing soft about a Chanku bitch, especially when the chips were down. And she loved Tia. He'd felt it last night, felt the deep range of emotion Lisa had broadcast without even realizing they could all read her like an open book. All her hopes and desires, her needs. He'd been there, a part of what she needed to make her happy. So had Tia and Luc. Maybe, just maybe, things wouldn't have to change all that much.

If she thought their packmates might not want to help out, it was obvious she hadn't fully grasped the complexity of the mating bond. She had to learn to embrace all their packmates completely, the way Tinker knew they would embrace Lisa. Somehow, she had to accept that Luc and Tia, even Mik and AJ and Jake, men she'd never met, were more than just friends, more than mere temporary lovers.

They were family. Family with privileges? Tinker chuckled as he headed south along the highway. It could get confusing, now that Lisa's brother and sister were part of the pack, but they'd work through that. For all their sexual freedom, incest definitely didn't fly among the Chanku.

They passed a Colorado state patrolman headed the opposite direction on his motorcycle. Tinker checked his speedometer. They were cutting the time close to the raid, but the last thing he needed was a speeding ticket. He glanced to his right and saw that Lisa had rolled to one side, as far as her seatbelt would allow. Her eyes were closed. He took her coffee cup from her hand and set it in the cup holder so it wouldn't spill. He hoped she'd get a little sleep before the shit hit the fan. He had a feeling it might get real ugly today.

The sun still hadn't come up, but the sky was growing light in the east. Tinker whistled quietly as he headed toward the sanctuary. All they had to do was get through one more day, and all would be well. Once everything was taken care of, there was that little bit about satisfying Lisa's wishes.

Thinking of making love to Luc with the girls watching was a marvelous way to take Tinker's mind off the events waiting for all of them at the High Mountain Wolf Sanctuary.

Chapter 13

Luckily they had time to stop at the cabin for a change of clothes and a quick breakfast, but Lisa almost wished she hadn't eaten when they pulled into the parking lot at the sanctuary. Her stomach immediately tied into knots. As early as it was, not even seven, Hal Anderson's car was in front of his office, and it looked like Seth's mom had just dropped him off as well.

When Lisa saw the teen, she had to consciously unclench her fists. Her hip still hurt where he'd shot her with the tranquilizer dart two days ago.

"Okay." Lisa took a deep breath. "I can do this."

"Of course you can," Luc said. "Just remember, Tia and I are friends of yours and Tinker's, here for a visit. If things go bad, you're on assignment and you work for me."

Lisa nodded. She fully expected things to go bad. Didn't they always?

"Okay. Let's go." Tinker climbed out of the SUV and stretched. The sound of the car doors closing seemed to echo across the parking lot.

Hal Anderson charged down the stairs. "Quinn! Where the hell have you been? Did you forget you have a job here?"

Lisa felt a sense of calm settle over her shoulders as the little man stopped on the bottom step and glared at her.

Obviously he'd try anything to give himself more height when he was around her. "Good morning to you, too, Hal. I would have called, but as you know, I don't have a phone in my company-owned cabin."

Tinker, Luc, and Tia had arranged themselves behind Lisa. She wondered if her sense of confidence and well-being originated with them.

Hal sputtered and opened his mouth, but no sound came out. He stared beyond Lisa and the others, and his face went deathly pale. He grabbed the stair railing as if for support.

She turned to see what had caught his attention. At least a dozen sheriff and state trooper cars were pulling into the road leading to the parking lot. Lisa spotted vehicles from other legal agencies as well. "Looks like we've got company."

Visibly upset, Hal brushed by her as Seth came running. The teen looked absolutely stricken. "What do you think they want?"

Lisa glared at him. "I imagine we'll find out real soon, don't you agree?"

A white, unmarked sedan pulled into the parking spot closest to the office. A tall man in a business suit got out and talked quietly with Hal for a moment, then handed him a sheaf of papers.

Hal turned around and pointed directly at Lisa. Three sheriff's deputies approached. One asked, "Are you Lisa Quinn?"

"Yes, sir, I am." She folded her arms across her chest and smiled at the deputy.

"We're investigating reports of wolves from the sanctuary ending up at an exclusive hunting club as prey. Mr. Anderson suggests you might be involved."

Lisa nodded. Was Hal trying to turn suspicion away from himself? Obviously, there was only one way past this roadblock. "In a way, I am. Let me introduce Tia Mason, Lucien Stone, and Martin McClintock. We're all with an investigative agency known as Pack Dynamics. We're here investigating the same reports."

"Pack Dynamics? Really?" The deputy shook his head. "Amazing group. We heard you had operatives inside the compound last night. Did everyone get out okay?"

Luc stepped forward with his ID in his hand. "Yes, we were successful. Thank you. I understand arrests were made?"

The deputy nodded as he looked over Luc's identification, then handed it back to him. "There were, and it's going to be all over the news later today. We've kept it as quiet as possible using this raid as an excuse, but when you've got a well-known senator, shots being fired, and illegal hunting of more than one protected species, well, the media's going to have a field day."

He stared back toward Hal Anderson, who remained with the other deputies. "We know Anderson is clean, but that doesn't explain why he's so insistent you're part of this. He actually reported the missing wolves a couple years ago when the first one disappeared. He's continued to keep us informed when others went missing. Your name, Ms. Quinn, has been in every report."

Luc stepped up. "We know Lisa's not involved either." He glanced around at the small group of curious volunteers standing off to one side, watching all the commotion. "However, it's definitely an inside job. I'd appreciate it if you'd keep our participation in this under wraps. We try our best to keep a low profile."

The sheriff nodded, but there was a curios gleam in his eye. "You wouldn't know anything about the death of a murder suspect we've been hunting for the past couple of years, would you? Found his body stuffed in a freezer at the hunting preserve. Not sure how long he's been there. Strange injuries to his throat. Looks like a wild animal got him."

Luc shook his head. "No idea. Did they have any big cats on the property? Those things can be nasty."

"Actually, they did. A couple of tigers and a leopard. Must have been one of those." The sheriff nodded in agreement, as if filing that bit of information away. "We'll keep your group's involvement quiet. No problem with that. Have you had any luck with your investigation? If Ms. Quinn's not involved, we still don't have the link between someone working here at the sanctuary and the wolves showing up at the preserve."

Lisa turned toward Seth. She stared directly at the teen when she spoke. "Actually, the person responsible for trapping and delivering the wolves is here. He tranquilizes them, stuffs them in a cage, and leaves them in an old barn on the north end of the property. Dunlop or his employees would collect them."

The color completely drained from Seth's face. Before Lisa had time to react, his arm snaked out and wrapped around her throat. He held a knife in his other hand. "Stay away!"

Lisa tried to jerk out of his surprisingly strong grasp, then felt the sharp pressure of the blade beneath her jaw.

Walking backward, pulling Lisa with him, Seth moved toward the old pickup. Lisa felt his hot breath on her neck and the knife blade biting into her skin. "Seth. What the hell are you doing?"

She reached for his arm with both hands, but he increased the knife pressure against her throat. Lisa felt the bite of the blade and the hot welling of blood. Black spots danced in front of her eyes as the teenager dragged her closer to the car.

Suddenly, there was a roar, a scuffle, and Lisa was down with Tia holding a cloth to her throat while Tinker grabbed Seth by the neck and held him off the ground in a stranglehold. Luc got in one punch before the deputy shouted, "Put him down!"

Tinker dropped him none too gently and raced back to Lisa. Officers moved in and cuffed Seth. A paramedic on hand for the raid arrived.

Two of the deputies grabbed Seth. One said, "Did you see those guys move? Damn, they're fast. I didn't even have time to pull my gun." He used plastic ties to cuff the teen.

Tinker pulled Lisa into his lap and held her close. "I'm okay," she said, but her hands shook, her body trembled, and tears ran down her cheeks. She felt stupid for crying, but she couldn't seem to stop. Tinker was in her head, his mental voice an agony of regret. She let him know she was okay, but he didn't believe her.

The paramedic lifted the cloth away from the knife wound. "Doesn't appear too deep. I'll clean it out and use a couple of sterile strips. Should heal without any problem, but you might want to see a doctor for a tetanus shot."

It only stung a little when the man cleansed the inch-long slice just beneath her jaw, closed the cut with his finger-tips, and held the edges together with the adhesive strips. "Looks good," he said, admiring his handiwork. "Now keep it clean and it should heal just fine."

Deep, wracking sobs caught Lisa's attention as the paramedic packed up his equipment and left. She turned and realized the sound came from Seth. The teen was curled up on his side, his hands and feet restrained with plastic cuffs. A deputy rolled him roughly upright. Seth buried his face against his knees and cried.

Lisa pulled away from Tinker's embrace, marched angrily over to Seth, and hunkered down next to him. "Why? You said you loved the wolves. Why would you send them to die? Why would you want to hurt me? I thought you were my friend."

Seth wiped his streaming eyes against his knees, then looked up at Lisa. His voice cracked and wavered, but Lisa was certain he spoke the truth. "The man who hired me, Mr. Smith, told me he worked for people who ran a breeding farm. That's why he wanted the best. Not to kill them, but to breed them. He said he wanted wolves to run free again. I didn't know anyone was hunting them. I didn't know! I'm sorry, Lisa. I panicked. I'm sorry I hurt you."

She sat back on her heels. "I'm sorry, too, Seth. You said you had no choice. Why?"

His head snapped up. "How do you know what I said?"

"I was there, in the barn. I heard you. So did Tinker."

Seth shook his head, then took a deep breath. "My dad ran out two years ago. I help support my mom and little sister. Mr. Smith paid me a lot of money for the wolves. I thought they were going to be free. God, I was so stupid."

Lisa nodded. "Yeah, Seth. You were. And ya know what? There's always a choice. It's not always easy, but it's up to you to choose right or wrong."

Tinker helped her up. The deputies were making a cursory check of the premises, but there wasn't much left for them to do now that they had Seth. He was the link who could tie Dunlop, through his employee Bill Smith, to the missing wolves here at the sanctuary.

Unfortunately, Tinker, Lisa, Luc, and Tia had only been on the preserve premises as wolves. There'd be no way they could testify against Dunlop.

Anderson brushed by Lisa on his way to his office. No comment about Seth's attack, no sign of concern for her injury. He glared at her but didn't say a word. Obviously, he'd been convinced she was behind the missing animals. It was just as obvious he didn't like being proved wrong, especially since Seth had long been his favorite. Lisa was almost sure Anderson planned to fire her. She figured that was coming as soon as he could do it without an audience.

Lisa leaned against Tinker. "He is such a jerk." She felt like crying. The thought of losing her job here was heartbreaking, but it was obvious things could never go back to the way they'd been. What would happen to the wolves?

Luc brushed the dust off Tia's butt and wiped his pants off as well. "Let us know what your duties for today are, and we'll help you get them done and get out of here. Are you okay?"

"I think she needs to see a doctor." Tinker's voice sounded as if he barely controlled his rage. He wouldn't even look at Seth.

Lisa stood on her toes and kissed him soundly. "No, she does not need a doctor. Thank you. You saved my life. I had no idea how fast you were. I knew you were strong, but you're very, very fast."

Tinker kissed the smile off her lips. "Not all the time. Sometimes I'm real, real slow."

Luc laughed, then leaned close and gave Lisa a quick hug. "I'm glad you're okay, but you're getting off the subject. Jobs?"

"Follow me. I'll show you what you can do while Tia and I make the roadkill run."

Tia made retching noises in the background. "Please tell me that's not what it sounds like."

Lisa laughed. She wanted to hug Luc and Tia and Tinker. Without them here, she had no idea how she'd handle something this awful. "You guys can clean out the quarantine pens. I think you two gentlemen can handle wolf-poop duty without supervision. Then, as soon as we're done, I want to go back to the cabin and sleep for a month. The docents and volunteer staff can feed the animals and take care of any visitors, and Hal will deal with the media. I imagine the reporters will be swarming once they realize this is connected with what happened with the senator and Charles Dunlop. Hal should be in his glory with reporters hanging on his every word."

They reached the pens, and Lisa pointed them toward the shovels. Tinker grabbed Luc's arm in one hand and Tia's with the other. "Now, aren't you sorry you asked how you could help?"

They both groaned.

* * *

"I can't believe you met Tinker while picking up flat-tened critters. That is just so gross!" Tia, riding shotgun in the old pickup, leaned out the window and let her hair tangle in the wind. Lisa kept picturing her as a wolf with her ears flattened in the breeze.

"It was pretty gross, but I guess if he can say he loves me after seeing what I do as part of my job, it might actu-ally be real love."

Tia pulled her head back inside the window and frowned at Lisa. "What do you mean, 'say he loves me,' and 'might actually be real love'? You act like you don't believe he means it."

Lisa glanced in the rearview mirror and shrugged. "I've only known him a week. You can't fall in love in a week."

"I disagree. You've bonded. You guys did the deep-link thing, didn't you?" Tia shook her head as if she couldn't believe what Lisa was saying.

"Yeah, but it was sort of by accident. I mean, the sex was so good, and I was on the verge of shifting for the very first time, and when it was all over, we were two wolves fucking, not two humans."

"Was it really great? Tinker's an amazing lover."

Tia sighed and Lisa burst out laughing. "Yeah, he is, isn't he?" This was all so odd, the way she actually felt comfort-able talking about Tinker's lovemaking with a woman who'd been his lover. Who would most likely be his lover again . . . and her own. Embracing her Chanku heritage had opened up an entirely new side to Lisa's normally monogamous nature, but it was all so new, so hard to understand.

Just as difficult to accept was the fact that she was at-tracted not only to Tia, but also to Tia's mate. It felt like the most normal thing in the world. Her memories of past relationships were so convoluted and painful. Now there was a lightness about love, about sex. It was suddenly a primary focus, yet as natural as breathing. One wanted, one loved. The old taboos were a thing of the past, no longer intruding on her amazingly healthy libido.

Shifting from woman to wolf was a huge change. Even larger was the absolute shift of her basic nature. So many changes, so many roads to travel, each welcoming her with something new, something different.

She'd noticed another change as well. This job she normally hated, driving along the road looking for animals that hadn't survived the journey across the asphalt, no longer seemed as onerous. In the past it had disgusted and saddened her. Now she saw herself as the one who fed the pack, the strongest, most capable, able to bring fresh meat to the rest.

She was Chanku. As much wolf as woman. Lisa turned and flashed a big smile at Tia. It still felt like a dream, but what an amazing trip it was.

The work was mundane enough that it gave him time to think. Tinker had to agree with Lisa. He still felt uneasy about Hal Anderson, but he couldn't put his finger on the reason. Other than the fact the man was a total loser, he hadn't been involved in Dunlop's plan.

So what kind of crap was he up to? Tinker's feelings were too intense to be wrong. He'd bet the farm Anderson was up to his scrawny little neck in something illegal, but what? All those nighttime forays into the woods had more to them than simple surveillance of the sanctuary.

Plus, he'd watched Anderson when the authorities pulled into the sanctuary parking lot. The man had looked like he might pass out. Once he realized they were here about the missing wolves, he'd gone back to his typical bravado.

Luc leaned on his shovel and stared at Tinker. "How long before the girls get back?"

"An hour. Maybe longer. Why?"

"I wish we could take a little run through the sanctuary.

Maybe a new set of eyes will provide a different perspective. There's something else going on here."

Tinker nodded. "You and I are on the same wavelength. I've been thinking the same damned thing . . . but we can't do it."

Luc frowned at him, obviously confused. "And why the fuck not?"

Tinker smiled, though he didn't feel much humor about the situation. "This is Lisa's quest, her problem to solve. The last thing I want to do is push her aside and do anything without checking with her first. It's too important to her. I realized that when she insisted on going back in the cage. She was scared spitless at being locked up in there, but she still did it. I can't do anything that will take the lead out of her hands."

Luc laughed and grabbed Tinker's hand in a firm handshake. "Welcome to the club, bro. You're figuring this out a lot faster than I did. You already realize if we go searching without her and find anything exciting, she'd kill us both without remorse. We'd probably end up with the roadkill."

"There is that." Chuckling to himself, unbelievably pleased with Luc's confirmation of his decision, Tinker finished up the last of the pens.

Lisa grabbed a couple of cold beers for the guys and sodas for herself and Tia, and walked outside to join them on the back deck. "Okay, everyone's had a shower and a change of clothes. No more excuses. What the hell were you guys laughing about when we got back?"

Tinker chuckled. "See? What did I tell you? If we'd followed up on any of our ideas, she would have been one pissed Chanku bitch."

"I still might be. Spill it." Lisa ruined the effect by sitting on the swing next to Tinker and kissing his chin.

Luc answered. "We talked about checking out the

empty pens, the larger ones in the hills, trying to find out what keeps drawing your scrawny little boss out to that area in the dark of night."

"And?"

"We decided to wait on you. You know the area better than we do, obviously. Besides, like Tinker said, it's your case."

Lisa blinked. Had she heard him right? Luc, the leader of the team, deferring to her? She glanced at Tinker, saw the full smile on his face, and knew he'd been the one to hold Luc back. She felt a blossoming of warmth that started somewhere suspiciously near her heart and ended in whatever part of her brain was in charge of tears. Her eyes burned. She had to get away—now—or she'd make an absolute fool of herself in front of them all.

"Thanks." She barely choked the word out, her throat felt so tight. "Just a minute." She practically ran from the room. As she turned to close the door, Lisa caught Tinker watching her. He looked confused, even troubled. She felt him touching her mind, but she slammed her thoughts down as best she could and closed the door behind herself.

It took Lisa a moment in the bathroom, splashing cold water on her face, to regain her composure. They'd waited on her. They hadn't gone off on their own, intent on finding answers without her. Tinker had wanted to wait. He actually understood!

She opened her closet door and dug through the stacks of books and papers on the floor, found what she was looking for, and headed back out to the others. "I've got this. It might help." She unrolled a large map, hand-drawn on butcher paper, and spread it out on the picnic table.

"I made this last year when the second wolf disappeared. I was trying to figure out if there was some way for them to escape, some sort of pattern to their disappearance. I'm not sure if it's much use, but it might help us figure out what Anderson is up to. See anything?"

Lisa had carefully drawn a map of the entire sanctuary, including all the larger, fenced enclosures. She grabbed a handful of pebbles out of a potted plant and placed one in the center of each of the inhabited paddocks.

Luc studied the map. "What's this little squiggly thing?"

Lisa bit back a laugh. "Are you insulting my artwork? That's a creek. This is a spring, these are rocky outcroppings, and these lines denote canyons."

"These are the service roads?" Luc tapped the red lines running between the enclosures. Lisa nodded.

Tia leaned over the map. "It looks like they all have creeks or springs."

Again, Lisa nodded. "All the enclosures have year-round water supplies. We check them regularly, but there has to be a natural source of water for the wolves in case the pumps fail."

"This is terrific. You've done a beautiful job." Tinker brushed Lisa's hair back from her forehead and planted a kiss on her temple. "Okay, we've got at least half a dozen uninhabited enclosures ranging in size from ten to twenty acres, fenced, with easy access, but secluded from the general public. Is there power?"

Lisa shook her head. "No. No need for power. There's a pump closer to headquarters that provides the supplemental water supply, and the entire area is plumbed, but it's run off the main power near the office buildings."

Tinker nodded. "Luc and I both agreed there's more to your slimy little boss than a personality disorder, and it's got to be connected with his late-night forays into this area." He pointed at the more isolated pens where Lisa had spotted Hal Anderson on more than one occasion. "I think we need to slip in and take a look. First, though, we need a meal and some rest."

"I agree. It shouldn't be too hard to get inside." Lisa sat back on the swing with Tinker. He wrapped his arm around her, and she leaned against his chest. He felt warm and good and so right in her life. Every one of them had so quickly become important to Lisa.

Unfortunately, it scared the crap out of her. When had she let them into her life? How could it have happened so quickly, and how would she survive when they left her?

Tinker turned and gave her a long, pensive look. "You're broadcasting angst again, sweetie. It's not becoming—and it's not fair. We're not leaving. None of us would dream of turning you loose."

"How the *hell* do you do that?" How could he just wander through her thoughts like that? It wasn't fair! Lisa tried to pull out of Tinker's embrace, but he held her tightly against him.

"Let me go, damn it!"

"Not gonna happen." Tinker leaned close and kissed her.

Lisa ground her teeth in frustration.

They wouldn't stay. No one ever stayed, and it was going to hurt so badly when they left! Her thoughts weren't even her own. She couldn't even be miserable without broadcasting everything that went on in her head. It wasn't fair!

Tia came over and knelt in front of Lisa; she took one of her hands and cradled it in both of hers. "Honey, it's okay. You've got to remember, you might be a grown woman, but you're just a baby Chanku. You have so much to learn, so many things yet to experience. Tinker said you've never even mated as wolves, which means your bond might not have given you a lot of the lessons we share so easily—like blocking your thoughts. Give it time. Accept your heritage, the love of your mate, and the love of your packmates. Don't be afraid it won't last. That's one thing I can promise. The love of a Chanku man for his woman is to the death. It's solid gold. So is the loyalty and love of the pack."

Lisa looked into Tia's amber eyes, so filled with love and hope, and did the unthinkable.

She burst into tears.

Tia scooted up on the swing next to Lisa and wrapped

her arms around her. "You. Men. Leave now." Tinker and Luc grabbed their beers and headed for the smaller deck at the front of the house. Lisa might have laughed if she wasn't crying so hard.

"It's okay, sweetie. You've had a shitty week, and they haven't got a clue." Tia brushed Lisa's hair back from her forehead and held her in a loving hug. "When guys first shift, they just learn to go from man to wolf. It's really cool, but no big deal in the scheme of things. Guys are horny all the time, anyway, so the nutty libido doesn't seem like a problem. I think they love it. When a woman makes the change, everything is different. It affects our menstrual cycle, our ability to conceive, our sexuality. Most important, it affects the way we perceive other people."

Lisa struggled for control while she listened to what Tia had to say. "What do you mean? The way we perceive . . ."

"I bet you've always been a good girl, right? Rarely stood up for yourself, let people push you around because you're a woman? When the guys refer to us as Chanku bitches, it's a term of respect. Somehow, when you're taking the supplement and able to shift, it's like you're stronger. More determined, more self-assured. Not really a bitch, but not a pushover either. I think of it more as setting our inner bitch free."

Lisa found a tissue in her pocket and blew her nose. "My inner bitch probably needs therapy."

"Nah. She's doing just fine. Believe me, I was a wreck when I first made the shift, but there was so much crap going on in my life. Did you see my background when you bonded with Tinker?"

Lisa had, but she'd hesitated to say anything. "Luc killed your mother. I saw that in Tinker's memories."

Tia nodded. "Yeah. It was pretty bad. He shot her when he was just a rookie cop, and she was a young mother out doing her wolf thing in a public park during the day. Not a smart move on her part. Luc lived with that guilt for twenty years, even though he was just doing his job when he shot her. He still lives with it, though he wants me to think he's past it. The point is, by the time we learn we're Chanku, we've usually managed to totally fuck up our lives. I'm hoping the children we raise will have a better start than we did."

"Children? Are there any?"

Tia laughed. "Not yet, but soon. Anton Cheval, that wizard we keep calling on? He's mated to my cousin, and Keisha's pregnant. So is their packmate Xandi. She's Stefan Aragat's mate. They're both due around the same time, in June, I think. It's a beginning, actually. An entirely new generation of Chanku, but they'll grow up with parents who understand the way of the pack, who can teach them the way we were never taught."

Lisa leaned back against the swing. "I hope I get to meet this infamous wizard someday."

"Oh, you will. Luc and I are actually getting married in a fairly traditional wedding next month. Everyone's invited. Your brother and sister are coming, and I certainly expect you and Tinker to be there."

Lisa thought of all the others she'd finally meet, including Tia's father, the leader and founder of Pack Dynamics. "Your mother and father were both Chanku. How come you didn't know?"

"That's another story altogether. When my mom died, my father went into total denial. Chanku children don't make the change until they hit puberty, and I was only six when she died. Plus, it only happens if they're getting the nutrients. I wasn't given the supplement and didn't have a clue about my heritage. It wasn't until I came back to teach in San Francisco and got involved with Luc. It was actually planned by my father, that Luc would be the one to tell me. Essentially, my father chose my mate for me."

Lisa laughed at the thought of someone choosing her lifetime companion for her, then realized someone had—

Luc was the one who sent Tinker to her. Thank goodness the match worked.

"I just realized Luc chose my mate for me."

Tia squeezed her hand. "He couldn't have chosen better. Neither could you. Wait until you see your sister and her guys! Of course, now we need to find someone for your brother."

Lisa sat on the swing with Tia next to her, listening to stories of her own family, of Tia's family. A sense of warmth settled in her soul. The belief that maybe Tia was right. Maybe she really did belong to a most amazing family.

For keeps.

Packmates. Lisa rolled that one around on her tongue for a while. It was definitely going to take some getting used to. She'd dried her eyes, felt as if she'd regained at least marginal control of her wayward emotions, when Tinker wandered back out onto the deck.

He knelt between the two women. Patted Tia on the knee with loving familiarity and took Lisa's hand in his. "Sweetie, are you okay?"

Not quite sure if she could talk without bawling again, Lisa nodded.

"Everything's going to be fine," he said. "Trust me on that one. In the meantime, Luc and I thought we'd help take your mind of all the crap that's been happening. We've got hours before we can check on Anderson. C'mon."

Lisa flashed a questioning look at Tia. Tia shrugged and the two of them followed Tinker inside. The guys had been busy. One of her favorite CDs played quietly. The gentle woodwinds and classical guitar reminded Lisa of the sound of wind in the trees. It was one of the CDs she liked to listen to when stuff bothered her. Had Tinker learned what music soothed her when they linked?

Lisa put that thought aside and simply stared at her once simple front room. The guys had taken the mattress off her bed as well as the one from the guestroom. It was only a double, but with her queen, the entire front room floor was covered with mattress.

For one ridiculous moment, Lisa wasn't sure if she was going to do her watering can routine again or break out in giggles. Only a guy would think of solving her angst with sex.

Chapter 14

"Is this where we're supposed to ask exactly what it is you have in mind?" Lisa glanced to her left, at Tia standing beside her with twinkling eyes.

Tia turned to Lisa and said with great seriousness, "I think they expect us to have figured it out. Let's see . . . does it perhaps require getting naked?"

Tinker didn't say a word, but he grabbed both women by the hands, waited while they kicked their sandals off, and walked them across the navy blue sheets covering the tops of the mattresses to the couch on the far side of the room. "No. It merely requires that you two sit and get comfortable while Luc and I get naked."

Tia sat down and glanced up at Luc. "What? No popcorn?"

Luc shot a dramatic glare at Tinker. "You forgot the popcorn? Martin, how could you?"

Tinker shrugged his shoulders. "I have other things I prefer to put in my mouth. Sorry."

Lisa felt as if she'd stepped into some sort of alternate universe. Tia grabbed her hand and tugged her down to sit beside her on the couch. "You mean they're just going to . . . ?"

"Fuck like bunnies? I hope so." Tia curled up in the corner of the couch. "They do it so well."

"That's a phrase I've heard before." She thought back to that first day, to Tinker's outrageous suggestion they fuck like bunnies when they'd known each other for less than an hour. Thought also of her outrageous action in agreeing. She glanced up and realized Tinker watched her with a tender smile on his face. Was he remembering the same thing? Still not quite sure what to expect, Lisa slid to the opposite end of the couch and tucked her feet under her.

Tinker pulled the shades closed, and the room fell into almost total darkness. Luc turned on a low-wattage floor lamp and tilted the shade, throwing a beam into the center of the larger mattress like a pale golden spotlight. The music played quietly in the background, and both men stood in the shadows.

In a matter of a few seconds and a few simple alterations, Lisa's simple cabin had become an eerily seductive stage. She glanced at Tia, who focused all her attention on the spot of light at the center of the room. As if waiting for a movie to begin, Lisa turned and made herself comfortable. She whispered to Tia, "What are they doing now?"

Tia laughed quietly. "Probably making sure they've got enough lube where it's needed."

"Oh." Her mind spinning with possibilities and her sex growing dangerously wet, Lisa turned back around. She heard a quiet rustle of clothing, saw the corner of the mattress dip as Luc and Tinker approached the center from opposite sides. As if they choreographed every step, the two men met in the middle and stood facing each other, not more than four feet from where Lisa and Tia sat.

They were entirely out of reach but close enough to see every bit of their perfect bodies in stark relief under the golden ribbon of light.

Neither man moved. Like statues of living marble, they held their position, facing each other, mere inches apart. Almost equal in stature, they could have been cut from the same mold.

Even their cocks appeared similar in size. Neither was totally erect, but neither were they flaccid. The crowns of their cocks touched, the only connection between them. Their beautiful bodies were a contrast of dark and fair. Caught from the chest down in the beam of light, they appeared an almost perfect match in every other way than color.

Lisa felt her breath catch, an amazing physical response from merely sitting here in the shadows, comparing the two. Broad chests with well-defined muscles, perfectly sculpted pectorals, light glinting off corded arms held loosely at their sides, off muscular thighs. Tight, sleek buns and thick mats of black pubic hair.

Black on black. Black on white. The contrast was perfect, arousing. Absolutely beautiful. As Lisa watched, their cocks expanded, extended, rose out of their dark nests. Pressed harder, one against the other, without any movement by either man. She wondered what kind of restraint it must take, to stand immobile while the slight pressure of contact aroused them to full tumescence.

There was something utterly fascinating, watching the slow expansion of two absolutely perfect cocks, one almost black, the other a deep, dark red. Light glinted off each man. Veins enlarged, pumping more blood into organs already hard and full.

Rising up now, erections brushed against each other, forming an X when viewed from the side. Neither man had moved, yet their tableau continued to change, slowly, inexorably as their arousal increased. Lisa realized her heart was pounding, knew her sex was wet and swollen. A throbbing deep in her womb matched the pounding rhythm of blood in her chest, the brush of nipples against her soft T-shirt had her rolling her shoulders in response. Her clothing felt uncomfortably tight.

As she watched intently, Lisa noticed a bubble of white slowly forming on the dark crown of Tinker's cock. Her tongue swept her upper and lower lip, as if she tasted the familiar flavors. The brush of her tongue tickled—her lips were so unbelievably sensitive. Lisa shot a quick glance at Tia. She'd already removed her clothing. Naked, Tia slowly rubbed light circles across her breasts with both hands.

Lisa tugged her shirt over her head and slipped out of her pants. The cool air in the cabin raised goose flesh across her chest, and the muscles between her legs clenched spasmodically. She didn't touch herself. Chose instead to test her body, to test her limits of arousal.

Luc's cock was covered now in a stream of pre-cum, flowing slowly from the tip of the broad crown. Lisa wondered if the men could reach climax, standing there like statues while their erections continued to grow and curve upward.

Suddenly, one dark fist and one light slipped out of the shadows. Tinker wrapped his long fingers around Luc while Luc did the same to Tinker. Each man carefully spread the other's fluids, lubricating the massive, deep-veined cock he held.

Sitting this close, Lisa realized how highly aroused both Luc and Tinker actually were. Their hands trembled. She tried to read their thoughts but discovered solid blocks. Did they communicate mentally on some sort of private band, or was every move, so perfectly duplicated, managed merely by touch?

Her questions fled as Luc and Tinker began to slowly stroke one another. Right hands only, their fingers slipping back and forth over slick, hard flesh. Muscles in thighs and buttocks quivered and clenched, and the golden light played over the changing shadows. They'd held perfectly still until now, but the almost imperceptible rock and sway of hips hinted at increasing desire.

Tia moaned. Lisa bit back her own whimper of need and thought of sitting on her hands to keep from touching herself. She wanted to let the fever build, slowly. Wanted it to grow merely from watching the men.

Tia had no such intention. Lisa glanced regretfully away from Tinker and Luc when Tia groaned, and almost came undone. Tia had hooked one leg over the broad arm of the overstuffed couch and slowly but surely was bringing herself to climax. Her fingers circled her engorged clit; the other hand tugged at the nipple on her right breast.

Lisa squirmed in her seat but kept her hands away from her body. Her skin practically hummed with growing need, but watching was amazingly arousing when she knew she wasn't going to touch herself. She forced herself to look away from Tia and slowly shifted her focus.

Turned back to the men.

Luc and Tinker appeared on the edge of climax. Muscles across their chests quivered, their legs trembled. Each man had his head thrown back, eyes closed. Sweat covered chests, backs, and legs, and they glistened in the mellow light.

Suddenly, they paused. Luc turned Tinker loose, wrapped his hands around Tink's hips, and dropped slowly to his knees. He licked the very tip of Tinker's cock, dipped his tongue into the tiny eye at the end, then wrapped his mouth around the upper third and sucked.

Lisa realized she was holding her breath, watching the dark hollows in Luc's cheeks when he tilted his head and sucked Tinker deep, so deep he had to swallow in order to take the full length. His throat convulsed with the size of Tinker's cock; his cheeks hollowed, dark and feral.

She let her breath out with a *whoosh* when Luc backed away. His lips dragged the full length of Tinker's massive cock, catching on the ridge just before the crown. Lisa licked her own lips, remembering how Tinker tasted, how it felt to circle the smooth head with her lips and tongue. She practically tasted his fluids, sensing in her mouth the bitter yet somehow addictive taste of his cum.

She swallowed back a whimper. Her breasts ached, her uterus ached, her entire body pulsed with need, and she wondered if she could come, just sitting here watching, not touching. Wondered if the men, with their heightened senses, could smell her arousal. Wondered if they even cared, so caught up were they with each other.

Luc used his hands to control Tinker's hips, pressing him close as he swallowed his cock, moving him away as he slipped his lips back, almost to the tip. Tinker's arms stayed at his sides, his hands clenched into tight fists, the veins across the tops of his hands and along his forearms highly distended.

A muffled cry to her right told Lisa that Tia had taken herself over the edge, but Lisa didn't look away from the men. She couldn't. Tinker suddenly pulled his cock out of Luc's mouth. His chest heaved with each deep breath, but he seemed to gain enough control that he didn't come.

Lisa didn't think she'd ever seen his cock so big, so hard. Glistening black and shining in the pale light, wet from Luc's mouth, wet from the fluid flowing slowly from the tip. Luc raised his head and grinned at Tinker, who slowly knelt facing Luc. They embraced, kissing long and deep, their mouths open, their cocks once again rubbing against each other. Now, though, the pre-cum was thicker, more evident, their movements jerky, more frantic.

Suddenly Luc grabbed Tinker in a wrestler's hold and attempted to throw him. Tinker responded with a defensive move that rolled Luc to his back. Lisa pulled her feet up out of the way when they tumbled closer to the couch.

Tia giggled and raised her fist in the air. "Go get him, Luc. Take him down!"

Still caught in her body's need for release, Lisa watched, open-mouthed, as the two men wrestled for the superior position. Tinker appeared to have the advantage; then Luc broke his hold and managed to roll Tinker onto his back. Grunting with effort, Tinker used his powerful legs to gain leverage. He lifted Luc and threw him to his belly, then rolled over on top and held him down with his own weight.

Both men were gasping with their efforts, but they appeared more aroused than before. Tinker's hips rode Luc's ass, though he'd not penetrated. Still, the threat was there, the power play of one man dominating another.

Lisa realized she had her fist shoved in her mouth to keep from screaming. They weren't really fighting, were they? It looked deadly serious, but there was no anger in the room, no sense of anything other than unimaginable lust and the male need for conquest.

Luc fought Tinker's hold, using his hips to try and buck him off his back. Advantage again went to Tinker. He reached beneath Luc and lifted his hips. Their bodies were sweat-covered, their cocks oozed fluid, and hot breath huffed from their lungs. In one swift move, Tinker reached around Luc's waist and grabbed Luc's testicles with his left hand. Luc went still just long enough for Tinker to grab his own cock in his right hand, position himself, and drive into Luc's well-lubricated ass with a single, harsh thrust.

Luc snarled and tried once more to dislodge Tinker, but there was no question who was victorious in this particular battle. Once Luc accepted defeat, it was obvious he thoroughly enjoyed the consequences of losing. Tinker was breathing as if he'd run a mile, but it didn't keep him from plowing hard and deep inside his partner.

He'd released his grasp on Luc's balls and now held him by the cock, both fists wrapped around Luc's hard length. Tinker fucked him hard and fast. He slid his hands back and forth, matching the steady rhythm of his cock, and his balls hit Luc's on every downward thrust.

Lisa was trembling, her entire body shaking as she watched the men's faces, watched the way their muscles stretched and contracted, the way they grunted and groaned with their efforts. She tried once more to read their thoughts and, without warning, stumbled into a blind haze of unimaginable lust.

She was Luc, her ass on fire from the powerful thrusts of Tinker's huge cock, the pain as exciting as the tight clasp of his hands around her straining erection. She almost climaxed, so sudden was the sensation, so amazing the myriad impressions stuffing her mind, just as Tinker stuffed Luc.

Luc came first, almost without warning. Lisa slipped out of his thoughts just in time and searched for Tinker's. Luc's body arched against Tinker's, and she felt his cock jerk in her own hands. Tinker had one fist covering the top of Luc's cock, and thick white streams leaked between his fingers with each jerk of Luc's body.

Lisa felt the hot, wet ejaculate spurting out of the end of Luc's cock, forced against her palm, leaking out between her fingers. The sharpness of detail, the strength of the sensation took her even higher. Luc's hand brushed Tinker's thigh, and she felt the pressure where he touched. Then he wrapped his fingers around Tinker's sac and squeezed lightly, his gentle grasp at odds with the tension in Tinker's body. It was all Tinker needed. All Lisa needed.

Tinker threw back his head and cried out. His hips thrust forward, almost driving Luc to the mat. Lisa felt her own muscles flex, so caught up in Tinker's thoughts that it was as if she drove into Luc, as if her cock were trapped tightly by his clenched muscles.

Tinker seemed to come forever, buried deep inside Luc. Lisa jerked with each thrust, each ripple of flesh as Luc's muscles contracted tightly around Tinker's cock. Her fluids ran along her inner thigh. No matter how much she'd not wanted to touch herself, Lisa realized her fingers were jammed deep inside her sex, trapped by her own spasming pussy.

Tia sprawled beside her, limp and grinning broadly. "Well, you wanted to see the guys together. What do you think?"

Lisa had to catch her breath before she could answer. She turned away from Tia, turned her attention back to the men. They had collapsed on the mattress. Tinker still impaled Luc, but he had a strained expression on his face. Luc was grinning like the cat that ate the canary. Lisa looked closely and burst into giggles.

Luc still held on to Tinker's balls. He glanced at Lisa and winked.

It took her a moment to get her laughter under control. "Luc, you remind me of that cartoon of the frog getting swallowed by the bird, and the frog has his little fists wrapped around the bird's throat, strangling him." She glanced at Tia and asked dryly, "Do those two *ever* give in?"

Luc answered, "Never. Right, bro?"

"Right. Now turn my balls loose before I bust yours."

Laughing, Luc let go. The two of them disentangled themselves and, slapping each other on the arms like a couple of ornery kids, headed for the bathroom to clean off.

Lisa sat staring at Tia for a moment without saying anything. There really were no words. Her body still thrummed with latent arousal; her breasts were tight, taut peaks, so sensitive they responded to the slight currents of air. She shook her head, laughing quietly. "Are they always like this?"

Tia snorted. "Always. Seriously, they love each other. They make love a lot. It's never just sex with those two, not like it can be with a lot of Chanku. The drive, the need for sex, is so powerful in our kind, but Tinker and Luc truly have a special relationship." She shrugged her shoulders. "Like Tinker keeps telling you, we're family. We all love one another, make love to one another."

No matter how often she heard this, Lisa wondered if she would ever truly understand or accept it. Family . . . her own was so splintered. It had always been so, though now there was a chance to reconnect with her brother and sister. She still wasn't sure how she really felt about that. "Will your marriage to Luc make a difference?"

"I hope not. Just as I hope Tinker's love for you won't make a difference." Tia looked away, as if unable to meet Lisa's direct stare. "I was so afraid when he came out here looking for you. I thought that if Tinker found someone for himself, he wouldn't need Luc and me anymore. Lisa, we still need him. We need both of you. I hope things won't change, other than you becoming another part of our family."

As much as she loved Tinker, as much as she thought she loved Tia and Luc, Lisa couldn't answer. She honestly didn't know yet how she'd feel when all of this finally sunk in. So many changes in one week. Would it ever make sense?

Tia waited for her to say something, but when Lisa didn't, Tia didn't push. She merely smiled, leaned close, and kissed Lisa very gently on the mouth. Then she settled back and tucked her feet under herself, waiting for the men to return.

Tinker was the first one out of the shower. He walked straight up to Lisa and kissed her on the mouth, hard. Water from his wet hair sprinkled her, and she pushed him away, laughing. "Cocky, aren't you? Did Luc let you win?"

"Let me? You're kidding, right?" Tinker glanced up as Luc walked into the room. "Hey, Luc. Did you let me win?"

"Hell no, and I've got the sore ass to prove it. You just got lucky. Next time I'm on top."

"In your dreams, man."

Luc sidled up close to Tinker and ran his hand down Tinker's chest, all the way to his cock. "You got that right."

"Okay, you two. Cut it out. It's our turn." Tia grabbed Luc's hand and flattened his palm across her breast. "Remember these?"

"Oh yeah . . ." He squeezed her breast, and Tia arched into his touch. Lisa heard the breath hiss out between her teeth. Tinker grabbed Luc's arm and pulled him away from Tia.

"Not now. No time. We need a plan if we're going to figure out what's going on at the sanctuary."

"What?" Now it was Lisa's turn to act indignant. "You get us all wound up and then you decide you need a plan? What happened to winging it? I don't think so." She folded her arms over her bare breasts and glared first at Tinker, then at Luc.

Luc grinned, grabbed Tia, and pulled her to her feet for a quick kiss. "Sorry, girls, but we're going in as wolves. It's a long run from here, and we'll need to eat first."

"Besides," Tinker added, "a little sexual frustration is good for you. Keeps you on your toes."

Lisa gave him a long, slow, appraising look. Then she grabbed Tia's hand and dragged her toward the bedroom to dress. She still wasn't too crazy about cooking naked. "They're gonna pay for this. You realize that, don't you?"

"Oh yeah. It appears great minds think alike."

The bandage strips fell off the wound on her throat when she shifted. Tinker growled at the four strips lying on the ground, then licked her throat. The slice from Seth's knife didn't even sting anymore.

Chanku definitely healed fast. *Is it bleeding?*

No. I can't really see it beneath your fur, but it looks as if it's healed. I should have killed the little bastard.

That would have been difficult to explain. Lisa nipped at Tinker's shoulder. *He's just a kid who screwed up. He thought he was helping the wolves.*

Holding a knife to your throat goes a little beyond screwing up, don't you think? I didn't find it at all helpful.

Lisa relaxed at the dry humor in Tinker's mental voice. At least he didn't sound as furious as he'd been earlier. She whirled around and headed toward the dark band of trees.

Tia raced beside her. Tinker and Luc followed close behind. Tinker was definitely right about one thing: Sexual frustration made her senses sharp. Lisa couldn't recall the scents of the forest smelling as pure as they did tonight, the sounds as clear. Once again she was struck by the surrealistic nature of the seemingly simple act of racing through the forest on four legs, the way her sharp nails dug into the hard ground, the way the air felt, rushing through her thick, coarse coat.

She felt it, the sense of power, the strength of the pack. Her packmates ran beside her. Behind her. It was all connected, this wolven body, this group of beloved packmates. Family.

After dinner they'd napped. All of them had sprawled together on the mattresses, but there'd been no sex. Now they set a fast pace and reached the series of fenced enclosures in a little over half an hour. Lisa felt ready for just about anything.

Except rounding a corner at a full run, right into the path of three large trucks running without lights. Three long-bed pickup trucks, loaded with men and guns, led by Hal Anderson.

Like ghosts in the dark, the four wolves slipped into the heavy brush alongside the road. Lisa's heart pounded frantically. Had anyone seen them? The moon was only half full tonight, but the sky was clear, and the silver glimmer of light might have been enough.

It had certainly been enough for wolven eyes.

What do you think? Lisa, did you get a good look at any of them?

Luc didn't sound the least bit concerned. Maybe everything was okay. *Just Hal. He was in the lead truck. Not driving. It might have been one of the new volunteers driving. I couldn't tell.*

I counted at least a dozen men, Tinker said. *Two in the cab of each truck, four riding in the back of the second truck, two in the back of the last truck. Rifles visible with a couple of them. Not sure about small arms.*

No dogs.

Thanks, Tia. I totally missed looking for dogs.

What now? Tinker sniffed the air.

Luc answered, *We follow them. See what's going on. Lisa, have you seen this kind of activity before? A group this size, armed?*

I've seen Hal out at night a lot, but not like this. I wonder if he figures now he's safe? The deputies didn't do much of a search once they got Seth. I heard Hal was really helpful, taking them to the barn where the transfers were made.

Convenient, don't you think, added Tinker, *that he was so willing to lead the deputies in the opposite direction of where he's headed now?*

Sneaky little bastard, isn't he?

Lisa snorted. Leave it to Tia.

They followed in the dark, padding silently along through the heavy brush at the side of the road. The trucks moved beyond the first inhabited wolf enclosure. The second was inhabited as well, but the third one, empty as far as Lisa knew, proved to be their destination.

She'd not had any reason to come this far for the past few weeks. There was a new lock on the gate and fresh tracks leading beyond where there shouldn't have been any activity at all. Hal got out and opened the gate, and his companion drove the first truck through. The other two followed. They left the gate open and unlocked.

Four dark wolves slipped through the open gate and trotted along behind the trucks, staying to the shadows. Their dark coats blended perfectly. Even Lisa had trouble seeing her packmates.

When the trucks veered off to the left in the direction of a large meadow, Lisa led the wolves along a trail to the right. They climbed to the top of a small bluff covered in scrub and twisted, burned trees from a long-ago fire. Threading their way carefully through the tangle, they reached a spot overlooking the area where the men now worked under portable lights.

What the hell are they doing? Luc raised up for a better view.

Looks like they're planting something. Or weeding . . . Gardening at this time of night? Tinker sat back on his haunches.

Lisa watched, fascinated that an idiot like Hal managed to keep something this big under wraps. *I think it's a pot farm. They're actually working on the drip system. Look over there.* She pointed in the direction of a couple of men who carried large rolls of black tubing. *He's growing marijuana. I'm almost positive. What do you want to bet he's got patches in each of the empty pens?* She stopped to do some calculations. *From the size of this one, and figuring the number of empties, he could have close to fifty acres under cultivation under all the trees and native plants. He's got water, and the land is fenced and private. It's perfect.*

We'll need to take a better look during the day, but I bet you're right. Tinker stretched. *There's not much we can do without evidence. Are the plants up yet?*

It's too early. They harvest in the fall. Probably just getting ready to plant. They'd need to get the drip system in first. This operation looks pretty sophisticated. I imagine photos would help. Once he plants, there'd be seed. We might have to sit on this for a while, until the plants are up.

Tinker turned and looked at Lisa. *You seem to know a lot about this.*

She sighed. *You were in my head when we linked. Don't you remember my previous living arrangements? I lived under a bridge in Florida for a while. Drugs were a way of life. There's no reason to hide what I did, but I'm not proud of it.*

Guess I missed that.

Lisa heard him sigh and saw him look away. Was he regretting that bond? Did Tinker wonder what kind of nutcase he'd hooked up with?

Luc turned around and headed back through the brush. The others followed. They slipped through the open gate and headed back toward Lisa's cabin, but everyone seemed unusually quiet tonight.

About a mile from her cabin, Tinker stopped and turned to Tia and Luc. *You guys go on. I want to talk to Lisa.*

Tia and Luc headed down the trail without comment. Tinker sat and watched Lisa without saying anything, then suddenly shifted. She did as well, though it was cold out tonight. She wrapped her arms around herself and shivered, but it was as much from nerves as the cold.

"Okay. You want to talk. What about?"

Tinker stood apart from her, hands on his hips, held tilted to one side as he studied her. Lisa had no idea what he was thinking, what he wanted from her. Finally, he smiled, sort of a lopsided grin that told her he was every bit as confused as she was.

"Do you love me?" he asked. "I mean, really love me in the way of two people who plan on spending a lifetime together?"

What a stupid question! "Of course—"

"No." Tinker held up his hand. The smile was gone. "I

want you to think about it. Don't just say what you think I want to hear. Think about what Lisa Quinn wants."

She felt a chill run along her spine. There was something so deadly serious about Tinker. So final. "Does it really matter? We've linked. Doesn't that mean we're mates no matter what?"

"No." He stepped back, putting more space between them. "Our link wasn't complete. It happened before you shifted. As amazing as it was, I don't think it was anything near the link Luc and Tia shared. Not what other Chanku have described. I realized it, talking with Luc. You still have secrets. There are things you haven't learned. You don't know how to block your thoughts. That's something you would know after a complete mating link because it's something I know. Neither of us has totally bonded with the other. You still have a choice, Lisa. You could choose to go on without me. Start your life fresh without me in it. Think about it."

She stood there in the dark, shivering, her arms wrapped tightly, protectively, around her waist. Tinker waited with his arms at his sides, his body so dark he looked part of the night. She tried to imagine life without him and couldn't. Tried to remember her life before Tinker and realized it never truly existed.

For so many lost years, she'd been Lisa, the druggie under the bridge. The one who dulled her miserable life with whatever worked, until the wolves called her. Until she climbed out of her personal sewer and found a job, then took the money from that job to come to Colorado.

As much as she'd loved it here, she'd never felt as if she belonged. Not until Tinker came into her life did she truly find a home. It wasn't the place; it was the man. He was her home, her future, the one she wanted beside her.

Was there really any other answer? For once in her life, Lisa realized there were no more questions. Only answers, and they lay in the heart of the man she loved, in the wisdom and patience behind his amber eyes. She stepped forward and took Tinker's hands in hers. His were warm; hers felt like ice. His long fingers wrapped around hers, and he held her tight, but he didn't pull her close.

She looked up into his eyes, and their amber lights seemed to glisten in the moonlight. What could she say to him that would convey to him how much he meant to her? What words could convey the sense of love, of future, of hope she felt with him in her life?

Simple really, the words. Said with love, said in a way that told him she meant them. From her heart. With her mind.

I love you, Tinker. I need you. I can't imagine my life without you in it. I'm not perfect, and I'll never be as good as you seem to think I am, but I promise to be the very best I can be, for you.

He didn't say a word. He reached for her, and she merely flowed into his embrace. He kissed her, and Lisa felt as if this were the first kiss they'd shared. The first time he'd held her. His body was strong and solid against hers, his arms around her protecting, holding. Loving.

When he shifted, it was the most natural thing in the world to shift with him. When he nipped her shoulder, pawed her back, and growled in frustration, she turned to him in an instinctual move that left her ready for Tinker to mount her, ready to take the sharp thrust of his wolven cock deep inside her body.

The sensations were so different, but the feelings weren't. She loved him, whether human or wolf. She needed him.

His front legs caught her shoulders with sharp claws, and she whimpered with the force of his taking. She braced her legs to hold his weight and felt him deep inside, ramming in and out with pistonlike speed and strength, felt the solid knot of muscle that slipped past her vaginal opening, penetrated her sex, and locked them together.

Then it happened. There, with bodies tied and trembling at the perfect peak of their shared orgasm. The link that was so much more than the first one, so much sweeter because it was expected, planned, wanted. Lisa opened her thoughts and her heart, shared her memories, her needs, her desires.

As did Tinker. Thousands of bits of his past, her past, his lovers and hers. She truly understood his relationship with Tia and Luc, knew how much he loved Mik and AJ, and in the learning, Lisa loved them, too.

She understood the abilities she'd not learned before— the way to block her thoughts when she needed to and how to send to only one person. All this and more found its way from Tinker's mind to hers, became part of her thought processes, melded within her own synapses and knowledge.

Her legs collapsed beneath his superior weight, and Tinker tumbled to the ground with her, their bodies still connected, his cock locked in place, pulsing within her clenching, rippling sheath. Both of them panted, tongues lolling, eyes half-lidded. For a moment, Lisa let her mind go blank. She absorbed sensation without thought, the pulsing heat of an alien penis lodged tightly within her strange-feeling vagina, the unfamiliar reactions of her bestial body to that of her mate.

This was so different on so many levels. Sex for the sake of procreation, yet she'd not released an egg. Sex as dominance, yet he'd not tried to overwhelm her. Sex as a link that was more gift than anything, a key that unlocked so many different aspects of her new self.

That was the ultimate difference between this act and the one time they'd linked deeply before. This time it had been complete. A total fulfillment of needs, desires, answers.

Lisa stared into Tinker's amber eyes and felt his deepest thoughts, his desires, his love. It was eternal. Complete.

All for her. Erasing all doubts and removing the fears she'd harbored that this wouldn't last.

Couldn't last. How wrong she'd been.

As they lay there, linked physically and mentally, Lisa finally understood the concept of family. Finally understood the man who would be her mate, who would love her forever.

Chapter 15

It took a good twenty minutes before the knot in Tinker's cock shrunk enough that he could pull himself free. Lisa whimpered when he slipped away from her body. They could have separated earlier, had they shifted, but there was no reason, no desire. The mental connection disappeared when they moved apart, and she felt suddenly adrift. Alone. After experiencing a most amazing union, she felt suddenly alone, lying close to Tinker with the deceptively cheerful sound of crickets all around.

Lisa raised her head and looked into Tinker's eyes, and suddenly the bond was there, as fresh and vivid as it had been during sex. She'd shut him out without realizing.

Obviously, she still had much to learn.

He could lie here all night, staring bemusedly into the feral beauty of Lisa's amber eyes. She chose him! She'd not been tricked, surprised, or coerced. Of her own free will, she'd chosen Martin McClintock as her mate.

He tried to remember the times someone had changed his life by choosing him. First his foster parents, then Ulrich Mason. Twice in all his twenty-seven years, neither time at his request, though he was certainly grateful.

However, *grateful* didn't come close to explaining how

he felt about Lisa. How did he thank someone for completing him, for making a lifetime decision based on a week's experience? For loving him.

He felt something crack deep inside and wondered if it was the armor around his heart. Tears would have welled up in his eyes, but wolves don't cry. Instead, he stood up, pointed his muzzle to the sky, and howled.

Tinker's cry was torn from deep inside and echoed off the surrounding hills.

Lisa joined him. The somewhat higher pitch of her voice rose in counterpoint to his. Other wolves, the ones running almost free in the pens, joined in. Long, mournful cries, the occasional sharp yip, Lisa's voice.

He could pick hers out from among all the others, even if she hadn't been standing next to him. There was joy in her sound, love, and a bit of humor that they should be standing here in the dark, their noses pointed to the heavens, howling for all they were worth.

They both stopped at the same time. Shook themselves. Tinker gazed into Lisa's eyes and discovered she felt as shell shocked as he did. The howling from the penned wolves died down, faded away. Once again, the steady chirp of crickets rose to hide the silence. Lisa leaned close and licked his muzzle, swiping her tongue across his mouth.

This was good. Very good. Tail waving in the air, Tinker turned and trotted back to Lisa's cabin. She followed for a few minutes, then passed him on a wide spot in the trail and led the way.

Heart light, mind at ease, Tinker followed her home.

Tia and Luc waited on the back deck, freshly bathed and dressed, each of them with a glass of chilled Chardonnay. When Lisa raced up the stairs, Tia patted the spot next to her on the long bench where she sat.

Lisa shifted and, ignoring her nudity, sat. She grasped Tia's proffered glass and took a long swallow just as Tinker shifted and sat on the chair next to Luc.

"We linked. The first one must not have been as complete. This was—"

"Amazing," Tinker said. "Absolutely amazing."

Tia laughed. "Can you block your thoughts better?"

"Damn, I sure hope so."

"What now?" Luc stepped out of the shadows. "Do we report Anderson, or do we wait?"

"We need to report him. Thing is, I worry about the wolves. Even if we had the money to run it now that Dunlop's in jail, what if the authorities decide to shut this place down? What will happen to the wolves?"

"Don't worry yet. I've got Dad on it. He and Anton will let us know what they find out." Tia leaned close, took Lisa's hand, and kissed her on the cheek. She held out her other hand to Tinker, and when he leaned close, she kissed him as well. "I'm more worried about you two. When are you coming home to San Francisco? Luc and I have to leave by the end of the week. We don't want to leave you here, Lisa—not you or Tinker."

Lisa raised her head and looked into Tinker's eyes. "Don't worry," he said. "We'll work something out."

Lisa and Tia both laughed. Lisa shook her head. "Uh-oh. Looks like Tinker's planning to wing it again."

Lisa wandered out on the deck the next morning just after six. The others already sat outside, drinking coffee and talking quietly. Luc was holding court at the moment, waving his coffee cup around as he spoke. She was surprised to see them all so wide awake. They'd all slept together on the mattresses that still covered her front room, so exhausted they'd done nothing more than hug and fall asleep.

Her night had been totally dreamless. Refreshing. She'd

loved the feeling of sharing her bed with her packmates, with her one true mate.

"I'd like to talk to Ulrich about Anderson's little farming project, but I doubt we can reach him." Luc sat in a chair across from the porch swing; Tinker was in the chair beside him. Lisa kissed Tinker and sat down next to Tia on the swing.

Lisa sipped her coffee. It was strong and dark, the way she liked it. A lot like Tinker. She smiled at her own time-worn analogy.

Tinker cocked an eyebrow in question, but Lisa kept her thoughts to herself. Thank goodness she was finally getting the hang of it!

Luc said, "You guys up to contacting Anton?"

It was a simple matter, the four of them holding hands and reaching out to the wizard. Lisa glanced around the small group and snorted. "We look like we're praying."

Luc said dryly, "Well, Anton's a god in his own mind."

"That's not fair." Tia nudged him with her chin but didn't release his hand. "I'd like to see you say that to his face."

He just did.

Oh shit. Luc's face turned a dark red. Tinker laughed out loud.

You're getting better at this. I sense more strength in your link, in spite of Mr. Stone.

Even Luc managed a strangled laugh at Anton's dry comment. Lisa wondered if her stronger bond with Tinker helped boost their ability to transmit their thoughts. Anton's voice in her mind felt amazingly intimate, and his immediate grasp of the problems eased much of her tension. With a man this powerful on their side, they could do anything.

I'll get word to the DEA about Anderson's activities as soon as you have some solid proof, and I'll let Ulrich know what's going on. Lisa, you really need to think about getting a telephone out there.

Thank you. Tinker smirked at Lisa. *I've told her the same damned thing.*

Anton's laughter faded away as he ended contact. Lisa let go of Tia's and Tinker's hands and settled back in the swing once more. She wondered if she'd ever get used to what this body could do. Wasn't it enough that she could become an entirely different creature? Mindtalking was just one more miracle.

Tinker, of course, was the greatest miracle of all. Lisa wrapped her fingers in his and felt as if everything was going to work out. It had to.

She'd never, not once in her life, been an optimist. Was this a new side of her nature as well? She laughed.

Tinker tilted his head and grinned at her. "What's that about?"

"Everything. Nothing. All of this. I love you."

Tinker smiled at her, shrugged his shoulders, and looked over his cup of coffee at Luc. "I don't get no respect. She thinks of me and laughs."

Luc held his cup of coffee out in a toast. "Get used to it. You mated an alpha bitch." Tia punched his arm.

Lisa sat back and sipped her coffee. She'd crossed the greatest hurdle and come over it with a most amazing family in tow. Now all she had to worry about was the sanctuary, the fate of the wolves, Anderson's pot farm, and how she could stay with the ones she loved.

Hal had locked himself in his office with orders not to be disturbed, and Millie was busy on her computer when Lisa entered headquarters. She'd already sent Luc and Tia off to scour the roads and sent a couple of volunteers to cover Seth's jobs.

Tinker was headed out to the pens on the perimeter to check on the wolves with the goal of finding a pen for the animals still in quarantine. It was time to move them into a more permanent home, but it also gave Tinker a good excuse to see which enclosures were under cultivation. Thank goodness Anderson had stayed in his office.

"G'morning, Millie." Lisa nodded to the secretary, grabbed a cup of coffee, and sat down at her own computer.

Millie raised her head and smiled at her. "Hi, Lisa. Where's that man of yours?"

"I sent him out to find a new home for the four animals in quarantine. They're ready to be moved into one of the large enclosures. I hope that's okay?"

"Perfect." Millie rubbed her fingers across her forehead, obviously distressed. "This has been such a nightmare. I wonder what's going to happen to us now? Do you have any idea how Dunlop's arrest will affect the financing?"

Lisa took a deep breath. She knew Ulrich and Anton were working on something. "No. But I've got friends working on it." She leaned across the desk and patted Millie's shoulder. "I promise to let you know what they find out."

Millie's smile was grim. "Thanks." She glanced at Lisa's neck. "How's your throat?"

Lisa blinked. In the two years since she'd worked here, this was the longest conversation she and Millie had ever had. She touched the healing cut on her throat. The sterile strips had fallen off last night when she shifted. The cut didn't even hurt anymore and was already almost healed. "It wasn't nearly as bad as it looked. See? Almost gone."

Millie frowned. "My goodness, you heal fast. That did look worse than it is. I can't believe what Seth did to you!"

"I know." Lisa sighed. Seth was, in her mind, one of the biggest victims in all of this; he was basically a good kid led astray by bad people. "I feel so awful for Seth. He acted without thinking when he attacked me. That was stupid, but I think he totally flipped out when he learned the wolves were being hunted. All along, he really thought he was doing something good for them."

Millie nodded. "I agree. Does that mean you're not going to press charges?"

Lisa shook her head. "I wasn't planning to. That will be up to the authorities, I imagine." She glanced toward the supervisor's closed door. "What's Hal up to?"

Millie tilted her head in the direction of Hal's office, then leaned closer to Lisa and whispered, "Napoleon's in there planning his next Waterloo. I can't believe all that business with Mr. Dunlop was going on under his nose and he didn't know about it. The man's an idiot!"

Lisa slapped a hand over her mouth to muffle her laughter. Millie so rarely said anything at all, much less something derogatory about their boss. "In all fairness," Lisa said, "I work close to the wolves, and I didn't have a clue."

"Well, Mr. Dunlop handpicked Hal to run this place. That alone makes him suspicious to me."

For the first time since working at the sanctuary, Lisa saw Millie in a new light. "How long have you been here, Millie?" The woman was attractive and ageless, anywhere between forty and seventy with silver-streaked blond, shoulder-length hair. Usually she wasn't very talkative or even friendly, but she'd always been amazingly efficient. Lisa generally kept to the outdoor jobs and really didn't know the secretary all that well.

Millie looked up and smiled wistfully. "I managed the ranch before Dunlop bought the property and turned it into a wolf sanctuary. My uncle owned it and raised cattle. I grew up here. I stayed on in the office because it's the only home I've ever known. I was hoping for the supervisor's job, but Hal got it." Her eyes narrowed, and she took a deep breath. "Believe me, if I was still in charge, I'd sure do things a lot differently."

"Wouldn't we all?"

Millie laughed. "When all that commotion happened yesterday, I was actually hoping they'd arrest him."

Lisa glanced toward Hal's office and whispered, "Me, too."

Millie reached out and took Lisa's hand. "I'm sorry I've taken so long to get to know you. I think working here as hired help after so many years as the boss has turned me into a bitter old woman. You're a good girl, Lisa. Don't let Harold Anderson give you a hard time."

Lisa went back to work on her computer, but she couldn't get Millie's comments out of her mind. Maybe things weren't going to be as difficult as she'd thought. Smiling to herself, she went online to do some research. It never hurt to have a little extra knowledge.

They regrouped at noon, meeting near the picnic area set up for visitors. There were more people here than usual today, most likely a result of all the publicity from the raid.

Tinker opened the ice chest filled with sandwiches Tia and Lisa had packed earlier and passed them out. He checked to make sure no one was within hearing distance of their small group, thought better of it, and resorted to mindtalking. *I had a good chance to check the empty enclosures. Almost all of them show signs of cultivation. A few actually have plants coming up.*

That's all we need, isn't it? Luc nodded and smiled at an elderly man who passed by with two children, headed for the small on-site museum.

Are you ready to call Anton, let him know so he can get the DEA out here? Lisa took a bite of her sandwich.

Tia grinned and looked around, obviously noting the large number of people in the area. "Do any of you feel like praying?"

Luc glared at Tia. "Funny girl."

Laughing, remembering Luc's major faux pas this morning, they clasped hands around the picnic table and bowed their heads. No one would disturb them now. Tinker glanced at Lisa and realized she was doing her best not to giggle. He squeezed her fingers, and they brought Anton Cheval into their group.

Praying? I could get used to this approach.

Luc blushed, but he didn't say a word. Their conversation was brief but productive. Tinker passed on his information regarding marijuana cultivation and Hal Anderson's involvement. When Cheval ended the contact, they all raised their heads.

"Is it getting easier to contact your wizard or is that just my imagination? I keep wondering if the fact Tinker and I have a stronger bond helps." Lisa finished her sandwich and wrapped her leftovers for the trash.

Tinker cocked an eyebrow at her. "It's getting easier because of all that sexual tension, we're supposed to work off of. If I get any more tense, I'm going to explode."

"Same here." Luc stood up and brushed the crumbs off his lap.

"Men." Tia grabbed Lisa and hauled her to her feet. "What are we doing next?"

"Well, if Anton's right, nothing will happen until this evening, after the crowds leave. DEA won't plan a raid until then because of the risk to public safety. All we have to do is make sure Anderson is still on-site." Lisa stretched and stared in the direction of the four wolves in their temporary pens.

"I say we talk to him about moving the animals from the quarantine pens to larger enclosures. As supervisor, he has to authorize which pen they go to. It's going to be interesting to see what he says, considering that all the available ones appear to be under cultivation."

* * *

Tinker grabbed Lisa's hand as they walked over to the quarantine section. He had to know what her plans were, no matter how painful it might be. She'd still not said a word about returning to San Francisco with him.

"Anton doesn't see a problem with the sanctuary remaining open," he said. "It sounds as if everything was put into trust as a tax shelter, so Dunlop's arrest shouldn't affect funding." Tinker stopped walking and pulled Lisa around to look at him. Her fingers felt warm and strong and absolutely perfect grasped in his, and it took all Tinker's willpower to ask the question. "Once Anderson is gone, though, who's going to run the sanctuary?"

Lisa grinned at him and squeezed his fingers. "Don't worry. I've got a plan."

"Are you sure?"

She stood on her toes and kissed him. "I can always wing it."

He pulled her into his arms and kissed her again. "No. Not with something this important."

Smiling mysteriously, her thoughts totally blocked, Lisa led him across the parking lot to check on the wolves.

Tinker couldn't help but believe he'd liked it better when Lisa had accidentally broadcasted her every thought.

The four of them met with Hal Anderson near the quarantine pens shortly after closing. He'd been reluctant when Lisa asked him for a few minutes of his time, but she'd finally convinced him.

When two unmarked cars pulled into the parking lot, Hal turned a questioning eye on Lisa, though he didn't appear overly concerned. "Any idea what this is all about?"

Lisa took her time studying the two cars and the four men who climbed out of them. When they were merely a few feet away, she said, "I imagine it has something to do with the marijuana farms in the empty paddocks, but I could be mistaken."

Anderson's face lost all color. He turned as if to run, but Tinker blocked his escape. Luc wrapped his fingers around Anderson's upper arm. Tia and Lisa moved aside to give the agents room to work.

A helicopter roared in over the treetops and landed in the empty parking lot. Lisa shielded her eyes from the blowing dust as a tall, dark-haired man climbed out, ducked beneath the spinning blades, then headed in the direction of their small group.

One agent held Hal's hands behind the little man's back, which were secured in plastic cuffs. Another read him his rights. Luc, Tia, and Tinker watched intently as Hal at first struggled, then glared sullenly at his captors. The helicopter rose into the air and headed toward the areas under cultivation. Lisa realized she was the only one who watched the man coming toward them. Tall and lean with his long, dark hair tied back in a queue, he looked like he should be dressed in a tuxedo, not in snug jeans and a loose cotton shirt. Lisa knew she'd never seen him before, but there was an odd sense of familiarity about him she couldn't explain.

Until he joined their small group and held his hand out to her. As she grasped his hand, he said, "Lisa Quinn? I'm Anton Cheval."

So this was the great Chanku/wizard. His grasp was strong and sure, his amber eyes twinkling with good humor. He was not at all what Lisa had expected, yet he was so much more.

"Hey, Anton!" Luc turned around and greeted him.

Anton Cheval cocked one winged eyebrow almost regally at Luc. "God to you, Mr. Stone." Then he turned to Lisa and, smiling broadly, leaned over and kissed her. Still in shock, she kissed him back.

"No discipline in that San Francisco pack," he said. "None at all." Laughing now, Cheval greeted Tinker and Tia, then nodded to one of the agents. "Thank you for the flight in. If you don't mind, I'd like a lift back to the airport when you're through here."

"No problem. I'll have the chopper swing back over and pick you up, Mr. Cheval." He grabbed the radio off his belt and gestured to the other agents to bring Anderson and follow him back to the car.

Lisa and the others watched as they marched Hal over to one of the unmarked cars and shoved him unceremoniously into the backseat. Tinker turned back to Cheval and laughed. "Okay, you've established your divinity, but I want to know why the DEA is taking orders from you?"

"Over here." Cheval led them to an empty picnic table. Once they were seated, he explained. "Ulrich and I pulled some strings and got me named as the temporary director of the sanctuary. Dunlop was removed from the board immediately after his arrest. Within the terms of the trust, a new, temporary director could be brought in under the discretion of the bank holding the trust. It so happens I'm on the bank's board of directors."

"That's handy." Luc grinned at Lisa and Tinker.

Anton bowed his head. "Yes, quite convenient." Smiling, he turned now to Lisa. "The problem is, we're going to need someone on-site to run the place. You, Ms. Quinn, are the obvious choice, but I imagine that's not something your mate wants to hear."

Lisa glanced at Tinker and saw so much pain in his eyes. She shouldn't have kept her idea a surprise. She realized now how unfair she'd been. "Actually," she said, looking back at Anton Cheval, "I don't want the job. There's someone else here who is much better qualified. Besides, the reasons that brought me here two years ago don't really exist anymore."

"What reasons?" Tinker reached across the table and took Lisa's hands in his. His grip was strong, reassuring, and terribly loving. "What brought you here?"

"I was looking for answers. I thought the wolves could show me the way. In that respect, I was right. Wolves truly did show me the way." She swallowed back the sudden lump in her throat. "I can't stay here, Tinker, because I could never ask you to leave your packmates and the life you had before we met. And face it"—her voice cracked, and she took a shuddering breath—"there's no way in hell I'm ever letting you go. You're stuck with me. All of you are."

Tears were running down Tia's cheeks, and even Luc looked touched by her words. Lisa kept a tight grip on Tinker's hands, but she turned to Anton. "Millie West, the secretary here, used to be the ranch manager before this became a sanctuary. She loves the wolves, she's an ardent conservationist, and she's even more qualified than Anderson. She should have had the job all along. Come with me so you can meet her."

They all trooped over to headquarters. Millie was just locking the front door. She smiled at Lisa when she looked up. "I told you he was in there plotting his own private Waterloo. A very nice gentleman just came in and confiscated Napoleon's computer. He had a search warrant, and I told him to take whatever he wanted. What happened?"

"We suspected Anderson was growing pot on the property. Turns out we were right, which leaves a big gap in management. Millie, I'd like to introduce you to a very good friend and the new director of the trust that controls the sanctuary. This is Anton Cheval."

Anton took Millie's hand in his. His eyes widened and then he smiled. Lisa turned to leave, but Anton stopped her with his free hand. "Lisa, you have no idea what an excellent suggestion you've made for the new supervisor's position. Thank you very much. Ms. West, do you have time for a chat?"

Looking almost mesmerized by Cheval's intensity, Millie turned around and unlocked the door. Anton raised his hand in a farewell salute. "Take care. I'll be in touch. And, Lisa, thank you again."

They lay together in a tangle of arms and legs and bedding. Tomorrow Tia and Luc would be gone, heading home on a flight back to San Francisco. Tinker planned to help Lisa pack her few belongings, and then the two of them would drive west. She wasn't quite ready to part with her beloved Jeep.

Lisa stared at the ceiling, ticking off all the things that needed to be done before they could leave. The wolves from the quarantine pens had been safely moved into one of the larger enclosures after the marijuana had been removed. She'd left her forwarding address with the authorities in case they needed her testimony in Hal Anderson's case.

Seth was back on the job already. When he learned Lisa didn't intend to press charges his relief had been almost humorous, but he still had much to atone for. Hopefully, this had been a very hard but long-lasting lesson for him.

Millie had moved into Hal's office immediately after her discussion with Anton. That had been an inspired suggestion on Lisa's part. She'd had no idea, though, just how inspired.

"How do you think she's going to take the news?" Luc's voice sounded groggy from sleep, but the contact they'd just had from Anton still reverberated in their minds.

Tia raised her head. "She won't know until someone tells her, and that won't happen for a while. At least not until after the wedding. Anton thought maybe Dad should be the one. They're about the same age."

Tinker rubbed his fingers over Lisa's nipple, and it immediately sprang to life. "How do you feel about that, Tia? Your dad and Millie."

"Good. I feel good about it. He's been lonely too long. I know my mother would approve."

"I can't believe Millie is Chanku." Lisa grinned into the darkness that wasn't nearly so dark. Damn, she loved the night vision she had now. Loved the strength, the powerful senses, the man. She found Tinker's fingers, brought them to her lips, and kissed each one. "She's a nice lady, but she's always seemed so bitter. Now I know why. It's sad that she's missed so much, but once she learns who and what she is . . ."

"It's going to be like a rebirth." Tinker rolled over until he was on top of Lisa. His cock was already hard, which was totally amazing, as they'd spent hours making love, the four of them, before finally falling into an exhausted slumber.

Until Anton's mental call. As a wizard, he was truly amazing, but as far as Lisa was concerned, his timing sucked. On the other hand, it wasn't bad to wake up to this.

Tinker slipped inside her wet and ready sex and sighed. Lisa searched his mind and found his thoughts, open and filled with love—and a lot of fiendishly wonderful ideas. *What do you think you're doing?*

Making love to you. See, Luc and Tia think it's a great idea, too.

Lisa rolled her head to one side and realized Luc and Tia were doing exactly the same thing. *It's almost like you planned this,* she said, rolling her hips to take him deeper.

Tinker kissed her. A long, slow meeting of mouths and tongues, lips and teeth. Finally Tinker came up for air. *No plan, my love. None at all. I'm winging it.*

I heard that. Tia's voice slipped into their silent, very private conversation. *I'd watch him closely, Lisa. Look what happened the last time he took off without a plan.*

Lisa turned her head and winked at Tia. Then she placed a very strong, very effective block in her mind. At the same time, she opened a narrow channel that let one man into her thoughts, and one man alone.

Tinker pushed himself up with his powerful arms and thrust his hips forward. *It's about time you figured out how those blocks work.* He leaned close and kissed the very tip of her nose, then moved his lips over hers.

Blocking out everything and everyone but Tinker, her heart filled with love and her head filled with plans, Lisa kissed him back.

Turn the page
for a sizzling preview of
THE SUPPLICANT.
On sale now!

Chapter 1

In the cool shade of the adobe wall, the knife blade in Sureya's hand glittered madly, dangerously. For a heartbeat she thought she heard the impossible, her little brother's gurgling coo. Careful of the thorns, she looked up from the blood-red roses expecting to see one of her charges.

Instead, she gasped. A second sun burned on the horizon—a lava-red heart surrounded by a halo of deep blue. Two icy white tails trailed behind, long and bright against the summer sky.

A strange sensation pervaded her senses. Between her thighs a rhythmic pulsing began, matched by the throbbing of the heart in the sky. She became aware of the length of her neck, the weight of her breasts, the curve of her lips.

A catty voice from the cherry tree in the distance caught her attention. "Oh, no," it said. Had one of the children climbed the tree?

Looking across the courtyard, she saw no child. Her employer, Risham, was plucking the last fat cherries of the season. He cupped several in his hand, and he looked like he was holding something precious. Even in her confusion, her nipples hardened with desire. He was supposed to be in town, with his wife.

"Risham," she called.

With a dark look, he strode toward her. He looked purposeful and strong. Knowing she shouldn't, Sureya admired his lithe movements, his fine features.

"Risham," she breathed as he moved into her space. The musky scent of him swirled around her, luring her toward him. Wordlessly, he cupped her cheek in his hand, his eyes locked on hers. She recognized desire. He burned with it, just as she did. "What are you—"

But he raised his sun-soaked fingers to her lips, and brought the warm, succulent fruit to her mouth. The sweet juice kissed her. The moment ripened in her mind. She could turn away now. She could leave Risham to his wife and children.

Instead, she opened her mouth, accepting his gift.

His finger brushed against her lip as she took the cherry, sending electric jolts through her. The tangy sweetness spread over her tongue, delighting her senses. Putting his hand on the curve of her waist, he pulled her toward him. Closing her eyes, she yielded to his touch.

"Oh, no," she heard again from the branches across the courtyard. The voice sounded husky, almost feline.

She opened her eyes and found Risham gone. Had he even been there? Alarm flooded through her. What was happening? And where were her charges?

"Nika!" she called. "Dayy! Lulal!"

Across the courtyard, gray feathers fluttered among the leafy branches. A catbird struggled in its nest, shoving something around with its beak. "This just won't do," the bird called to her, and then it meowed.

Sureya blinked, and the new sun shifted in the sky again, lurching its fiery heart closer to the horizon.

Standing in the cool shade of the fat adobe wall, Sureya's nipples hardened, almost painfully. Her breasts were tight,

longing for something to loosen them—a hand, lips, fingertips. Anything would be better than this unfamiliar longing.

"Nika! Dayy! Lulal!" she called.

"These won't do at all," the bird said in its catty voice.
It tossed its eggs—glossy and blue—out of its nest and into
the air.

Sureya gasped, wanting to catch the eggs, wanting to
return them to the feathery safety of their nest. She ran,
hands outstretched, knowing she wasn't close enough to
help.

But as the eggs fell, they hatched. Naked chicks covered
in feathers squeaked indignation at their early flight. Midair,
they flowered into frothy blossoms and floated softly to
the ground.

The chicks, Sureya thought as a bloom caressed her cheek.
Fighting a growing panic, she looked around the courtyard for the children in her care, the children of her heart.

They stood right before her.

But the yard, filled with the happy screams and laughter
of older children just moments ago, was eerily silent. Nika
and Dayy eyed the sky, oblivious of the catbird in the
cherry tree, to chicks that turned into flowers.

Ignoring the throbbing between her thighs, hoping the
sensation would go away, Sureya watched the red heart
pound on the horizon.

"It's beautiful," Dayy said.

"But so strange," Nika added.

The children were enthralled. Watching the new sun,
awe etched in their plump expressions, they stood rapt.
Only the youngest child still chattered at her side, happily,
thoughtlessly.

The throbbing between Sureya's thighs matched the
pulsing on the horizon beat for beat. Sureya sighed, getting a hold of her strange emotions.

She set aside the basket of roses she and the youngest
child were cutting. Over the thick peach adobe wall, fields

of artichokes and grapes spread before her, just as expected. No talking birds. But the brawny peasants had stopped their work to stare at the horizon, pale-skinned hands on their white foreheads to better see the new sun.

Little Lulal grabbed Sureya's skirt and tugged. Sureya ripped her gaze away from the new sun and looked down, amazed even now at how much the girl's eyes looked like her father's. Her skin was as dark as her father's, so beautiful. So unlike her own. Affection for the girl surged through Sureya's heart.

She ignored the liquid silk flowing between her legs. She ignored her aching nipples, the way she felt suddenly aware of the fullness of her lips.

"Why's everyone quiet all of a sudden, Miss Sureya?" Lulal asked. Sureya realized the little girl couldn't see above the wall. She picked up her beloved charge and balanced the girl on her hip. Lulal clung to Sureya's side like she belonged there.

"Now you can see it," Sureya said, pointing to the bizarre sky. The warm comfort of Lulal's body soothed her jangling nerves. The child smelled like her father.

"What is it?" Lulal asked. "The sky looks so weird."

"I don't know, little girl. It's probably nothing."

But the plaza bells started ringing wildly, off kilter and chaotically, as if to contradict her calming words. Someone in town was yanking on the tower ropes, randomly and hard.

Hard.

Hard hands. Hard mouths. Hard bodies pounding into hers.

What was happening?

For a frantic moment, Sureya wondered whether she should run, take the children and go someplace safe. The mountains, maybe. But how would the children's parents find them? She couldn't leave without Risham—without his shiny brown hair and his deep, lambent eyes. She'd miss the burning look he sometimes gave her across the dinner table, while he sat next to his wife and their children.

And how could she outrun the sky?

"Let's go inside," Sureya said to the older children over the resonating clanging. Her charges looked at her blankly, and Sureya realized they couldn't hear her over the cacophony.

"Into the house!" she shouted, pointing to the door with her empty hand. The two older children ran inside, their hands over their ears, screaming. Nika was crying, her face pink in anger and fear. Sureya cursed the bells. The new sun was frightening enough without their riotous racket.

Sureya's upper thighs slid together as she fled into the house. An image—a woman's dark hair and skin, crimson nails—danced through her mind. The woman carried a scent of sun-ripe mulberries, a dangerous aura of sensuality.

The thick adobe walls of the house muffled sound and cooled the hot summer air, but her small charges were staring at her with terror-struck eyes.

"Shh, my little girl," she said, petting Nika's forehead. "Don't fret so. It's a little nothing."

"What is it?" asked Dayy, worry etched on his eleven-year-old face. "What is it, exactly?" He raised his voice slightly to overcome the pealing bells.

Sureya ignored the question. She ignored the swollen pearl between her thighs. Still carrying Lulal, she closed the door behind them with her foot. Then she walked around the house and shuttered the windows.

What would Risham do, if he were here with his children?

Sureya knew the answer—he'd pretend everything was normal. He'd make things customary with his calm attitude.

"Now," she said in a steady voice as she closed the last shutter, "we'll be able to hear each other." Maybe it would shut out some of the afternoon's evil, too.

"But what *is* it?" Dayy asked again.

Sureya put Lulal down on the floor and stroked her head. "Lulal, my love, why don't you go with Nika and ask Cook to prepare tea and cakes for us?"

"Yay!" Lulal chirped. She grabbed her sister's hand and dragged her toward Cook's lair. Trailing behind her little sister, Nika shot a look at her nanny. Sureya read reluctance to leave the safety of her nanny's side.

"But what—" the boy said again.

"Dayy!" Sureya said. "I heard your question, and I don't know the answer."

"But you always know the answer," the boy said, his green eyes shining in dismay. He looked more like his mother than the other children did, and Sureya had to remind herself that she had nothing for which to feel guilty.

Except . . . she'd eaten a summer cherry from sun-soaked fingers. And the catbird had fed her eggs to the wind.

Images of a woman's dark hand sliding over her white breast skated through her mind: long, tapered nails over her hardened nipple. The area between her thighs ached for—for something she couldn't name.

What was wrong with her?

"Miss Sureya!" the boy said.

"I'm sorry, Dayy," she said, shaking herself from her inappropriate thoughts. "I don't know what that thing is in the sky, and I just wish those bells would stop ringing—"

Just then, the bells fell silent.

"How'd you do that?" Dayy asked.

Sureya laughed, sounding nervous to herself. "I didn't do it!" She wiped her damp palms on her skirt and said, "The priests probably stopped the village madman from pulling the ropes."

"Do you think they know about the new sun—the priests, I mean? What will they do?"

"Dayy, my love, I just don't know. The holy fathers probably have to make a sacrifice or two and say a whole bunch of prayers. Then it'll probably leave."

"But it's a new sun," the boy said. "How can anyone make the sun leave?"

The girls burst into the room before she could answer, and Sureya breathed a sigh of relief.

"Look! Cook gave us honey!" Lulal said. Nika hurried back to the dining room with a kitchen servant in tow. The sweet scent of almond cakes filled the room, warm and delicious. The servant set out a pot of honeyed *khal* and plates for the rolls.

"Thank you, Weset," Sureya said to the servant, and to the children, she said, "Sit, please."

Sureya placed the last roll on Dayy's plate just as the door swung open, wafting hot, dusty air over them. "Risham!" Sureya said, resisting the urge to throw herself into his strong, safe arms. "Daddy!" the children shouted.

His gaze flew over the children sitting around the table eating almond cakes. "Thank the One God, the children are safe!" Finally, he looked at his nanny. "Thank you, Sureya." He sounded surprisingly relieved.

Sureya blinked. His fingers dripped with what looked like cherry juice. Had there been a real danger?

But when his eyes locked on hers, she felt a different hazard. Her knees tingled and her stomach fluttered. "You're welcome," she said.

"What's happening, father?" Dayy asked.

"And where's Momma?" Nika asked.

The front door opened again, this time smacking the adobe wall behind it with a loud crack.

"Momma!" Lulal cried, rushing from the table and flinging herself into her mother's arms. Nika did the same. Even in the chaos, Sureya caught Dayy's look. He dearly

258 / *Lucinda Betts*

wanted to find comfort in his mother's arms, but he didn't want to look like a baby. Sureya stepped behind him and surreptitiously put her hand on his shoulder.

Fajal closed the door and paused to pet her girls. Sureya watched the woman close her eyes as she ran her brown fingers over the silky hair of her children.

She squashed a jagged pang of jealousy. Of course the children loved their mother. They might also love Sureya in their own way, but she would always be hired help. She would always be white.

Watching the mother's fingers as they stroked her child's heads, Sureya wondered whether it were Fajal's hand she'd imagined skimming under her chemise, hardening her nipples. What would it feel like if Fajal actually touched her like that?

But somehow the thought didn't seem . . . accurate. Fajal didn't smell like mulberries. The scent of ginger wafted around her employer.

Sureya shook her head. Why was she thinking such absurd and disturbing things?

She snuck a gaze at Risham and found him looking at her. Was that burning intensity she saw, or was it her heated imagination? His fingertips were stained a cherry red, and her mouth watered for sun-soaked summer fruit.

Silly girl, she chided herself, ignoring her wobbly knees. *Stupid girl.* She would always be in the peasant class. Her skin color ensured it. Risham belonged to his wife, and no amount of longing would bring him to her.

Sureya shook her head. She'd never do anything to hurt this family. They were all she had. The bloody barbarians had orphaned her; only Risham's and Fajal's kindness redeemed her.

Fajal untangled herself from her brood and straightened. Then she walked over to the heavy door and locked it, making butterflies flutter through Sureya's stomach. Why would the door need locking in the afternoon?

Then Fajal looked right at her, as if the older woman could read all the longing Sureya felt, as if Fajal could sense the strange magic pulsing through her thighs and breasts and lips and fingers.

"Children," Fajal said, "I want you to play by yourselves quietly for a few moments—in the cellar."

"But Momma!" Lulal objected. "It's dark down there. And stinky."

"Sureya will light a lantern for you—no, two lanterns. Grab your paints and your books if you want them, Nika, and yes, Lulal, you may bring your stuffed pony. Be quick."

Why did Fajal want them hidden in the dark amongst the roots and apples? Squashing her growing alarm, she turned to usher the children to the cellar.

"Sureya," Fajal added.

"Yes, ma'am?"

"Please return to the study immediately after you get them settled."

"Yes, ma'am."

"You'd better hurry," her mistress added in her smoky voice. "I want to talk to you."